"Maybe we should just hike to civilization,"

Kate suggested.

"With three babies?" Matt asked. "You expect them to hike with us?"

"We could carry them."

"And food? Diapers? Bottles? Formula? Get serious."

Okay, so it was a lousy idea. But the thought of spending three or four days in a run-down shack with Matt Sullivan and three infants had her making desperate suggestions....

Dear Reader,

Welcome to Silhouette **Special Edition**...welcome to romance.

Fall is in full swing and so are some of your favorite authors, who have some delightful and romantic stories in store.

Our THAT SPECIAL WOMAN! title for the month is *Babies on Board*, by Gina Ferris. On a dangerous assignment, an independent heroine becomes an instant mom to three orphans in need of her help.

Also in store for you in October is the beginning of LOVE LETTERS, an exciting new series from Lisa Jackson. These emotional stories have a hint of mystery, as well...and it all begins in *A Is for Always*.

Rounding out the month are *Bachelor Dad* by Carole Halston, *An Interrupted Marriage* by Laurey Bright and *Hesitant Hero* by Christina Dair. Sandra Moore makes her Silhouette debut with her book, *High Country Cowboy*, as **Special Edition**'s PREMIERE author.

I hope you enjoy this book, and all of the stories to come!

Sincerely,

Tara Gavin
Senior Editor
Silhouette Books

Please address questions and book requests to:
Silhouette Reader Service
U.S.: 3010 Walden Ave., P.O. Box 1325, Buffalo, NY 14269
Canadian: P.O. Box 609, Fort Erie, Ont. L2A 5X3

GINA FERRIS
BABIES ON BOARD

SPECIAL EDITION

Published by Silhouette Books
America's Publisher of Contemporary Romance

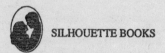

SILHOUETTE BOOKS

ISBN 0-373-09913-4

BABIES ON BOARD

Books by Gina Ferris

Silhouette Special Edition

GINA FERRIS,

who also writes as Gina Wilkins, declares that she is Southern by birth and by choice, and she has chosen to set many of her books in the South, where she finds a rich treasury of characters and settings. She particularly loves the Ozark mountain region of northern Arkansas and southern Missouri and the proudly unique people who reside there. She and her husband, John, live in Jacksonville, Arkansas, with their three children, Courtney, Kerry and David.

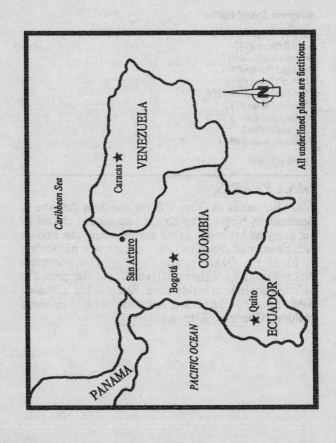

All underlined places are fictitious.

Chapter One

Kate Hennessy didn't even have enough breath to curse when she saw the press bus speeding away from the rendezvous point, leaving billows of dust in its wake. Sweating, gasping, aching beneath the heavy load of her backpack, tote bag and camera equipment, she stamped a booted foot in frustration, wondering what in hell she was going to do now.

Though muffled by the dense forest surrounding her, the sound of gunfire was getting louder, closer. She couldn't just stand here, couldn't risk being discovered by those who viewed every American as a potential political weapon. She turned to run, hoping she'd find shelter with a sympathetic local before she collapsed in utter exhaustion. Then she'd decide what to do next.

"Hey, you! Over here! Hurry up!"

The shout—in American-accented English, thank God—brought her head sharply around. Another bus, this one a rickety old specimen that looked barely roadworthy, had slammed to a stop, the heavy dust still swirling thickly around it. Through the dry, brown cloud, a masculine arm waved for her attention, signaling her to climb aboard.

"Get it in gear, dammit!" that same gruff voice yelled. "We've gotta get outta here."

Amen to that, Kate thought, and thanked the guardian saint of reckless photojournalists for providing rescue. She sprinted toward the bus as another ominous blast sounded behind her—but not nearly far enough behind her. That male arm grabbed her and hauled her unceremoniously onto the bus just as it squealed into motion again. Her feet had hardly cleared the ground before the bus was moving.

Kate's head made solid contact with the low doorframe as she was yanked into the bus. She grunted in pain, automatically closing her eyes against the sudden explosion of fireworks.

The man who'd pulled her on steadied her until she regained her balance. With her eyes still tightly closed, she registered the jerking and rattling of the bus beneath her feet. The engine whined and complained at the strain of being so roughly used. Funny, she thought dizzily, she could almost believe it sounded human. Rather like a baby crying—several of them, actually.

She must have hit her head harder than she'd thought.

Great. A concussion. Just what she'd needed to top off one royal bitch of a day. And it was only a couple of hours past noon.

"You okay, Hennessy?"

In response to the low growl, Kate dared to open her eyes a fraction of an inch. The sight of the face in front of her made her close them again with a heartfelt groan.

Oh, no. Not *him.*

Given a choice, she would have preferred a concussion, she thought, resignedly opening her eyes again.

"It's me or them," Matt Sullivan said with a jerk of his head toward the back of the bus to indicate the fighting they'd left behind. "Take your pick."

She wondered almost absently if he'd read her mind. It wouldn't have surprised her if telepathy was among multiaward-winning newspaper correspondent Matt Sullivan's many vaunted talents. "Just this once," she said coolly, "I'll take *you.*"

He grinned. "Trying to surprise me with a rational decision rather than one of your usual reckless, dangerously impulsive acts of defiance?"

She stumbled as the bus made a leaning, two-wheeled left turn. Matt's strong, tanned arm shot out to steady her again. It annoyed her that she had to accept the assistance or fall on her face—and wouldn't *that* have amused him?

Before she could think of a suitably cutting reply, she was distracted by the sound she'd heard before—the one that eerily resembled crying babies. She turned toward the passenger section of the bus, and her jaw dropped.

"Oh, my God," she said with a gasp. "Where did you get *those?*"

"*Those* are babies," Matt answered, mocking her tone. "And they came with the bus. It's an orphanage evac mission. I flagged down the driver just outside of town."

She stared at the three car seats strapped onto the shabby benches lining the sides of the bus. Each car seat held a tiny, squalling occupant. After a long, stunned moment, Kate slowly dragged her gaze away from the babies to examine the remainder of the cramped interior.

Piles of boxes filled the back of the bus, their contents rattling and clanging, adding to the chaotic noise level. A large, folded item that appeared to be made of aluminum, vinyl and netting rested flat against the emergency door at the back of the bus, thumping rhythmically with each bump in the road. Kate thought it looked like a playpen.

She turned slowly back to Matt. "Shouldn't there be a nun or someone taking care of them?" she asked dazedly. "Is the driver the only one with them?"

"The other kids in the orphanage were being evacuated to a nearby convent, farther away from the violence. The nuns had to go with them. These three were to be transferred to San Arturo, anyway. According to the driver, they have families waiting to adopt them—if they get there safely," he added. "The driver's a volunteer—I think he said he was a groundskeeper for the orphanage. One of the nuns was supposed to accompany him to San Arturo, but she was injured and forced to stay behind. He promised her he'd get the kids out himself, somehow."

Kate glanced doubtfully at the back of the driver's head, amazed that he'd volunteered to take care of three infants on the road by himself. It certainly wasn't something she would have done! "So what are you doing here?" she asked Matt. "How come you weren't on the press bus?"

Matt grimaced. "Same reason you weren't. I missed it."

"One more story," she said with a roll of her eyes.

He cocked an eyebrow toward her camera bag. "One more photo."

"Touché." Sighing wearily, she slid her bags to the floor and kicked them under the nearest bench, clinging to a metal pole for balance as the bus jerked and swerved in the rutted road. "Why aren't we going the same direction the press bus went?"

"They're on their way to the nearest airport. It's in the opposite direction from the orphanage at San Arturo."

Kate shoved a dirty hand through her short, wildly disheveled cinnamon hair. "Terrific."

He shrugged. "We can arrange transportation from there. At least it's away from the fighting."

She nodded. "Do you have any idea how long it will take us to get there?"

"Not counting unforeseen circumstances—a couple of days."

A baby screeched as if in protest of the estimate. Kate groaned in sympathy. "A couple of days?" *On a bus with three infants and Matt Sullivan?*

No guardian saint of reckless photojournalists had sent *this* bus, she thought grimly. This one had come straight from journalism hell.

"Look, can't you do something with them?" Matt asked, waving toward the crying babies. "I feel kind of sorry for them."

She planted both hands on her hips to stare at him in disbelief, then had to grab again for the pole when the bus rounded another corner with heart-stopping speed. "What do you expect me to do with them?"

"I don't know." Matt shrugged helplessly. "Pat them or something."

"They're babies, not puppies!" she shouted, thoroughly exasperated.

"Well, damn it, you're a woman. Don't you know anything about kids?"

"Yes. I know you put stuff in one end and it comes out disgustingly at the other. I know they need lots of care and attention, but I haven't the faintest idea what that entails. And I damned well know that I'm not taking care of these three by myself for the next two days!"

Scowling, Matt met her determined glare for several long moments. And then he exhaled gustily and turned toward the benches. "All right. I'll see what I can do with this one. You try to do something with those two."

Kate started to vent her feelings with a string of choice epithets. Then, thinking of innocent young ears, she bit her tongue and moved toward the nearest car seat with the same reluctant caution she might have displayed toward a ticking bomb.

Red-faced from crying, the baby was chubby and olive-skinned, with a thatch of straight black hair and huge dark eyes swimming in tears. The open mouth revealed two tiny teeth. How old were babies when they got teeth? Kate made a shaky estimate of somewhere between six months and a year. The child was firmly strapped into the shabby car seat and dressed in a disposable diaper and a faded yellow T-shirt that gave little clue to gender.

Kneeling awkwardly in front of the car seat, Kate hitched up her jeans and shoved the sleeves of her khaki shirt up her forearms before reaching out tentatively to the baby. "It's okay, kid. Don't cry," she said.

The baby kicked its tiny bare feet and screamed.

"Oh, *that* helped," Matt grumbled, looking up from the baby he was crouching over.

Kate returned the look scornfully. "You aren't doing any better," she pointed out. "Yours is still crying, too."

Matt expressively turned his back to her and started talking in a low, soothing growl to the other baby.

Kate took a deep breath and turned back to her task. She reached out to pat the soft little head—just as she would have patted a puppy, she thought in resignation, remembering her heated retort to Matt.

"Come on, kid, you're making me look bad," she murmured, knowing Matt couldn't hear her over the other noises. "Stop crying, okay?"

A flash of color caught her eye. Investigating, she found a pacifier dangling from a red ribbon that had been pinned to the baby's outfit. With a surge of hope, she poked the rubber nipple into the gaping little mouth. "Here you go," she said brightly, and mentally crossed her fingers. "Take your frustration out on this thing. Give your mouth a workout."

The baby quieted magically. Its mouth closed around the pacifier and began to work it furiously. Wet-lashed, swollen little eyes drooped from exhaustion as the baby visibly relaxed, its breath catching in heartrending whimpers.

Matt looked over his shoulder, and his narrowed gray eyes were beginning to look harried. "How did you do that?" he demanded, still busily patting his own bawling charge.

"See if there's a pacifier pinned to its shirt."

He checked the faded blue garment. "Yeah, there is," he said, extracting it from the car seat straps.

Thank you, Sister Whoever, Kate thought without levity. She sent up a quick prayer that the good nun would recover from her injuries.

While Matt continued to soothe the second infant, Kate turned to the third. Smaller than the others, this one looked only a couple of months old. Its head moved with little muscle control as it squirmed against the bindings of the safety seat, too tired to make more than a few mewling sounds as it cried.

Kate felt her chest tighten. For the first time in her life, she wished she'd spent more time baby-sitting when she was a teenager and less time hanging around her uncle's newspaper offices. Maybe then she wouldn't feel quite so useless and ineffectual right now. These kids deserved better care than she knew how to offer, and obviously Matt was as lousy with them as she was.

Again, a pacifier worked wonders. The baby was asleep within minutes after comforting itself with its suckling.

Two asleep, one to go, Kate thought rather smugly, turning to help Matt. And then she grinned wearily. "That is *not* a pacifier, Sullivan."

Matt glared at her. "I'm aware of that," he said coolly. "But the pacifier didn't work with this one."

Kate looked expressively at the expensive, leather-band watch the child was examining with such enthusiasm. "I hope it's waterproof," was all she said as the baby took an experimental lick.

Keeping a close eye on his watch, Matt winced. "I didn't have anything else for it to play with," he muttered.

She sank heavily onto a narrow open space on one of the crowded benches and propped her feet—damn, but these boots were heavy!—on the bench opposite her. "I haven't had any sleep in two days," she murmured, leaning her head against the cracked vinyl and closing her eyes. "Wake me if we're in imminent danger, will you?"

"Wait a minute. You can't just—"

But she tuned him out with practiced ease and allowed herself to slide gratefully into unconsciousness.

Matt stared at Kate in exasperation. It didn't particularly surprise him that she could fall asleep so quickly in a jerking, springless, wheezing old bus, racing down a rutted dirt road in a South American country that had just erupted into violence following yet another leftist guerrilla uprising. After all, she was a journalist. They learned to get their sleep when they could.

No, what annoyed him so greatly was that she'd fallen asleep *now,* when he could have used her help with this watch-eating kid.

He should have known Kate Hennessy would be as incompetent as he was when it came to babies. He'd never denied that she was one hell of a photojournalist, but as far as he could tell, she was a washout when it came to anything feminine.

Despite having big, sooty-lashed green eyes, an intriguingly full mouth, a nice, if somewhat thin figure and legs that looked disproportionately long in contrast to her just-below-average height, Kate Hennessy was one of the *least* feminine women he'd ever known. He'd told her so on more than one occasion during their few encounters in the past couple of years. In response to which, she'd royally cussed him out and told him exactly what he could do with his opinions, effectively dampening those momentary flashes of attraction he'd occasionally felt for her, before reminding himself that she represented everything he did not like in a woman.

Okay, so maybe he *was* somewhat sexist, as she'd so heatedly accused him of being. He just happened to think women should be a little more—well, womanly. And Kate, with her sailor's mouth, dangerously reckless pursuit of her career, hair-trigger temper and damn-your-eyes independence, just didn't fit his vague ideas of what was womanly. Based, most likely, on memories of his sweet old grandmother and happily domestic mother.

Trying to keep one eye on his watch—damn, the little brat had slobbered all over the band—he slanted one more brooding look across the aisle at the woman sleeping so soundly between the two dozing infants. Her red brown hair, which she wore shorter than any other woman he knew, was standing every which way, giving her a gamine, tousled look that just might have been cute on someone he didn't know as well as he knew Hennessy.

She wasn't wearing any makeup, as usual, so the smattering of golden freckles over her nose was visible through the smudges of dirt she'd acquired in her hasty escape from the war zone. Her lips were parted just a bit, showing a glimpse of tongue and white teeth—which might have looked inviting to an unsuspecting stranger. Her stained, wrinkled khaki shirt was pulled tightly across her chest by her slouched position. She was on the small side, but that wouldn't have mattered had she made any effort to maximize her assets.

As for those long, denim-cased legs stretched across the narrow aisleway... Well, he *might* have been interested if they'd belonged to any other woman. But not Hennessy.

A gurgle of sound got his attention just as the baby tried to shove the entire watch in its avid mouth. Matt retrieved it hastily—after all, he wouldn't want the kid to choke. Immediately, the round little face screwed into a mask of displeasure beneath a mop of dark brown curls, and the tiny mouth opened to express extreme indignation. Matt groaned and tried the pacifier again. The baby spat it out in utter disgust and started to cry.

Matt gave momentary consideration to joining in before taking a long, deep breath and trying again to soothe the kid.

I will *repay you for this, Hennessy.*

Her cheap, dependable watch told Kate she'd been asleep for an hour when she opened her eyes to check. She could use another eight hours in a soft bed, but she didn't waste time on futile daydreams. She'd take what rest she could get.

Something told her she was going to need it before this trip was over.

A perfunctory glance to either side reassured her that both babies were still sleeping. A look across the aisle showed her that Matt was, too, his arms crossed over his chest, his head nodding. The baby beside him was still wide-awake, though no longer crying. It was holding a battered teddy bear, which it whacked enthusiastically against the padded bar across the front of the safety seat. With a slight smile, Kate wondered where Matt had found the bear.

Her sleepy attention turned back to Matt. The lanky reporter looked like a trail-weary cowboy in his faded denim shirt with the sleeves rolled up on his forearms, well-worn jeans and slant-heeled boots. No jungle fatigues for *this* stubborn Texan, she thought with a slight sniff. All he lacked was a ten-gallon hat pulled low over his face while he dozed. Instead, his dark-coffee-colored hair fell in a shaggy forelock over his tanned forehead, drawing her gaze to the almost-ridiculously long eyelashes fanning his lean, brown cheeks.

His was an arrogant face, in need of a shave at the moment, with a strong nose, firm mouth and stubborn chin. Kate had always thought his overbearing personality could be read right there in his features. Still, she guessed she could understand why some of the women she knew found him attractive.

As for her, she was usually too mad at his sexist, condescending, completely tactless remarks to spend time admiring his masculine attributes, though she was rather sheepishly aware that she had certainly noticed those attributes on occasion. *Rare* occasions, she reminded herself firmly.

Matt suffered from a severe, chronic case of the dreaded LWS—Little Woman Syndrome. And Kate had learned from hard, painful experience to avoid that disorder as carefully as she did any other disease that could prove hazardous to her health and well-being.

She glanced toward the front of the bus. The so-far-nameless driver was still pushing the old vehicle as hard as he could. The back of his dark head was the only part of him she could see. It didn't surprise her that Matt had neglected to perform introductions. Social niceties were no more his forte than child care.

She squirmed into a slightly more comfortable slump and closed her eyes again. Why was she wasting time thinking about Matt Sullivan when she had an opportunity, no matter how brief, to grab some Zs?

The jarring stop threw Kate from her seat, bringing her abruptly awake. She landed on her hands and knees on the grubby floor of the bus. Matt came down on top of her, knocking most of what remained of her breath from her lungs.

"Oomph! Get off me, you—"

"All right, I'm trying, for Pete's sake," Matt grouched, scrabbling for footing.

Still safely strapped into their seats, the babies started to cry again, a trio of startled displeasure. Kate groaned and pushed herself upright, ignoring Matt's extended hand. "*Now* what?"

Another hour had passed since she'd last checked. Any signs of civilization had long since been left behind as the sorry excuse for a road had wound its way into the heavy forest. The towering trees surrounding them blocked so much light that it could well have been late evening rather than midafternoon. The bus had come to a stop on the side of the road, the wheels on the right side leaning precariously into a shallow ditch. The driver wasn't behind the steering wheel, where Kate had last seen him.

"If he slammed on the brakes and woke up these babies just so he could take a leak..." she muttered, shoving her hand through her hair and trying to see through the dirty windows.

Matt gave her a look of distaste. "Real nice, Hennessy."

"Oh, excuse me," she said with a roll of her eyes at his priggishness. "I mean if he slammed on the brakes just to answer the call of nature, then I'm going to be a tiny bit piqued with him. Does that satisfy your delicate sensibilities, Sullivan?"

He ignored her. Pointedly. Heading for the open door, he tossed over his shoulder, "See if you can do anything with the kids. I'll find out what's going on."

If Kate had been holding anything, it would have hit him square in the back of his dark head. As it was, she took a very deep breath, counted to thirty-six—she wasn't nearly calm enough by the time she reached ten—and then turned to the babies, wondering what in hell he thought she was going to do with them.

The baby in the yellow shirt—the one she'd quieted first earlier—settled down as soon as she retrieved its pacifier. The child across the aisle—the one she'd started to think of as Matt's baby—took a bit more work. Rejecting the pacifier and the teddy bear, it continued to cry until Kate dug out a package of somewhat stale chocolate-chip cookies from her bag. The baby made a grab for the one Kate experimentally offered and shoved it in its mouth, gumming the snack with enthusiasm.

"Don't choke, okay? Please." She took some reassurance from the child's apparent familiarity with cookies. Surely that meant it had eaten them before—and survived.

The smallest baby was wailing around the tiny fist it had shoved into its mouth. It stopped every few moments to suck hungrily at its knuckles, then broke into screams again when it received no reward for its efforts.

Even Kate could figure out that baby body language. "You're hungry," she said. "You want something to eat, right?"

The baby cried harder, as if in confirmation.

Kate looked around wildly for something to feed it. There were still several cookies left in the package, but it was pretty apparent that this baby was too little for solid foods. This one needed milk or formula. Surely the nun had sent provisions for the trip, if only Kate knew where to find them among the supplies crammed into the bus.

Matt climbed back inside, ducking beneath the low doorframe. He looked in approval at the two babies who'd stopped crying, then frowned at the little one. "What's the problem?"

"It's hungry."

Matt shrugged. "So feed it."

She really was going to have to hurt him soon, Kate thought dispassionately, taking another one of those steadying breaths. When she could speak without shrieking, she said, "I don't happen to be lactating at the moment. Are you?"

She hated him for breaking into a grin. "No," he replied. "I'm not. Might I suggest a bottle?"

"Might *I* suggest that you get your butt back here and help me find one?" she asked much too sweetly.

His grin faded. "Jeez, Hennessy, can't you handle anything by yourself? I need to give José a hand outside. That's what I came in to tell you. Something's wrong with the engine. José's trying to figure out what it is, and I told him I'd be right back to help."

"Do you *know* anything about bus engines?" she asked.

He cleared his throat and shuffled his boots against the floor. "Well, no, but..."

Having gummed its cookie to unappetizing pulp, the baby next to him started to cry again.

"You help me feed these babies, Matthew Sullivan, or so help me, someone will find your lifeless body hanging from one of these trees. Is that clear?"

His face darkened with his scowl. "Now, wait just a minute, Hennessy...."

The stereo crying had startled the yellow-clad baby, who joined in the fray. Matt's eyes glazed. Kate started to shake.

"I need your help!" she shouted above the din, furious that she had to ask. "Dammit, Matt, I need your help with this!"

He closed his eyes, rubbed his temple with a dirt-streaked hand and nodded. "All right," he said, then opened his eyes and dropped his hand. "Let's check those boxes."

Chapter Two

They found empty plastic bottles packed in one box, jars of baby food in another, diapers and tiny T-shirts in others. Nothing that looked like it belonged in a baby bottle. Kate was starting to panic when she finally opened a box and found cans marked Infant Formula.

"Thank God," she breathed, and held one up to show Matt, whose own digging had turned frantic as the wailing from behind them intensified.

He relaxed visibly. "Great. Let's pour it into the bottles and—"

"Oh, no."

He grimaced at her tone. "What?"

"It's powdered formula. It has to be mixed with water."

Matt's curse was rough and expressive.

"Oh, very nice, Sullivan," she said, mocking his earlier remark to her. "*You're* the one cussing in front of the kids."

"They only know Spanish," he grumbled, though he looked quickly and rather shamefacedly, at the crying trio. "Keep looking. Surely the sister packed water for the formula."

Had the next box not held jugs of sterile water, Kate might well have burst into tears for the first time in recent memory. She snatched one of the bottles and hugged it to her chest. "I found it."

Matt looked as relieved as she felt. "Great. All right, let's get it mixed."

"How much of each?"

"How should I know? Read the label on the formula can."

Luckily, the instructions were written in Spanish *and* English. "Half and half."

"Good. We can estimate that without worrying too much about the measurements." Holding a plastic bottle in one hand, he held out his other hand for the formula can. "I'll dump in the powder, then you pour the water in and shake it up to mix it."

She nodded, but frowned as her gaze fell on his outstretched hand. His very dirty outstretched hand. "Don't touch the nipples, okay?"

Lifting an eyebrow, he let his gaze drift idly down her shirtfront. "Don't worry, Hennessy. You're completely safe from me."

Angered by the ill-timed barb, she bared her teeth. "Of all the juvenile—"

Realizing that she was only amusing him with her flare of temper, she bit off the rest of the words and shoved the formula can into his hand.

Fortunately, the oldest baby—the two-teeth one in the yellow T-shirt—was old enough to hold his—her?—own bottle. Eager hands reached out to grab the bottle almost before Kate could offer it, and the little mouth closed proficiently around the reasonably sterile nipple. Glancing across the aisle, Kate noted that Matt's baby was taking its own formula with only token help from Matt's supporting hand.

The smallest baby was different. Kate tried kneeling by the car seat and supporting the bottle, but the bobbing little head was difficult to follow and Kate's legs had already started to cramp from the awkward position. Both she and the baby were getting frustrated before even an ounce of the formula was gone.

"You're going to have to hold that one," Matt said with a frown at her ineffective efforts.

"But I'm filthy."

"And the kid's hungry. A little dirt won't hurt it. It needs to be held."

"You do it, then."

He smiled blandly and indicated his own charge. "Sorry. I'm busy."

She knew he was right. She just really hated admitting it.

Sighing, she set the bottle aside, then spoke hastily when the baby immediately protested. "Okay, hold on a minute," she said, fumbling with the straps and buckles of the car seat. "I'm trying. Cut me some slack, will you?"

When the straps were all unfastened, she reached into the seat to pick up the baby, trying to look more confident than she felt. Maybe babies were like dogs and horses, she reasoned. Maybe they sensed when someone was terrified of them.

"Don't forget to support its head."

"I know that much," she snapped in response to Matt's unsolicited advice. She slid a hand behind the baby's downy head, regretting that she hadn't had a chance to wash up. She hoped Matt was right about the dirt not proving harmful. She'd thought of using some of the bottled water to wash her hands, but she didn't know how much longer it would take to reach the orphanage—especially now that they were having engine trouble—and she certainly didn't want to risk running out of supplies for the babies.

She settled onto the bench with the baby in her arms, trying to support its head and body and retrieve the bottle at the same time. She thought she saw bewilderment in the baby's dark eyes. "Yeah, I know, kid," she muttered, poking the nipple back into the rosebud mouth. "You don't quite know what to make of me. Well, join the club."

The baby sighed around the bottle and settled in for some serious suckling, looking more content than it had since Kate had first seen it.

"All right, Hennessy," Matt said approvingly. "I think you're getting the hang of it."

The smile she gave him felt decidedly smug. "Piece of cake."

"So don't they have to be burped or something?"

Her smile vanished. "Uh, I don't know. Maybe." *When? How?*

As if in answer, the yellow-shirted baby lowered its bottle for a moment, belched noisily and stuck the bottle back into its mouth.

Matt grinned. "Way to go, kid. D'you all do that for yourselves?"

Kate shook her head. "I don't think so. If they did, why would everyone make such a fuss about burping the little ones?"

"Mine looks big enough—maybe," Matt decided, eyeing the curly-haired tot beside him. "How old would you say they are?"

"Beats the hell out of me."

"Make a wild guess."

She shrugged. "The oldest one over here must be close to a year. Maybe ten months. It has a couple of teeth and seems pretty handy with the bottle. Yours is probably a couple of months younger."

It occurred to her that they'd apparently split temporary ownership of the babies—and she'd come out with one extra. She'd have to see that Matt shared duty with her when it came to this little one. That thought made her glance back down at the baby in her arms, who was still nursing contentedly. "I don't know about this one. It couldn't be more than a couple of months old."

"Wonder if they're boys or girls."

"Didn't José tell you *anything* about them?"

"He doesn't know anything about them. Apparently, the nuns loaded the kids on the bus and José just drove off with them without asking too many questions."

"I'm sure we'll be finding out genders soon," she said with a grimace. She knew that diaper changes were rapidly becoming inevitable. The kids were probably all wet now. She just hoped that was all they were.

"Your baby's had half the bottle already. You'd better burp it."

Again, Matt's suggestion only annoyed her. For one thing, she was beginning to feel more incompetent by the moment. She hadn't the faintest clue of how to burp a baby, other than a hazy knowledge that it had something to do with patting it on the back. "How?"

"Throw it over your shoulder. That's what my sister did with her baby."

Kate's head came up sharply. "Your sister has kids? Then you should be the one taking care of this! You have experience. I don't have any siblings, so no nieces or nephews, either."

"The hell I have experience. I said my sister had a kid, I didn't say I'd ever fed it or burped it or anything. I held it a couple of times."

"It? You don't know if it's a boy or a girl?" she asked snidely.

He glared. "Girl. It—she's a girl. Melanie."

"You even know her name. I'm impressed, Uncle Matthew."

His glare deepened. "I don't get back home much, okay? I only see her a couple of times a year. Now, would you burp the kid before it explodes or something?"

Kate abandoned the stalling tactics, and pulled the bottle out of the baby's mouth with a soft pop. Very carefully, she lifted the squirming body to her shoulder, and winced when the little head bumped a couple of times against her. "Easy, kid," she murmured, gingerly patting the tiny back through the soft white cotton of its too-big shirt. "Come on, now. Burp."

"I think you have to pat harder. Carolyn—my sister—really whomped Melanie."

"I'm not 'whomping' this baby," Kate snapped, though she increased the pressure of her pats a bit. "It's too little. I could—oh, *yuck!*"

"What?"

The warm, sticky, regurgitated liquid oozed over Kate's shoulder and trickled down her back. "It threw up."

"Oh." Matt tried unsuccessfully to hide a grin. "I forgot to warn you. They do that, sometimes. Carolyn always put a cloth diaper over her shoulder when she burped Melanie."

"Thanks a lot, Sullivan. *Now* you tell me. Oh, God, that smells awful."

"Give it a couple of hours to ripen."

No way. She was digging out a clean shirt immediately after this baby was back in its car seat, even if she had to change right in front of Matt, José, the babies, God and everyone, she decided, lowering the baby again and sticking the bottle back into its mouth.

The baby was asleep before the bottle was completely empty. Sighing in relief, Kate returned it to the car seat, relieved when it didn't awaken. "We should probably check diapers."

Matt stood. "They're all asleep. Let's wait a few minutes. I want to see how José's doing."

"But won't they get diaper rash if they sit in wet diapers?"

"They're all wearing disposables for the trip. They keep the babies drier."

Kate looked at him skeptically. "How do you know that?"

"I watch TV commercials."

"Oh, that's—"

"Look," he interrupted impatiently, holding his voice down with obvious effort. "They're all quiet for once. Do *you* want to get them stirred up again?"

She bit her lower lip, torn between concern for the babies' well-being and her own need for temporary peace. "No..."

"I'm going out. You do whatever you want." He ducked out the door before she could reply.

Muttering imprecations beneath her breath, Kate dropped to her knees and dragged her tote bag out from beneath the bench, then dug out a clean T-shirt. The sour-milk smell was starting to turn her stomach. She stayed on her knees as she rapidly stripped out of the soiled khaki shirt and tugged the clean red T-shirt over her head. It would have been nice to have a bath first, but at least she no longer smelled like baby puke.

"If you're saying your prayers down there, Hennessy, see if you can arrange for this tired old engine to last until we get to San Arturo, will you?" Matt suggested, appearing in the doorway. "José isn't sure it's going to make it."

"What's wrong?" Kate asked.

"What *isn't* wrong?" He shook his head and dropped onto his former seat on the bench while José returned to his place behind the wheel. The engine started with a noisy protest. To Kate's untrained ears, it sounded as if they'd be lucky if the thing ran for another ten miles.

Maybe she *should* have said her prayers while she was down on her knees, she thought grimly, climbing back onto her own bench between the largest and smallest sleeping babies.

She glanced at her watch. It was nearly 4:00 p.m. She hadn't eaten since breakfast, and that had been only an overripe banana and a cup of coffee. She thought of finishing off the stale cookies, but then decided to save them for the babies in case they got fussy again. "I don't suppose we'll be passing any fast-food restaurants soon."

Matt made a face. "We won't be passing *anything* soon. José just told me we're on an old abandoned logging road. Hardly anyone uses it anymore, but he thought it would be the safest passage for us and the kids. We're a good two days away from anything."

"Oh, terrific. And if the bus breaks down for good while we're two days away from anything?"

"Bite your tongue, Hennessy. I don't even want to think about that right now."

Neither did she. She pushed that worry aside for a more immediate complaint. "I'm hungry."

"José said he has some sandwiches stashed around here somewhere. As soon as he thinks we've gone far enough for safety, we'll stop and have something to eat."

Her mouth watered at the mention of food, but she could see the logic in making sure they were safe before stopping. She'd photographed enough violence in the past few days to know what could happen should they run into a group of power-pumped guerrilla soldiers or drug runners. Americans were hardly their favorite people at the moment—and journalists were even farther down on their lists.

She'd done her job, dutifully recorded the local situation for the edification of safely isolated newsmagazine readers. Now it was time to move on, preferably in the same healthy condition she'd been in when this assignment had begun.

"After we eat, what then?" she asked. She wasn't turning the planning over to Matt, but she'd rather make conversation than sit there brooding about everything that had gone wrong that day—and everything that could still go wrong before she made it onto a plane home.

"Then we get back on the road. José and I agree that we should keep moving. We're going to take shifts driving."

"I can drive, too. I'll take a shift at the wheel."

A fleeting frown crossed his face. "We thought you'd take care of the babies while we handle the driving."

"Think again. I've already made it clear that I'm no expert on babies, nor should you expect me to be just because I happen to be a woman. We'll take shifts driving *and* baby-sitting—is that clear?"

Matt scowled. "I should have known you wouldn't make this ordeal any easier."

"I'll do my share, Sullivan. You just worry about pulling your own weight."

He didn't bother to respond—maybe because she'd left him nothing to say.

It was after six when they finally stopped. The engine had been making such terrible noises that Kate had ridden for the past half hour with her fingers crossed. She breathed a sign of relief when José explained that he'd stopped only because they needed a rest and food. He believed the bus would run again when they were ready to move on, he explained.

Kate's Spanish was poor—strictly high school level—but Matt's was excellent. He served as translator and, to his credit, did so without making Kate feel stupid for not being bilingual herself.

José had pulled the bus to the side of the rutted road. He and Matt disappeared separately into the forest before eating, responding to the demands of nature. Kate needed to go, too, but wasn't too keen on wandering into the brush alone. The sun was setting, and the thick foliage overhead cast long, dense shadows all around them.

Kate looked at one particularly dark shadow and wondered if she saw eyes glaring back at her. She gulped.

"Don't go far, Hennessy," Matt warned, following her gaze. "You never know what's out there."

She briefly debated staying right where she was, but knew she couldn't ignore her bladder forever. She sighed, lifted her chin and made a silent vow that she wasn't going to look like a coward. "Don't worry about me, Sullivan. I can take care of myself."

He snorted and turned away, leaving her to wonder whether he'd been expressing skepticism or was simply annoyed at the knowledge that she was right.

They washed as best they could using sparing amounts of bottled water, and then José dragged a small wicker basket from beneath the driver's seat. Sitting at the end of one of the crowded benches, he opened the basket and pulled out thick sandwiches of sliced ham on homemade bread smeared with spicy mustard. The food had probably been intended to last him for the entire trip, but he generously divided it into three equal portions. He seemed grateful to have Kate and Matt with him.

Kate wondered how in the world José would have managed to drive and take care of the babies by himself for at least two days. Not that she doubted he'd have coped somehow. There was something about the dark little man that made her suspect he usually accomplished whatever he set his mind to doing.

She took a bite of one thick sandwich and almost moaned in pleasure. "Good," she told José when she'd swallowed. *"Bueno."*

He nodded, and what might have been a faint smile fleetingly softened his lined face.

Matt had opened another bottle of distilled water. He took a long swallow and passed it to Kate. "You don't have any communicable diseases, do you, Hennessy?"

"No. You?"

"Not a one."

She nodded and drank from the open bottle, as he had. Satisfied she'd demonstrated that she could be as nonchalant as Matt about handling primitive conditions when necessary, she passed the bottle to José.

The two older babies woke while the adults were finishing their meal. The curly-haired one strained restlessly against the bindings of his car seat. The biggest baby sat still, but expressed displeasure with a few pitiful whimpers.

"They're getting tired of the seats," Kate surmised. "Probably want to stretch a little." She knew the feeling. She was tired of the bus herself. She tried not to think of how many more hours she'd be spending on it.

"Guess we could take them out and walk around with them for a few minutes," Matt suggested. "Maybe after that they'll go back to sleep when we start moving again." He repeated the suggestion in Spanish for José, who nodded and said something back in the same language.

"He's going to look at the engine again while we walk the kids," Matt translated.

Kate stood. "Which one do you want?"

"I'll stick with the little watch-eater," Matt said resignedly. "He and I are starting to communicate, I think."

"He?"

Matt shrugged. "Looks like a boy to me."

"Don't you think we'd better change them now? They have to be soaked."

Matt grimaced. "Yeah. Let's just hope that's all they are."

Kate crossed her fingers again.

Matt dug through the supply boxes while Kate fumbled with the straps of the biggest baby's car seat. He tossed a disposable diaper onto the bench where she'd been sitting. "You change that one. I'll see what I can do with this one."

Kate nodded, relieved that they weren't going to have another argument about who should be handling this particular task. She wouldn't have been at all surprised if Matt had asserted that it was a woman's job to change diapers! He probably would have tried it if he hadn't known exactly how she would have responded.

She moved the baby carefully from the car seat to the bench and peeled away the tape above one chubby thigh.

"I've got a boy," she announced a moment later, removing the saturated diaper.

"Congratulations."

She made a face at Matt's back and slid the fresh diaper under the baby's round bottom. Apparently pleased to be dry and naked, the child kicked and babbled in front of her. She dodged his little feet as she tried to position the diaper. Since the tapes on the other diaper had been fastened back-to-front, she made sure the new one fit the same way. It wasn't easy holding the sides together when the baby kept moving, but she managed, though not as neatly as she would have liked.

"Hey, I was right. This one's a boy, too," Matt said from across the bus.

"Bet the little one's a girl."

Matt glanced at the tiny infant still sleeping in the third car seat. "I think you're right. It looks like a girl. Pretty little thing, isn't it?"

"They all are," Kate commented, glancing from the straight-haired baby lying in front of her to the curly-mopped tot Matt was awkwardly diapering. "I'm sure their adoptive families will be pleased."

"Let's just hope we get them delivered safely."

"We will," Kate said firmly, lifting the squirming little boy again. He settled comfortably against her shoulder, apparently trusting her, a complete stranger, to take care of him. His innocent faith gave her a funny little feeling inside. If she hadn't known herself better, she'd have thought it was a latent maternal instinct showing itself for the first time.

They were ready to leave by seven. As Kate and Matt had hoped, the boys were satisfied—at least temporarily—by the short walk outside and they settled back into the car seats without much protest. The smallest baby woke just as they were about to get on the road again. Kate changed its diaper while Matt and José prepared three bottles of formula. As they'd guessed, the baby was a girl.

"We're outnumbered, kid," Kate murmured as she lifted the child back into her arms. "We'll have to stick together against all these males."

"Don't start indoctrinating her with your feminist chip-on-the-shoulder attitude, Hennessy. She's too young."

"Never too early to start getting prepared for the real world," Kate answered blithely, settling back against the seat. She took the bottle Matt gave her and offered it to the baby, who accepted it eagerly.

Kate and Matt held their breath when José tried to start the bus again. It took three tries, but finally sputtered into life. Kate let out her breath in relief, hearing Matt do the same across the aisle.

Kate held the little girl until she'd finished her bottle, then carefully strapped her back into her seat. Matt had supervised the boys as they'd downed their own formula. All three were soon asleep again.

"The formula may not hold the boys long," Matt warned, glancing at the cases of baby food. "I'll bet they're both on solids by now."

Kate frowned. "Didn't I read somewhere that they're supposed to stay on formula for the first year?"

Matt shrugged. "My niece was eating baby food before she was a year old. Maybe they're supposed to be a year old before they switch to cow's milk."

Kate hated feeling so ignorant. Had she known what to expect, she would have read a few infant-care manuals before she'd left the States. But how could she possibly have ever imagined she'd end up on a bus in the jungle with three infants?

* * *

Sometime in the middle of the night, she woke from a restless sleep to realize that the bus had stopped again. Wearily pushing her bangs out of her eyes, she squinted through the darkness toward the steering wheel. There was no one sitting in the driver's seat. Nor could she find Matt.

She heard some thumping noises coming from the front. Great. Must be another breakdown, she thought glumly.

She stood, deciding to find out for herself just what was going on. The moon was almost full, its colorless illumination making it easy enough for Kate to see her way. The hood of the old bus was open and two male rear ends protruded from beneath. A flashlight glowed between them.

Swatting absently at a small, night-feeding insect, Kate noted—quite objectively, of course—that Matt's rear wasn't at all bad. Lean, tight, firm. His best side, she thought, biting the inside of her lip against a smile.

"What's the prognosis?" she asked.

Matt bumped his head on the hood. "Damn it, don't sneak up on me like that!"

"You're expecting a rear ambush?" she inquired idly, looking over his shoulder at the mysteries of internal combustion. "What's wrong with the engine?" she asked before Matt could respond to her mocking comment.

José said something in Spanish. It didn't sound promising.

Kate looked to Matt for a translation. "Did I hear him use the word 'dead'?" she asked in trepidation.

Matt nodded glumly. "'The engine, she is dead.'"

"Oh, God. Now what?"

Matt exchanged a volley of rapid Spanish with José, who responded with a glum shake of his head and expansive arm motions.

"What?" Kate demanded when Matt turned back to her.

His expression wasn't encouraging. "It's not good."

"Considering the way my day has gone so far, I didn't expect it to be. Okay—what's the plan?"

"First thing in the morning, José goes for help. We stay with the babies."

Kate shoved her hands into the pockets of her jeans and swallowed hard. "How far away is help?"

"By bus, a day and a half or so. On foot—three or four days."

Her breath caught hard in her throat. "There's nothing closer? How could we be that far from anything? We're on a road!"

"A back road," Matt reminded her with a wave of his hand to indicate the potholed dirt road surrounded by dense forest. "There's no civilization for miles, other than the guerrilla-held town we left this afternoon. And neither of us wants to go back there, do we?"

She closed her eyes in a brief spasm of defeat. "No."

And then her eyes opened again. "But how can we take care of three babies on a bus? They can't stay in car seats for three or four days! They're already getting restless when they're awake. We'll all go crazy."

José said something else in Spanish.

Kate waited impatiently for the translation as Matt nodded and replied to the driver's words before turning back to Kate. "There's a house—an abandoned shack, really—a couple of miles from here. José discovered it one night when his car broke down on this road. He was able to fix the car the next morning and make it back to the convent. He says the shack's not much, but it would probably beat staying in the bus. He'll help us get the babies there tomorrow, before he strikes out for help."

"Maybe we should just hike to civilization with José."

"With three babies? You expect them to hike with us?"

"We could each carry one."

"And food? Diapers? Bottles? Formula? Get serious."

Okay, so it was a lousy idea. But the thought of spending three or four days in a run-down shack with Matt Sullivan and three infants had her making desperate suggestions.

Oh, God, why had she taken those last few photos? Why couldn't she have been content with the rolls of film she'd already shot? She could have caught the press bus, would have been on a plane to the States by now.

And Matt would be alone here in the wilderness with three helpless babies. Maybe he deserved it, but the poor kids didn't. She sighed. "All right. What do we do first?"

Matt gave her a nod of guarded approval and turned back to José. They decided to rest until daylight, then push the bus into the forest and do their best to conceal it from casual passersby—not that they expected any for the next few days. This road to nowhere-in-particular was of little interest to either government or leftist forces, since the strategically useful points were along the main roads.

José explained that the old logging road wasn't even utilized for moving illegal drugs, since it wasn't close to water ports or airports. It had originally been used for minor logging operations before the forest in this area had been cleared of almost all the desirable hardwoods, leaving only the less-valuable softwoods behind.

He added that even when he'd broken down the last time here, he'd passed no one for days along this arduous trail that had long been abandoned in favor of the more modern byways. He'd chosen it, he added, only because he enjoyed the solitude.

Kate had already pegged the guy as a loner. Probably in his early fifties, he was small and wiry, with lanky black hair and inscrutable dark eyes set into a lined, expressionless face. "How do we know he'll come back for us?" she asked Matt in a low voice.

"I weel come back for bebees," José said flatly, with no apparent offense at the question.

"I'm sorry," Kate muttered. "I didn't know you spoke English."

"*Un poco.* Seester Maria tell me take care of bebees. I weel come back."

Matt rested his hands on his hips and tapped one booted foot. "If you're satisfied," he said to Kate, apparently annoyed with her for doubting José, "we'd better try and get some rest. We all have a long day ahead of us tomorrow."

Feeling unaccountably contrite, Kate nodded and turned back to the bus.

Chapter Three

The hours until dawn passed slowly and with little rest for any of them. As accustomed as she'd become to sleeping in strange places in her career, Kate had never tried sleeping sitting up on an uncomfortable cracked vinyl bench, with José snoring in the driver's seat, Matt squirming restlessly across the narrow aisle, three babies making funny little noises and occasionally waking with demands to be fed and the sounds of a dark, unfamiliar forest closing in around her. She was heavy-eyed and aching all over by the time the sun finally rose.

Kate, Matt and José each changed and fed a baby before trying to accomplish anything else. Kate didn't complain that the men assumed she would be the one responsible for the tiny girl. She'd found the little one easier to take care of, actually, since it wasn't as active and restless as the bigger boys.

They'd eaten all the sandwiches the night before, but José had a small bag of fruit on hand that they split for breakfast.

"What will we eat until he comes back for us?" Kate asked Matt with some concern. "How are you at trapping food, Sullivan?"

José spoke, and Matt translated. "There's food at the shack. Canned emergency supplies. He says there's enough to last until he comes back for us."

"What about you?" Kate asked José, not certain whether he could understand her. "What will you eat while you're walking for help?"

José shrugged. "I get by."

She had to accept his air of confidence. Obviously he knew this land better than she did.

After breakfast, they strapped the babies into their seats, then went outside to decide what to do about the bus. Although José repeatedly assured them that the chances were slim anyone would be along to disturb the bus before he returned, he agreed that it was probably best to move it off the road and into the brush.

A shallow ditch ran alongside the rough dirt road, clogged with brush and dead wood. Matt and José cleared the area directly in front of the vehicle, then spent nearly an hour pushing the bus into the brush and concealing it as best they could. Kate did her best to help with the bus and with the babies during that hour. All three adults were a bit frazzled by the time they decided they'd done all they could with the bus.

The next task to be faced was the transfer of the babies and their supplies to the shack, which José insisted was approximately two miles deeper into the forest.

"I sure hope he knows what he's talking about," Matt muttered at one point to Kate.

She looked from him to José's calm, unreadable face. "Something tells me he does," she said, hoping her faith in the odd little man was well placed.

It was obvious that they couldn't carry supplies and babies all in one load. They discussed taking the babies first and then having two of them come back for supplies. José vetoed that idea. He wanted to make sure the shack was free of intruders—human or otherwise—before taking the babies there, he insisted.

Kate gulped. "Sounds like a good idea to me. I'll stay with the kids."

Matt snorted. "*Now* you offer to baby-sit."

She cleared her throat and turned her back to him.

After some discussion, Matt and José began to assemble a makeshift litter out of blankets, tree branches and fronds. They piled it as high as they dared with baby supplies, topping the wobbly stack with the folded playpen.

"We'll drag this to the shack and then come back for you and the babies," Matt said to Kate, wiping his sweating forehead with a shirtsleeve.

She could have suggested, of course, that Matt or José stay with the babies while she helped transport supplies, but was rational enough to admit that her smaller size made her a much less effective pack mule than either of the men. And, to be honest, she wasn't enthused about the idea of checking the shack for intruders. Not that she was any more thrilled with the idea of staying here alone with three babies in a broken-down bus.

She sighed at the contradictions. This must have been the way prehistoric women felt when the men ran off to chase food, leaving the women in the cave with the kids!

Matt took a step away, then turned, looking a bit worried. "You'll be all right?"

Her chin lifted. "Of course."

He ran a hand through his hair. "There probably won't be anyone through here to bother you. Even if anyone passes, they'd have to really be looking to see the bus. Still—"

"I can take care of myself, Matt. Now go—we haven't got all day."

"Stay on the bus."

"I will. Give me a break, Sullivan. You don't really think I'd leave the babies alone, do you?"

He didn't look entirely comfortable with the question, which made her mad all over again. Just how low *was* his opinion of her, anyway? "Haul the stuff to the cabin and hurry back here, will you? I'd like to get there sometime before dark."

He nodded curtly and turned to join José at the front end of the precariously stacked load of supplies. Watching their halting, stumbling progress forward, Kate closed her eyes and pressed both hands to her temples. Oh, God, it was going to take them hours to pull that stuff a couple of miles like that. And she was stuck here, alone. . . .

Well, not quite alone.

She looked at the bus and swallowed hard.

It would have been better, as far as she was concerned, if she *had* been alone!

Tired from traveling and the unsettling changes in their routines, the babies slept most of the time the men were gone. The little one woke once, but quieted down when Kate patted it and softly sang the only song that popped into her head at the moment. "Jeremiah Was a Bullfrog" was hardly a classic lullaby, but it worked. She sighed in relief when the button-black eyes closed again.

Kate stretched and checked her watch for about the fiftieth time since Matt and José had disappeared into the jungle. It had been well over an hour. How long would it take to drag the supplies a couple of miles, clear out the cottage and then hike back for her and the kids?

She winced at the knowledge that it could well be another hour before she saw them again. What would she do if the babies all woke at once, wanting to be fed and changed?

Hurry it up, Sullivan.

Just to have something to do to keep her hands busy, she pulled out her camera and snapped a couple of shots of the outside of the bus and then of the babies sleeping inside. She'd need pictures, she decided, when she told this story. If she didn't have proof, her friends would never believe she'd taken care of three babies. She could almost hear their scoffing disbelief now!

Matt's baby came awake with a start and a whimper just as Kate was storing the camera away again. She rushed to his side, patting the curly brown hair, murmuring soothing inanities, doing everything she could think of to keep him from waking the other two. But the baby refused to go back to sleep. Instead, he strained restlessly against the car seat straps, arms extended demandingly toward Kate.

His message was clear. He wanted out.

Swallowing a groan, she loosened the straps and hefted the baby onto her hip. "I can't keep calling you 'Matt's baby,'" she said when the child grasped her shirt and looked her over with friendly curiosity. "Since I don't know what the nuns have been calling you, I guess I'm going to have to come up with something for the next few days. I guess it should be a Spanish name, huh?"

The child grinned, obviously enjoying the attention and just as obviously not understanding a word she was saying. Unconsciously rocking her upper body, Kate kept talking because her voice seemed to hold the baby's interest. "How about Miguel? Carlos? Julio?"

The baby frowned comically.

Kate lifted an eyebrow. "Sorry. My selection of Spanish names is limited. I guess I could call you an American name, instead. It's not like it really matters—in a few days your new family will give you an all-new name. How about Mickey? Or Steve? Or Bubba? No, you don't look like a Bubba."

The baby laughed and stuck his fingers in her mouth as though trying to capture her fascinating voice to examine more closely.

Kate smiled and caught his hand in her own. "I guess I should check your diaper. It's been a while, hasn't it? To be honest, I'm a little afraid of what I might find in there. It isn't easy changing diapers in a bus, especially for someone whose experience is as extremely limited as mine. Let's just hope there's some sort of furniture in the shack. A bed would be nice. A couple of chairs. A table. Hot water..."

Her voice drifted off wistfully.

The baby pulled his hand from hers and grabbed her nose. He was obviously growing restless, ready for more interesting entertainment. And the bigger baby was beginning to stir in his car seat, looking as though he could wake at any minute.

Sullivan, get your butt back here! Quick! I'm out of clever tricks.

Matt pushed past a heavy green frond and increased his speed toward the bus, which he figured was only a couple of hundred yards away. He'd hurried back as quickly as he could, not wanting to leave Kate and the babies alone for any longer than necessary.

Not that he was worried about Hennessy, of course. No woman he knew was more capable of taking care of herself. As for taking care of the babies . . . well, that was another story.

It was with some relief that he found the bus exactly where he'd left it. The door was open, as were the windows that hadn't long since rusted shut. Kate's voice drifted softly toward him—singing? That rather surprised him. Even more surprisingly, she sang very well, her voice pleasant and mellow. No wonder the kids were being so quiet. He was tempted to stop and just listen a minute himself.

And then he heard the words. *Poor boy, you're bound to die.*

"What the hell kind of lullaby is that?" he asked himself with an exasperated shake of his head, hurrying his steps again.

"'Tom Dooley'?" he demanded, ducking through the low doorway into the bus. "You don't know any nice, happy songs?"

Kate looked up with a frown. "It's the only song the kid really likes, okay? I've tried about a hundred others and my repertoire was running out!"

Only then did Matt really look around him. Kate was sitting on the far bench, one leg bent in front of her. The curly-haired baby he'd taken care of earlier was perched on her lap, clutching her T-shirt in chubby hands and bouncing in apparent demand for her to continue singing. The oldest baby was still strapped in his seat, working at a cookie with his two sharp little teeth. The little girl lay in her own seat, looking around in bemused silence as she worked the pacifier in her tiny mouth.

Matt couldn't help grinning. "Looks like you've got everything under control here."

Kate's hair was even more tousled than it had been when he'd left an hour and a half earlier—as though she'd been running her hands through it, or maybe clutching it in her fists. "What took you so long?" she asked in a tone that let him know the peacefulness in the bus had been hard earned.

He shrugged. "It takes a while to drag a makeshift litter of supplies two miles through uncleared jungle."

"Where's José?"

"He's gone. For help," he added when Kate's eyes widened.

"Already?"

"Yeah. He didn't want to waste any more time. I tried to talk him into resting awhile first, but he wouldn't consider it. Said it was too risky for the babies."

"How are we supposed to get them to the house by ourselves?"

"I wouldn't exactly call it a house," Matt muttered, wincing in memory. "A hut, maybe."

Kate closed her eyes and her lips moved silently. Matt guessed she was counting.

Before she'd reached ten, he said, "We'll just have to do our best, Kate. I'll try to carry two of the kids, and you can take the other one. José figured we could handle it. Let's just hope he was right."

The baby on Kate's knee bounced again, imperiously, and said something that could have been a few words of Spanish, or maybe just baby babble. None of it made any sense to Matt.

Kate stood abruptly, unceremoniously pushing the child into Matt's arms. "I'll start getting my stuff together."

Hastily balancing the squirming baby in one arm, Matt lifted an eyebrow. "You can't take much on this trip. Don't forget you'll be carrying a baby. I can come back later for anything else we need.''

He was getting tired, figured he'd be even more so after trying to carry two babies through a couple of miles of forest, but he wasn't about to admit his weariness to Kate. He was, after all, a man.

Kate only nodded and started rummaging in her bags, taking some stuff out of her backpack, replacing it with items from her tote bag and then stuffing her camera in on top of that.

"The camera can wait," Matt protested. "I'll get it later."

She gave him a stubborn look. "I'm not leaving my camera in this bus. I can handle it."

"Look, didn't you hear me earlier? This is not an easy little stroll we're about to make. It's dense forest. It's tough-going. And you'll be carrying a kid."

"I can handle it," she repeated flatly. She pulled the backpack straps over her shoulders as she straightened. "Which baby do you want me to carry?"

"You are the most obstinate, hardheaded, single-minded female I've ever met."

"So you've said before. Now, which baby do you want me to carry?"

Letting out a pent-up breath, Matt shoved the happily babbling child he held back into Kate's arms. "Take this one. I'll get the other two."

Kate settled the baby on her hip with more determination than skill. The baby didn't seem to mind her awkwardness, but gave her a slobbery grin and grabbed her shirt again for balance.

Kate winced, moved one little hand from her breast to a more innocuous position and looked at Matt. "We'd better get started."

Dragging his eyes away from the soft mound the baby had so innocently groped, Matt cleared his throat and turned toward the other two children. "Can you hold the little one in your other arm for a minute while I unbuckle the bigger one?"

"Yes. You know, we're going to have to call them something. This is getting awkward. I tried to think of some names while you were gone, but I couldn't decide."

Matt was working at the buckles on the smallest baby's seat. "Doesn't matter. We'll come up with something later if we need to. After all, we'll be taking care of them for several days."

Kate swallowed a groan, but Matt heard it.

"Looks like we're going to be playing mommy and daddy for at least a few days." He knew he must look as dazed as he felt when he turned to carefully rest the tiny baby in the crook of Kate's free arm. "Weird, huh?"

"You have no idea how weird."

He snorted at her dry tone. "Trust me. I know."

And then he turned back to the bigger baby, who seemed eagerly impatient to be released from his own bindings now that the others had been freed.

Matt sent up a quick prayer to whoever was listening that the helpless babies weren't in more danger now than they would have been had they stayed at the orphanage.

As Matt had warned, it wasn't an easy hike. Beneath the towering, sun-blocking trees, the ground was uneven and covered with snaky vines and roots that lurked in wait for an unsuspectingly misplaced foot. Kate had only made it a hundred yards or so before her back, arms and shoulders began to ache from the combined weight of her backpack and the squirming baby. Her red T-shirt was drenched with perspiration.

She peeked through her lashes at Matt, who carried the older baby on one hip and the little girl in the crook of his other arm. It had to be tough-going for him, Kate thought with a small ripple of sympathy. Especially since he'd already made this trek once.

"Wonder what our friends would say if they could see us now?" she asked, her voice annoyingly breathless.

Matt made a face. "I don't even want to think about it," he admitted. "I still can't believe I'm doing this."

"Has it occurred to you that we sort of got ourselves into this? I mean, it wasn't really necessary for us to ride with José. We could have found other transportation out."

"I guess we could have," he admitted, then looked at the helpless children he carried. "But once I realized that José was planning to transport the kids to San Arturo by himself, I knew I had to ride along and give him a hand. Now I'm glad I did. What would he have done if he'd broken down alone with them?"

Kate cocked her head in surprise, then winced when the little boy she carried promptly twined his chubby fingers in her hair and gave a gleeful tug. "Ouch!"

She disentangled his hand and popped his pacifier into his mouth, hoping it would interest him. He let it fall to dangle from its ribbon again. She didn't even know why this one had been provided with a pacifier. Of the three babies, he was the only one who'd shown absolutely no interest in one.

Remembering what Matt had said, Kate looked at him again as she carefully stepped over a small fallen tree in her path. "I didn't know you were such a good scout, Sullivan. You sound as though you voluntarily missed the press bus just to help José with the kids."

"I didn't, but I would have if I'd had to make the choice," he insisted. "Are you telling me you'd have abandoned the poor guy and taken the easy way out yourself?"

She opened her mouth to tell him she'd have done just that. And then the baby she held rested his head against her shoulder and gave a funny little sigh. Her throat tightened.

Would she have taken the easy way out if given the choice, or would she have been as unselfish as Matt had claimed to be and volunteered her assistance? As disconcerted as she was with her present circumstances, she couldn't bear the thought of anything happening to these babies. They were so little, and helpless, so dependent on the care of even incompetent strangers like herself.

"No," she said with wry insight. "I wouldn't have left them. Given a choice, I'd have had to offer help."

Matt looked oddly pleased—and a bit skeptical. She was well aware that the conversation was only hypothetical now, and that he had good reason to question what she really would have done if faced with a choice. She cleared her throat and shifted the baby to a more comfortable position on her hip. How could the kid have possibly gained at least ten pounds in the past fifteen minutes? Her arms ached, but she trudged on determinedly, trying to ignore the sounds of distant birds and heaven only knew what else calling through the trees.

The baby squirmed, pushing at her hand as though to move it to a more comfortable position on his back. "Please be still," Kate murmured, though she knew the kid didn't understand her. She certainly didn't want to drop him—or worse, fall on top of him!

Struggling to balance the two he carried, Matt glanced over at her. "You okay, Hennessy?"

She nodded grimly. "Fine." She didn't have enough breath to say anything else now.

The smallest baby had begun to cry. Matt made clucking noises and started walking a bit faster. Kate swallowed hard and picked up her own pace, placing her feet as carefully as she could to avoid a stumble.

She hoped that guardian angel of journalists was making note of Kate's first totally noble and unselfish behavior in quite some time.

She'd never been so glad to see anything as she was the shack, though to call it a cabin—or even a hut—was being generous. It was little more than a pile of splintered boards, but Kate didn't care what it looked like as long as she could get inside, drop the backpack, put down the baby and get off her aching feet for even a few blessed minutes.

All three babies were fussing now, tired and uncomfortable. Kate knew just how they felt. She ached all over, as though she'd been systematically beaten with heavy clubs. She felt as though she'd been walking for days, though it could only have been just over an hour since they'd left the bus. Matt didn't look to be in much better shape than she was.

She followed Matt through the shack's flimsy door. There was only one window, and that one so filthy that very little light penetrated the glass. The heavy shadows made the primitive, one-room hut look even gloomier than it should have. The only furnishings appeared to be a cot shoved against one wall, and a lopsided table and two rickety chairs in the center of the dirty hardwood floor.

Matt directed Kate to the cot, and instructed her to sit on the bare mattress with the babies while he lit the lantern sitting on the table.

There was a scrape of a match, the acrid smell of sulfur, and the lantern flared to life. Kate gulped at what it more clearly illuminated.

Okay, she thought with an attempt at optimism. So it wasn't the Ritz. It was shelter, a place to keep the babies safe until they were rescued. She couldn't—shouldn't—complain.

Matt stood in the middle of the floor, looking around with a deprecating expression, his thoughts obviously echoing hers. He met her eyes across the room. "Well..."

"It'll do," she assured him.

He nodded. "Yeah. Better than the bus, anyway."

"Right."

She looked from the lantern to the stacks of canned goods lining a couple of shelves that served as a pantry in the corner designated as a kitchen. A small, wood-burning stove and a rusty sink—no faucets—were the only kitchen furnishings. "Was José the one who left the lantern and the food here?"

Matt nodded. "Apparently, since discovering this place, José has been the only one to use it. He said he keeps it stocked with food and lantern fuel, and comes here occasionally when he wants to spend a few days alone—his vacation home, I guess. He told us to use anything we need until he comes back."

Kate was still looking at that faucetless sink as she thought of how dirty she was. Her vague fantasies of a hot shower seemed rather silly at the moment. "No water?"

"There's a well. The water is drawn from a hand pump out back. By the way, that's where the bathroom is, too. Out back. Let's just say it's, uh, primitive."

"Great."

She took a deep breath, then patted the smallest baby, who was still fussing. The other two were busy looking around at their new surroundings. The curly-haired one moved as though to climb off the cot. Kate reached out with her free hand. "We'd better change these diapers. They're soaked."

"I don't suppose you'd, uh . . ."

"No way, Sullivan. Haul it over here and help me."

Matt muttered, but pulled disposable diapers out of the pile of supplies he and José had brought from the bus and joined her at the bed. He caught the oldest baby, who was moving toward the edge. "Whoa, partner. Let's get that diaper changed first," he said.

"What part of Texas are you from, Matt?" Kate asked idly, pushing the hem of the little blue T-shirt higher on the baby's round tummy to give her better access to the tapes of the wet diaper.

"San Antonio. Haven't been back for a while, though." Matt was having a bit of trouble getting the biggest baby to lie still.

"You live in D.C. now, don't you?"

"Most of the time. Come on, kid, give me a break here. How am I supposed to change you when you're wiggling like a worm in hot ashes?"

There was no more time just then for conversation. Kate sighed, wondering how long it would be before she and Matt were back at each other's throats. Given the circumstances, she figured it was inevitable.

Chapter Four

When all the diapers were changed, Kate lifted the curly-haired, middle baby onto her lap. "I've decided to call this one Tommy," she announced.

The baby smiled as though in approval of her choice.

"Tommy?" Matt repeated. He'd been strolling around the shack, exploring the meager interior, the bigger baby balanced on his hip. In response to Kate's words, he turned to look at her. "Why Tommy?"

"He likes 'Tom Dooley,' remember? Besides, we have to call them something."

"Hmm." Matt sounded distracted again. He was studying the stacks of canned goods on the narrow shelves, a look of distaste on his face. And then he glanced back toward Kate. "Not much to choose from over here. But I guess we won't starve."

"That's all that counts, I suppose."

The baby Matt held jabbered a few syllables and then grinned as if proud of himself for articulating. Matt smiled automatically in response. "What are we going to call this one?" he asked Kate. "Any particular song he preferred?"

"Hmm." Kate thought about it a moment, studying the baby's straight black hair and serious dark eyes. "Charlie," she said finally.

Matt lifted an eyebrow. "Charlie?"

"He looks a little like a miniature Charlie Sheen, don't you think?"

Skeptically, Matt looked down at the baby. "If you say so. What about the girl?"

"Maria. After the sister who made José promise to get them to safety."

"That'll work."

The child she'd dubbed Tommy started to fuss, squirming in Kate's lap and making it difficult to hold him. Little Maria spat out her pacifier and whimpered, tiny fists flailing. As though prompted by the others, even more placid-natured Charlie started to look unhappy.

"I think they're hungry," Kate said.

"Yeah. I know the feeling." Matt looked across the room to the stack of baby supplies he and José had piled in one corner. "Maybe we should try feeding the boys some baby food this time. I don't think the formula is satisfying them."

"You're probably right. The only solid food they've had in the past twenty-four hours is cookies, and that's hardly healthy for them."

Matt nodded and moved toward the boxes. "I'll feed Charlie, you take Tommy and then one of us will give Maria a bottle while the other supervises the boys."

She smiled at how easily he'd reeled off her spur-of-the-moment names. "Your turn to feed Maria," she reminded him, remembering the unpleasant aftermath of the earlier feeding.

He shrugged and began to dig through the pile of supplies. They agreed that applesauce and strained carrots seemed like a nourishing meal, even though the carrots would have to be served at room temperature, since neither of them was ready to tackle the wood stove as yet.

"What?" Kate asked, bouncing Tommy on her knee in a futile attempt to entertain him until dinner. "No microwave?"

"Very funny," Matt commented without looking at her as he rummaged around in the boxes and then in the meager kitchen supplies. "I can't find any spoons."

"José doesn't have any here?"

"I've found a couple of forks and a knife and two large serving spoons. Nothing that would fit safely in a baby's mouth."

"There were none in the baby supplies?"

"If so, they're still on the bus."

Tommy was chewing on his fist now, looking very unhappy. Kate bit her lip. "What are we going to do?"

Charlie had started to cry. Matt offered the pacifier still dangling from the ribbon on his shirt, but the baby refused it.

Matt balanced the hungry child against his shoulder as he struggled to open a jar of applesauce. "We'll dip it out with our fingers. I'll try to find something to use for spoons later."

"Our fingers? Matt, that's gross."

Tommy added his wail to Charlie's. Maria whimpered again.

Matt thrust Charlie into Kate's arms. "Here, you hold him while I wash my hands. Then I'll watch them while you do the same. It's the best we can do, Kate."

While Kate wrestled with the two unhappy, wriggling boys, Matt washed his hands with some of the bottled water and a bar of hard soap he found by the sink. Then he took Kate's place on the bed while she washed up.

"I'll do applesauce, you get the carrots," he said when she rejoined him.

She watched as he dipped two fingers into the jar of applesauce and scooped a glob into Charlie's open mouth. The baby blinked, stopped crying and swallowed before eagerly opening his mouth again.

Tommy was still crying. Kate took a deep breath, coated two fingers with strained carrots—ugh, that felt disgusting!—and filled Tommy's mouth. He sputtered a moment, making her worry that he wasn't ready for solid food after all, but then he licked his orange-stained lips and looked at her as though to request more. She offered another scoop and he gummed it contentedly.

"They *were* hungry," she said in relief.

Matt nodded, still shoveling applesauce into Charlie's mouth, and making a nice mess of it, Kate noted critically. And then Tommy gurgled and a mouthful of orange goo spattered the front of Kate's T-shirt.

She groaned. Matt chuckled wickedly.

Maria continued to cry, but they had to ignore her for the moment. Kate promised the baby that she'd get a bottle as soon as the boys were fed. Maria wasn't notably appeased.

Kate and Matt switched babies when the baby food jars were half-empty, offering the boys the second courses of their decidedly casual meal. "Ouch!" Kate yelped when

Charlie's two sharp little teeth closed over the end of her finger. "That hurt."

"Gotta be faster than that, Hennessy. The kid's quick."

"Hasn't anyone ever warned you about biting the hand that feeds you, kid?" Kate asked Charlie, who only grinned and blew a carrot-tinted saliva bubble at her.

Maria had worked herself into a true tantrum by the time the baby food jars were empty. Matt quickly mixed up three bottles of formula. He fed Maria while Kate supervised the boys, who held their own bottles, their dark eyes drooping sleepily as they nursed.

The bottle finally emptied, Matt burped Maria—who, Kate noted in resignation, kept the formula down this time—then handed her to Kate so he could set up the folding playpen to use as a baby bed. He padded the vinyl bottom with one of the four worn blankets he and José had brought with the litter.

"Will it be big enough for all three of them?" Kate asked with a frown, looking at the mesh-and-vinyl cage.

"It'll hold the boys," Matt answered. "I don't want to put Maria in here with them. One of them might hurt her."

He scratched his chin as he glanced around the room, then set to work making a pallet on the floor next to the playpen. He folded one of the remaining blankets for a pad, and surrounded it with formula boxes to keep the baby from rolling off the blanket.

"She's too little to crawl, so this should contain her," he explained for Kate's benefit.

Kate nodded absently; she had already begun to wonder about her own sleeping arrangements. There was only one bed. Would Matt offer to join Maria on the floor?

Tommy was already asleep, and Charlie growing heavy-eyed. Matt transferred them carefully to the playpen, where they snuggled into the blanket-covered bottom without another peep. "With the lives they've led so far, they must be used to adjusting to new situations," Matt remarked, looking down at the sleeping babies with a thoughtful expression.

Kate nodded. "Poor things. I wonder what happened to their parents."

He shrugged. "Who knows? But José was certain that good families are waiting for all three of them. He said Sister Maria was very happy about it."

Kate cradled the nun's temporary namesake closer to her breast. "Then we'll just have to see that they make it safely to San Arturo, won't we?" she said, trying to sound matter-of-fact.

Matt looked at her in what might have been faint approval. "Yeah. I guess we will."

Their gazes held for a moment, and then Kate looked down at the baby again, suddenly feeling inexplicably self-conscious.

Matt cleared his throat and moved back toward the shelves of canned goods. He rummaged among the battered-looking stacks of cans, his eyebrow lifting as he pulled out a clear bottle filled with a dark amber liquid. Screwing off the cap, he took a sniff, then choked, his eyes watering.

"Whew! I don't know if José drinks this or cleans with it, but it's strong stuff." He replaced the bottle where he'd found it. "How about if I open a can of pork and beans for our lunch?"

"Yeah, sure. I'm hungry enough to eat whatever you find over there. I'll even eat it with my fingers, if necessary."

"That won't be necessary. We'll use José's forks."

Maria was sleeping soundly, so Kate stood very carefully and laid her on the pallet Matt had arranged. She let out a breath of relief when the baby settled into the blanket without waking.

Matt had found a crank-style can opener. He fumbled with the can, but managed to open it and split the contents into two battered tin bowls. "Wonder why José has two of everything," he said. "Think he brings his lady friends here sometimes?"

Kate made a face. "If so, I can't imagine he has many dates. This isn't exactly the most elegant romantic retreat I've seen."

"Seen a lot of romantic retreats, have you, Hennessy?"

She frowned expressively at him. "That's really none of your business, Sullivan."

"Hmm . . ." A note of amusement underlined the exaggeratedly nonchalant murmur.

Matt moved the lantern from the table and placed it on the stove to give them room to eat. The gaslight glowed brightly in the kitchen area, but faded into deep shadows in the corners of the hut. Kate filled two dilapidated tin cups with bottled water. She hadn't realized how thirsty she was until she took a sip.

"Do you think the water from the well is safe to drink?" she asked, thinking that they probably needed to conserve the bottled water for the babies.

"José probably drinks it," Matt answered. "But I don't think we should. There were several cases of bottled water in the bus. We should be okay as long as José doesn't encounter any problems in getting back to us."

The ugly possibility of José's not returning at all slithered into Kate's mind, but she refused to acknowledge it. She couldn't even bear to think about it. Instead, she concentrated on the meal, such as it was, scooping up cold, rather gelatinous pork and beans with the bent fork. She was hungry enough that they actually tasted pretty good.

Funny, she thought as a silence grew between her and Matt. There was an odd intimacy about dining together by lantern light, with the sounds of the forest and three sleeping babies for background.

She glanced at Matt through her lashes. The lantern light was kind to him, bringing out highlights in his dark brown hair, adding interesting shadows to his lean, tanned face. He looked tired, grubby and unshaven, but most women would probably think he was sexy as hell at the moment.

Unfortunately, Kate thought so, too. Which, she decided firmly, only proved that the stress of this misadventure was getting to her.

They rinsed the tin bowls with a little more of the bottled water. Afterward, Matt brought in a bucket of well water, explaining that it should be safe enough to use for washing if they boiled it first. He looked dubiously at the wood stove.

Kate had other things on her mind. "I don't suppose there's a light in the outhouse," she said.

"Nope. But it shouldn't be too dark inside during the daytime. There's no door to block the sunlight."

She groaned.

"Don't worry, Hennessy, you'll have plenty of privacy. I'll stay inside, and there aren't any other humans for miles. I can't guarantee you won't be watched by any four-legged voyeurs, of course."

She glared at him. "Oh, thanks so much for reassuring me!"

He chuckled. "Want me to escort you? I promise I'll turn my back."

It was tempting, but she shook her head. She'd been using the forest as a bathroom for the past twenty-four hours or so. How much worse could the outhouse be?

She returned in less than five minutes.

Crouched in front of the stove, Matt looked up when she closed the cabin door behind her with more haste than entirely necessary. "That was quick," he commented, grinning.

She made a face. "I didn't want to stay out there any longer than necessary. That outhouse is disgusting."

"I said it was primitive."

"You weren't giving it full credit."

He ignored her sarcastic tone and stood to rummage through the kitchen area again. "I hope José has some . . . oh, good. Here they are." He plucked a box of matches from behind the stack of canned goods.

"He really is a strange little guy, isn't he? I mean, using this dump as a retreat, keeping it stocked this way. I wonder if he has a family."

"He didn't say. I got the impression the guy's a real loner."

"Yeah. So did I. You *do* think he'll come back for us, don't you?" she asked, trying to sound only casually interested.

"He'll be back," Matt answered confidently. "He seemed almost fanatically loyal to the nuns."

"Maybe he considers *them* his family," Kate said, watching as Matt struggled to light the first match.

"Could be. Hope it doesn't get too hot in here with this stove burning."

"We could always turn on the air-conditioning."

"Funny, Hennessy. Damn, that match was a dud."

"Do you know what you're doing, Sullivan? Have you ever started a fire in a wood-burning stove before?"

"I've built plenty of fires," he answered defensively. "In fireplaces. Couldn't be all that different."

"You think not?" But Kate decided to let him find out for himself. She straddled one of the chairs and rested her elbows on the table, her chin propped on her hands.

Matt struck another match, stuck it into the kindling stuffed into the stove, then cursed when it promptly went out. "Do you have to sit there staring at me, Hennessy?" he asked crossly.

"Nothing else to stare at," she replied. "Want any help?"

"No. I can do it."

"Fine." She smiled to herself.

A moment later, Matt cursed again. "Damn it, why won't this fire start? Maybe the wood's too green."

"Sullivan, that wood has probably been sitting there for months. It's not green."

"Then the stove's broken."

She shook her head in disgust. "Why can't a man ever admit that there are some things he just doesn't know how to do?" She shoved the chair away from the table and stood. "Move out of the way. I'll light the stove."

"What makes you think you can do this any better than I can?"

"Just move," she said, thinking longingly of clean skin, teeth and clothing. If she waited for Matt to light the stove, she'd never have a chance to wash up!

Five minutes later, the stove was sending waves of heat through the tiny cabin. "I'll be damned," Matt said, hands on his hips as he stared at her. "How'd you do that?"

"My grandmother cooked on a wood-burning stove until my father threatened to put her in a nursing home if she didn't join the modern world and start using electricity," Kate admitted. "She lived alone on a mountain in

Colorado, in a cabin not a whole lot fancier than this one. She died in her sleep at the age of ninety. She was a tough old bird. Pioneer stock. Strong and stubborn and fiercely independent.''

"Sounds familiar," Matt muttered.

"I'll take that as a compliment. I always wanted to be like Granny Hennessy."

She dipped water into a badly dented tin pan and set it on the stove to boil. "You'd better open the door. It's going to get hot in here with this stove burning."

It took a while to boil water and then let it cool enough for bathing. In the meantime, Kate pulled clean under-things, T-shirt and pants out of her backpack, wondering how she was going to wash her hair. She supposed she could always hold her head over the sink and pour water over it, using one of the tin cups. Fortunately, there were a couple of travel-size shampoo bottles in her pack.

The boys were awake again by the time there was enough cooled water to satisfy her. They seemed content enough to remain in the playpen, Tommy with the battered teddy bear Matt had found on the bus the day before, Charlie playing with a colorful rubber Mickey Mouse figure that had been packed with the baby clothes.

Kate had assumed that Matt would wait outside while she washed and changed. She wondered if they could set the playpen outside, as well. She didn't mind having Maria inside, but the thought of stripping in front of Tommy and Charlie made her uncomfortable.

"Feeling shy, Hennessy?" Matt teased when she made the suggestion to him.

She set her jaw and refused to take the bait, knowing he was getting his revenge over the stove incident.

He exhaled through his nose and moved toward the playpen. "Okay. You watch the kids while I set this up outside."

She nodded, relieved that he wasn't going to give her a hard time about it.

Maria had fallen asleep on her pallet, so they didn't disturb her. Promising Matt that she would hurry, Kate closed the cabin door. She gratefully peeled off her dirty, carrot-splattered clothes and set to work with the hard soap, toothpaste and shampoo.

Lacking anything better, she was forced to use her discarded T-shirt as a towel. She then tugged on her clean clothing, noting with resignation that the cotton shirt clung to her still-damp skin.

Oh, well, she thought with a shrug. She was wearing a bra. Not that Sullivan would have noticed either way. She could well have been just one of the guys from the way he'd been treating her. Which, she assured herself hastily, was exactly the way she wanted it.

Making sure that Maria was still sleeping, Kate carried her comb outside with her. Matt sat in a patch of sunlight, carving on something with his pocketknife while the boys watched with apparent interest from the playpen.

"What are you making?" Kate asked, leaning over his shoulder.

"Spoons. Sort of."

He showed her how he'd cut a small plastic aspirin bottle into long, narrow scoops. They didn't look like spoons, but Kate agreed they'd work as well, or better, than fingers. "You didn't leave any sharp edges?" she asked.

He frowned at her lack of faith in him, but ran his thumb over all the edges to demonstrate that he'd left them smooth. "They'll need to be washed, of course, to get rid of any aspirin residue."

She sat beside the playpen, then started pulling the comb through her short, wet hair. "You'll have to heat some more water if you want to wash up," she said when Matt rose to go inside. "I used it all."

His jaw twitched and he shot her a glare, but he refrained from commenting.

Kate smiled to herself after he went inside. She'd thought about putting fresh water on to heat for him, but then she'd remembered his cutting, uncalled-for comments about her.

She'd always made it a practice to live up to the expectations of others.

Dinner was a can of unappetizing beef stew they heated on the stove before putting out the fire for the night. Kate thought it was one of the more revolting meals she'd ever eaten, but she kept her complaints to herself.

Griping wouldn't help anything, she decided, and this ordeal was no easier for Matt, who was managing to keep his complaints to himself. She could at least do the same.

They fed the babies their bottles, then put them down for the night, the boys in the playpen, Maria on her pallet. Kate let out a sigh of relief when all three settled into sleep. "At least they're down for the night," she murmured. "I can't remember when I've ever needed a good night's sleep this badly."

She had to make another trip to the outhouse before turning in. She opened the cabin door and looked out into the dark night. The looming trees and animal sounds gave an eerie quality to her surroundings, making her reluctant to walk outside alone.

She almost swallowed her pride and demanded that Matt go out there with her. But then she squared her shoulders and told herself not to be stupid. Clutching the flashlight Matt had given her, she stepped outside into the darkness.

She wasn't gone longer than necessary. Matt moved toward the door when she came back in. "I'll be back in a minute."

"Want the flashlight?"

He shook his head. "We'd better conserve the batteries as much as possible."

Kate checked the babies while Matt was outside. They were still sleeping deeply. She wondered when they'd need to be changed again. It had only been an hour since the last time, she reasoned. Surely they'd be okay during the night. She certainly wouldn't want to disturb their much-needed rest—or hers—just to check diapers.

And then she turned toward the solitary bed. Now, about *her* sleeping arrangements.

Matt came back inside and closed the door behind him. "No lock," he commented, glancing at the simple latch closure.

She shrugged. "Who'd be out there to break in?"

"Let's hope you're right." He moved toward the bed, sat on the edge and tugged off his boots. And then he looked curiously at Kate, who was still standing in the middle of the room. "Aren't you tired?"

"I'm exhausted. Uh—"

He glanced from her to the bed and back again. "Look," he said wearily, "I'm too tired to worry about social niceties tonight, and the floor's full. I'm sleeping on the bed, and I suggest you share it with me. I can assure you you'll be perfectly safe from me."

Something in his tone made her chin go up defensively. "You don't worry me, Sullivan. And I'm too tired to bother with a lot of coy foolishness. I expect you to treat me as just another journalist—another one of the guys."

"Yeah," Matt muttered, rolling onto his back on the bed, fully dressed. "Somehow I figured you'd say something like that."

She snorted and sat in a chair to unlace and remove her boots. She left her socks on. "What about the lantern?"

"Blow it out. I've got the flashlight within reach so we can check on the kids during the night."

The cabin lay in complete darkness when the lantern was extinguished. Kate made her way carefully to the bed, feeling with her hands to establish her location.

"Ouch! You poked your finger in my eye, Hennessy."

"So move over," she said unrepentantly, sliding onto the bed. She lay on her side, back to Matt, and pillowed her head on one curled arm. It felt strange to share a bed, when she'd long been accustomed to sleeping alone. But she was tired enough by now to sleep soundly on a bed of nails.

Soft baby snoring was coming from the direction of the playpen. Kate smiled sleepily and closed her eyes. It had been a long time since she'd been this tired, she thought, feeling her aching muscles slowly starting to relax. Tomorrow she'd be rested and refreshed and ready to face Matt Sullivan and their three tiny charges again.

Tomorrow, she thought, already drifting into unconsciousness.

Chapter Five

Morning did *not* find Kate rested and refreshed. She was little more than a glassy-eyed zombie by the time weak sunlight filtered through the cabin's one grimy window. If only she had known, she thought blearily, that babies didn't actually *sleep*. They dozed. Briefly. Waking every few hours to be fed, changed or comforted.

It had usually been Maria who woke first, wailing and sucking her little fist to indicate her desire for a bottle. Her crying, in turn, had awakened the boys, who'd decided that they, too, wouldn't mind a midnight snack. And a two o'clock one. And a four o'clock one.

Looking as haggard as Kate felt, Matt sat at the table, clutching his head and moaning while Kate fed Maria yet another bottle. Having just polished off jars of baby oatmeal—fed to them with Matt's makeshift spoon—the boys were in the playpen, Charlie playing with his toes, Tommy with the ragged teddy bear.

"What I wouldn't give for a cup of coffee," Matt groaned. "How do parents survive this stage?"

Stifling a yawn, Kate shrugged, jostling the nursing baby. "It's got to be easier having just one at a time. Not that I intend to find out for a long time. If ever," she added darkly, remembering the long, harrowing hours of the night.

"Just as well," Matt muttered from behind his hands. "I can't imagine any woman less suited to marriage and motherhood."

The comment stung. Hadn't she been coping just as well as he had with these three babies? Okay, so she wasn't June Cleaver or Carol Brady. But she hadn't actually done any harm, either. "I could really use some coffee," Matt said again a few minutes later, during which Kate had sat in sullen silence. "And breakfast. Eggs, ham, biscuits."

"A hot shower," Kate added wistfully, lifting Maria to her shoulder, which she'd prudently covered first with a scrap of terry cloth that might have started life as a dish towel. She'd found it in the rough cabinet under the sink. It was ragged and threadbare, but had looked clean enough to serve as a burp cloth. "Scented soap. Fresh fruit."

"A hot tub," Matt murmured, then rubbed his bristly chin. "A barber shave. Eight hours of sleep. Coffee."

Their gazes met across the table in a rare moment of agreement. Maria's resonant belch made them look away, smiling self-consciously.

Matt sighed. "What do you want for breakfast? We have canned fruit, canned soup, canned stew or canned beans."

She shuddered. "Canned fruit, I guess."

He pushed himself to his feet. "I'll get us some."

"Need help?"

He shook his head. "You baby-sit. To be honest, I'm glad to have something to do to take my mind off coffee."

"You're an addict, Sullivan," she accused him, though her mouth was all but watering for caffeine—coffee, tea, cola, she wouldn't have cared which.

"I know," he growled. "And I'm in bad need of a fix."

Kate moved to the bed to change Maria's diaper. "Yuck," she said, finding an unpleasant surprise. "Maybe you and I should change jobs," she said, watching Matt wielding the can opener.

He glanced her way, then wrinkled his nose. "Too late, Hennessy. I've already started . . . and so have you." He turned to lift something from the table. "Here, catch."

She deftly fielded the soft pack of premoistened disposable cleaning cloths he lobbed at her. "Thanks a lot, Sullivan."

He ignored her sarcastic tone. "You're welcome."

A few messy moments later, she returned the freshly changed baby to the barricaded pallet, then carried the soiled diaper to the box they'd set outside the cabin door for that purpose. Matt had set the bowls of fruit on the table and was pouring water into the tin cups.

Tommy started to fuss, wanting attention. Kate turned to look at him, then said in surprise, "Matt, look at Charlie!"

Matt glanced around. Charlie was standing on his little bare feet, clinging to the side of the playpen and watching them over the top, his double chin propped on the padded rail. "Well, I'll be damned. Did he do that by himself?"

"Yes, he must have. Looks like he'll be walking soon."

"He's pretty young to be walking, isn't he?"

"We don't know how old he *is*," she reminded him, lifting the fretting Tommy out of the pen. "And I'd bet you don't know any more than I do when babies are supposed to start walking."

"True," he conceded.

Holding Tommy on her knee, Kate ate her fruit with the dented fork in her free hand. Though he'd already had his own breakfast, Tommy seemed very interested in hers. She stopped occasionally to feed him a tiny bit.

"Don't let him choke," Matt warned. "Remember, he doesn't have any teeth."

"I'm aware of that, Sullivan. Give me a little credit, will you?"

He surprised her by apologizing. "Sorry. Lack of sleep and caffeine is making me surly."

She blinked, surprised by his sudden conciliation. "Oh. Well, that's okay."

He turned his attention back to his fruit. Kate wondered if sleep and caffeine deprivation actually *improved* his attitude. After all, he'd never apologized to her before for snapping at her—and heaven only knew he'd snapped at her plenty of times. She prudently kept the thought to herself. If Matt could make an effort to get along, so could she.

At least until the next time he annoyed her.

The babies kept Kate and Matt very busy this morning. It seemed as though something always had to be done with them.

They bathed them all as best they could, using dampened rags, more premoistened towelettes and the one hard bar of soap. They dressed them in diapers and clean T-shirts. Kate could see why the shirts had been selected as the most practical garments, since they couldn't be too selective about size. Charlie's was a bit snug and Maria's long enough to look like a nightgown, but they'd do.

Though Kate and Matt had agreed that they needed to conserve diapers as much as possible, it still seemed that one or the other of the babies always needed to be changed. Neither Kate nor Matt minded the wet diapers too badly; the dirty ones, however, caused some squabbling over whose turn it was to take care of the smelly situation.

Matt developed a caffeine-withdrawal headache during the afternoon. Kate dug over-the-counter painkillers out of her pack and offered him two, which he accepted with rather surprising gratitude. Feeling particularly generous just then, Kate even urged him to lie down for a few minutes to allow the painkillers to take effect.

She entertained herself for the next half hour by watching the babies and making personal observations about each of them. It intrigued her that even children so young had developed such different personalities.

Black-haired, black-eyed Charlie was quiet, rather serious. He studied everything around him with such intensity that Kate couldn't help but wonder what he was thinking. He seemed to enjoy standing in the playpen, watching Kate and Matt moving around the cabin. His pacifier was usually stuck in his mouth, and he worked it idly as he took in his surroundings. Kate found herself going out of her way to amuse him, and then feeling a funny, warm feeling inside when her efforts were rewarded with sweet, innocent smiles.

Tommy, on the other hand, was a restless bundle of energy. He couldn't stand as well as Charlie, though he was working hard to learn to pull himself up. He crawled around the playpen, wrestled with the teddy bear for brief interludes and then demanded adult attention. Kate knew Tommy would just love to get down on the floor and explore every inch of the cabin, but she was reluctant to place him on the grubby surface that was probably full of nasty splinters to pierce a baby's delicate skin.

Little Maria slept a good deal, but was a sweet baby when she was awake, with her funny facial expressions and jerky head movements. She, too, elicited odd feelings from Kate, especially when she snuggled her little face into Kate's chest and went to sleep after taking a bottle. Maybe she had more maternal instincts than she'd ever actually suspected, Kate mused at one point. Not that she'd mention that discovery to Sullivan, of course. He'd never let her live it down.

Some forty-five minutes after he'd fallen asleep, Matt came awake with a visible start. Kate had been sitting in one of the chairs, holding Maria, and had seen Matt's confusion upon awakening. She smiled. "Forget where you were, Sullivan?"

He yawned and stretched, then swung his feet over the side of the cot and sat up. "Something like that," he admitted.

"Headache better?"

He moved his head experimentally, one hand at the back of his neck. "Yeah," he said after a moment. "Much better. Guess I needed that nap. Thanks, Hennessy."

"No prob. The kids have been good."

He smiled at her, and Kate had to look away, turning her attention back to Maria. Something about that particular smile of Matt's made her react in a manner she'd just as soon hide from him. With his oversize ego, he'd probably think she was just like the other silly women who went all mushy at the sight of his killer smile.

Matt stood and rummaged around the cabin for a while, searching through the canned goods and bits and pieces of junk José kept in the shadowed corners of the room. He seemed pleased when he found an old, rusty can half filled with equally rusty nails. A few minutes later, Kate and the boys watched curiously as he climbed carefully onto one of the rickety chairs and, using a block of wood as his hammer, drove several nails into the ceiling.

"What in the world are you doing, Sullivan?"

He tossed her a grin over his shoulder. "Building walls."

She lifted an eyebrow. "Is that right?"

"Just wait." He leapt lightly off the chair and reached for the last unused blanket. With the use of the chair again, he hung the blanket from the bent nails. The rather threadbare blanket obscured the view of the bed from the rest of the cabin, providing a sense of privacy.

"Now you can change your clothes without me having to take the boys outside," he said with a rather sheepish half smile, motioning toward his makeshift "wall."

She found his gesture uncharacteristically sweet. Still mindful of that ego of his, she didn't tell him so, but simply nodded and said, "Thanks."

"You're welcome." And then he turned to respond to a babble from Tommy, and the brief moment of personal communication was over.

Having gotten so little sleep the night before, Kate and Matt were both exhausted again by the time all three babies were bedded down that night.

"How long do you think they'll sleep?" Kate asked in little more than a whisper.

Matt made a face and ran a hand through his tousled dark hair. "Judging from last night—two or three hours. Four, if we really managed to wear them out today."

"Hmmph. They're the ones who do the wearing out, not the other way around."

Matt smiled wearily. "True. So, are you ready to turn in?" They'd already eaten, having shared a can of stew that had been only marginally edible, even though they'd taken time to heat it.

Kate glanced at the bed. Last night she'd been too bushed to quibble much at sharing the narrow mattress, but now she found herself fighting an attack of self-consciousness at the thought of crawling back in beside Matt.

She cleared her throat and spoke brusquely to conceal her reaction. "Almost. I need to go outside for a few minutes first."

He nodded. "The flashlight's on the table."

She spent part of the short time while she was outside lecturing herself about retaining her objectivity where Matt Sullivan was concerned. Okay, she thought, so they were sharing a cabin—and, incidentally, a bed—for a couple of days. It wasn't as if they had any choice. God or fate or sheer coincidence had made them miss that press bus and end up on the ill-fated orphanage bus, and now the welfare of three helpless infants rested in their hands.

The fact that she and Matt had gotten along relatively well during the past two days could be explained easily enough. They'd been too busy with the kids to waste much time arguing with each other. Had they been stranded in this same cabin *alone* for several days—well, it would have been completely different, she reasoned, picking her way carefully around the outside of the cabin with the beam of the flashlight to guide her. Matt would have long since succumbed to LWS—Little Woman Syndrome—at which point, Kate would have been forced to hurt him. Simple as that.

She nodded decisively, but unwisely took her eyes off her path when she did so. Her right foot caught against something heavy and immovable. She fell heavily to her knees on the hard, damp ground, and the still-burning flash-

light rolled away from her as she landed with a choked cry
of surprise and pain.

The door to the cabin opened abruptly. "Kate? You
okay?"

"Yeah," she answered, thoroughly disgusted with herself. "Just fell over something."

"Damn. I hope you didn't break the flashlight," Matt
fretted, picking it up to check for damages.

"Well, thanks so much for your concern," Kate muttered indignantly, shoving herself rather clumsily to her
feet.

The flashlight illuminating his face, Matt lifted a quiz-
zical eyebrow. "You said you were okay, Hennessy," he
pointed out. "Unless you were hoping I'd rush out and
carry you solicitously inside?" he added, his tone blandly
mocking.

She flushed. Now *that* sounded more like the Matt Sullivan she'd come to know and dislike. "No! I certainly did
not want that," she informed him a bit too vehemently.
"In fact, you'd have been walking funny if you'd tried it."

"So what's the problem?"

"Nothing," she answered haughtily. "I'm going to bed
now." She swept past him toward the cabin door, her re-
gal manner a bit diminished by an awkward limp.

"I'll be in in a minute."

"Take your time," she muttered, firmly closing the door
behind her. "In fact, take the whole damned night."

But she knew he wouldn't, of course. She might as well
face it. She was about to spend another night in bed with
Matt Sullivan, annoying male that he was.

Her palms were dirty and scraped, but not seriously.
Kate washed them quickly and quietly, still muttering
about Matt's callousness. Not that she'd actually needed

him to rush out to her rescue, of course. But he could have at least pretended to be concerned, damn him.

Maria mewed and squirmed on her pallet. Holding her breath, Kate quickly stuck the pacifier into the tiny mouth. The baby settled down immediately, her tiny lips working the rubber nipple as she sank more deeply into sleep. Kate exhaled in relief and uncrossed her fingers, noting that neither of the boys had stirred. Thank goodness.

Levering her feet out of her boots, she dusted off the knees of her pants and climbed fully dressed onto the bed, moving as far to one side as safely possible. It would have felt wonderful to sleep in nothing but her T-shirt and panties, but of course she wouldn't. She could just imagine Sullivan's obnoxious comments about that!

Matt came back inside a moment later. He kicked off his boots, checked the sleeping babies, then blew out the lantern, throwing the cabin into darkness. They'd found a few candles among José's supplies; they used those rather than the lantern during the night when feeding the babies. Kate heard Matt fumble around on the table, checking to make sure the candles and matches were handy for later.

Matt moved around the blanket he'd hung beside the bed and climbed onto the mattress, managing to jab an elbow into Kate's side as he settled down.

"Oof! Sullivan, you oaf, move over, will you?"

"Look, it's not my fault this bed is barely big enough for the both of us. Cut me some slack, all right?"

She sighed loudly and squirmed a bit closer to the edge. Matt rolled onto his side so that they lay back-to-back. Kate closed her eyes, determined to ignore him.

A few moments later her eyelids popped open again. She was dead tired, but she couldn't go to sleep. The bed was lumpy and uncomfortable. Her palms were still stinging from her fall. The sounds of the forest outside seemed to have suddenly magnified. Her clothes felt tight and binding.

And then there was Matt, lying so close beside her, she could almost feel him breathing.

Funny how that blanket hanging from the ceiling gave a new sense of intimacy to the bed, simply by blocking the view of the rest of the cabin. Silly, of course. After all, it was only an old blanket. . . .

"What's the matter, Hennessy?"

She jumped at the sound of Matt's deep voice. "Nothing. Why?"

"You seem restless. You didn't really hurt yourself when you fell out there, did you?"

At least he'd finally asked, she thought grudgingly. "No, I'm fine. Just having trouble getting to sleep."

"Better take advantage of the quiet. It probably won't last long. Maria's going to want a bottle in a couple of hours."

She made a face. "I know."

"What do you do when you can't sleep at home? L.A., right?"

"Right. And I read, or watch television until I get sleepy. That doesn't seem to be an option at the moment."

"What sort of books do you like to read?"

"Why?" she asked suspiciously.

She felt him shrug. "Just making conversation, Hennessy," he replied irritably. "Maybe talking for a little while will help us relax enough to sleep."

Which must mean that he, too, was having trouble unwinding. Maybe a little innocuous conversation *would* help, she decided. If nothing else, it would take her mind off the awkwardness of the sleeping arrangements for a few minutes.

"I like thrillers," she said finally. "Real heart-stopping, breath-catching, page-turning stuff."

"Yeah? Me, too. Who are your favorite authors?"

Rather to Kate's surprise, their tastes in reading overlapped quite a bit. It was the same with films, they learned when they named a few of their favorites. However, Kate was a rock music fan and Matt admitted that he preferred country, a taste he'd developed growing up in Texas, he explained. That led to talk of their backgrounds—which, again, were surprisingly similar.

Though Kate had grown up in Southern California and Matt in Texas, they both came from traditional middle-class families. Kate had been an only child, while Matt had a sister, but both had been especially close to one grandparent and considered their childhoods happy ones.

"My mother's going to be worried that I'm out of contact right now," Kate admitted. "She'll be certain something has happened to me. She's not crazy about my job— she wants me to take up a safer career, like opening a portrait studio or shooting weddings."

"I can't see you snapping pictures of self-conscious families slicked up in their Sunday best and posing like department store mannequins," Matt said with a smile in his voice. "Or setting up romantic, soft-focus shots of dreamy-eyed brides and adoring grooms."

Kate shuddered dramatically. "Neither can I. What about you, Matt? Will your family be worried if they don't hear from you for a few more days?"

"They're getting used to it," he replied. "But, yeah— they'll probably worry."

Kate lay quietly for a few moments, lost in guilty speculation about her parents' concern over her carelessness in missing that press bus. She wondered if Matt was wrestling with the same remorse.

"So, have you got a boyfriend back in L.A. who's probably wondering where the hell you are?" Matt asked seemingly out of the blue, startling her.

"No. I don't seem to have much success with 'boyfriends,'" she said. "Guess I'm too busy with the career."

"Yeah, I know what you mean. Our job plays hell on a social life, doesn't it? I hardly remember the last time I had a real date."

She lifted an eyebrow in the darkness. Something told her Matt Sullivan didn't spend any nights alone except by his own choice.

He shifted onto his back. "I'd still like to get married and have a family someday—one baby at a time, preferably," he added wryly. "I just haven't found the right woman yet."

She sniffed. "I can imagine the type of woman you'd look for."

"Oh, yeah?"

"Yeah. A walking, breathing, talking—but not too much, of course—Barbie doll. One who'll keep your house, cook your meals, care for your kids and cheerfully kiss you goodbye when you take off on one of your news assignments."

"You couldn't be more wrong, Hennessy," he muttered, but something in his tone told her she hadn't been that far off.

"So what about you?" he demanded before she could argue. "Have you ever even been involved in a serious relationship?"

"Twice. One in college, another a few years later. They didn't work out. Both guys developed severe cases of LWS. I must be a carrier, somehow," she mused, staring at the dark wall beside the bed. "They never seem to suffer from it before I get involved with them, but after a couple of months, they fall prey to it."

And both times, she'd been crushed when it happened, which had left her all the more determined to protect herself from that sort of pain in the future.

"LWS?" Matt asked warily.

"Little Woman Syndrome."

"Ah. More of your feminist bull—er—jargon."

"I don't see what's wrong with wanting to be treated as an equal. Or with wanting to be free to pursue my own goals and challenges, and not just when it's convenient for some man. Not having to cater to some guy's fragile macho ego."

"Hennessy, you are one hell of a good photojournalist, but you've got a lot to learn about being a woman."

"I'm simply not interested in meeting anyone's preconceived notion of what 'being a woman' entails," she snapped back. "I'm a lot more interested in being seen as a competent human being!"

"If you'd only—"

Whatever unsolicited advice he might have given was interrupted by a quiet fussing sound from the floor. Matt sighed. "Sounds like Maria's lost her pacifier again."

Kate didn't move. "You're closer to her."

He lay still a moment in a stubborn, silent battle of wills. And then, he muttered a curse and rolled off the bed. Kate shifted onto her side and closed her eyes again, grateful for the distraction from their conversation.

She only wished she could shrug Matt's criticism off as easily as she had similar comments in the past few years. But for some reason, they'd stung...especially since she'd spent the past two days doing a damned good job of dealing with the responsibilities of three babies, she thought resentfully.

Sure, Matt had done his share, but she'd coped every bit
as well as he had. Could have handled it herself, if necessary. He really was a macho jerk, despite his momenetary
lapses of decent behavior.

That unflattering assessment made, she found herself
slipping into sleep. She didn't fight it. She certainly didn't
want to engage in further conversation with Sullivan tonight.

Whether because they really had been worn-out, or because they'd become a bit more comfortable with their
unfamiliar surroundings, the babies slept better that night.
Maria woke only once for a bottle, and Tommy took one
at the same time. Charlie never stirred.

Even after a relatively undisturbed night's sleep, however, Matt and Kate weren't in the best of moods the next
day. She was still brooding over his criticism, while he
seemed to be growing restless. Both were bored with the
bland, canned food and with the narrow confines of the
one-room cabin. The routine of changing diapers, washing and filling bottles and pacing with fidgety babies had
long since lost the advantage of novelty.

Matt pushed himself out of his chair after lunch. "I
think I'll take a walk and check on the bus. Need me to
bring anything particular back with me?"

Kate looked up quickly from the sink, where she was
washing bottles in freshly boiled water. "You're going
out?"

"Yeah. I'll only be an hour or so. Just want to stretch
my legs."

"What about *my* legs, Sullivan?"

He glanced automatically downward. "What about
them?"

"I'd like to get out of here for a while, too. Why don't *you* stay with the kids and *I'll* go check on the bus."

He shook his head. "No. I'll go."

"The hell you will!"

"Look, Kate, be reasonable," he said impatiently. "You don't need to go wandering off into the forest alone."

"You were planning on doing so," she pointed out.

"Well, yeah, but I'm—"

"A man," she finished for him in disgust.

He exhaled loudly. "Yes, damn it."

"Big hairy deal. I'm as capable as you are of walking to that bus and back."

Matt threw up his hands. "Fine. Great. We'll *all* go check on the bus. Me, you, and all three kids. Will that make you happy?"

"Yes," she answered recklessly. It wasn't that she particularly wanted to trudge through the forest again carrying a baby. It was just that she wasn't about to sit in the cabin baby-sitting while Matt went out and enjoyed himself. Talk about LWS!

"Fine."

"Fine."

They glared at each other a moment longer, and then Matt grumbled and shoved a hand through his hair. "Where's your backpack?"

"Why?" she asked, eyeing him suspiciously.

"Just empty it and bring it here, Hennessy. I need it."

She didn't like his tone but bit her lip to keep from starting another argument. She figured he must want to take the backpack along for bringing back things from the bus. Since she was wearing the last clean clothes she'd brought with her on the first trek, she got the pack for him without further resistance.

She gasped indignantly when he pulled out his pocket-knife and started making cuts in the thick canvas bottom. "What the hell are you doing?"

"Making a baby carrier," he replied without looking up.

She winced at the sound of ripping fabric. She'd ordered that pack out of an L.L. Bean catalog. It had cost her a fortune, dammit!

"You better know what you're doing, Sullivan," she muttered.

He didn't answer. A moment later, he stood, lifted Tommy out of the playpen and put the baby's bare little feet through the two holes he'd cut in the bottom of the backpack. "Help me get this on," he ordered Kate, turning his back to her.

She picked up the pack, baby and all, and helped Matt slide his arms through the padded straps. When they were finished, Tommy rested comfortably in the pack facing Matt's back. The baby grinned and tugged at a handful of Matt's hair, obviously liking the new game.

"Ouch! That hurt," Matt complained.

"It was your idea, Sullivan," Kate reminded him sweetly. And then she turned to the playpen before Matt could make a cutting reply.

Charlie sat in the center of the pen, holding his arms up demandingly. Kate smiled at him and picked him up. "Want to go for a walk, Charlie?"

The tot babbled something that could have been agreement.

Still grumbling beneath his breath, Matt picked Maria up from her pallet and cradled her in one bent arm. "All right," he said ungraciously. "Let's go before they all need to be changed and fed again."

Kate started to reach for her camera, then thought better of it when Charlie's eyes lit up at the sight of the expensive toy. "Okay, I'm ready," she said.

"I'm so glad," Matt muttered and stalked out the door. He might have looked more intimidating if he hadn't been carrying one baby and having his hair cheerfully mussed by another, Kate thought with a grin.

Chapter Six

The babies seemed to enjoy being outside. Even Kate and Matt started to relax once they were away from the confining walls of the shack.

"Charlie," Kate told the bouncing baby in her arms, "you are very heavy. Don't you think it's about time you learned to walk?"

"You could try setting him down and let him hold on to our hands," Matt suggested. "He could probably walk a while like that."

"But he's not wearing shoes," Kate pointed out. "He could step on something that would hurt him."

Matt conceded the point. "Don't worry, kid," he told Charlie. "Your new family will buy you some shoes. Then you can walk and run just like the big kids."

"I hope his new family is nice," Kate said, holding the baby more closely. "I hope they'll all be raised in happy homes."

"I'm sure the adoptive families have been carefully screened," Matt said encouragingly. "They'll be raised by families of their own ethnic and cultural background, which beats the heck out of growing up in an orphanage."

"True. I guess I'm starting to feel proprietorial about them."

Matt lifted an eyebrow. "Latent maternal instincts, Hennessy?"

She raised her chin. "You want to make something of it?"

"No," he said in conciliation. "To be honest, I know exactly how you feel. Despite the trouble, they're great kids, aren't they?"

"Yes," Kate said, dropping a kiss on Charlie's soft, dark hair. "They are."

Riding happily in the backpack, Tommy squealed and kicked and drooled down Matt's neck. Matt groaned and predicted permanent kidney damage from the busy little feet. Baby Maria lay contentedly in the crook of his protective arm, her huge dark eyes focusing blearily on the treetops passing over her head.

They found the bus just as they'd left it, half-hidden in the thick brush that grew along the excuse for a road, apparently undisturbed. "I've got a backpack in there somewhere," Matt said. "If I put a few things in it, will you be able to wear it and still carry Charlie?"

"Of course," Kate replied. "Or I could take Tommy and Maria, if you'd prefer."

He made a face and glanced over his shoulder at Tommy, who grinned wetly back at him. "It isn't Tommy's weight that's the problem. It's his activity that makes him so hard to balance. I'd better keep him. We don't need much—just a couple of changes of clothing. José and I hauled enough diapers and formula to last another day or two.''

Kate sincerely hoped it wouldn't be that much longer before José returned to rescue them. What if something went wrong with one of the babies out here in the middle of nowhere? She wouldn't have the faintest idea of what to do—and she knew Matt wouldn't, either.

Matt dragged a car seat out of the bus and set it in a shady spot on the ground, then buckled Maria into it. She sat contentedly in the seat, gumming her pacifier and looking around. Still carrying Tommy on his back, Matt then returned to the bus to locate his backpack, telling Kate he'd put a few of his possessions into it, and she could add a few things of her own afterward.

Kate sat on the ground beside Maria's car seat while Matt was inside the bus. Charlie stood on her knees, holding her hands and bouncing as he babbled in his funny mixture of monosyllablic Spanish and baby nonsense. Kate began to sing for him, and he gave a squeal of pleasure.

"You have a nice voice," Matt said when he rejoined her, interrupting her in midverse of "There Was an Old Lady Who Swallowed a Fly."

For some reason, Kate was embarrassed by the remark. She ducked her head and murmured, "Uh, thanks. Did you get everything you need out of the bus?"

"Yeah. Here, let me have Charlie and you can get a few things. Don't get too many or you won't be able to carry both the pack and the kid."

That brought her chin back up. "I'm not an idiot, Sullivan."

He didn't apologize this time, only shrugged and swung Charlie into his arms. Charlie and Tommy grinned at each other over Matt's shoulder.

Inside the bus, Kate unzipped her bag and pulled out two changes of underwear, a pair of slacks and a couple of T-shirts. Her mouth twisted wryly as she remembered packing in preparation for leaving the country with the press crews. If anyone had told her then how she'd actually be spending the next few days...

A baby started crying outside the bus.

"Hurry up in there, Hennessy," Matt called out impatiently. "The kids are getting hungry again."

She sighed and fastened the backpack. "Coming."

She'd thought they'd head straight back for the cabin. Settling Charlie on her hip, she wondered why Matt wasn't taking Maria out of her car seat. He knelt beside the seat, staring at the bus with a frown while Tommy nodded sleepily in the pack behind him. Maria had stopped fussing and had the pacifier in her mouth again, but still Matt made no move to take her out of the seat.

"Matt?" Kate asked. "What's wrong?"

"I wonder if I should push the bus a bit farther into the brush. The back wheels are clearly visible from the road where it sits now. If I move it another couple of feet, it would be better hidden."

"Who's going to see it?" Kate asked logically. "It doesn't look as though anyone has come this way since we broke down."

"Still," Matt mused aloud, "it would only take a few minutes for me to move it. I'd hate for anyone to make off with the rest of the orphanage supplies. They're probably needed in San Arturo."

Kate tried to argue, telling him that moving the bus a few feet wouldn't guarantee invisibility from the road. The brush wasn't all that thick, she pointed out, and anyone looking closely enough was bound to see something. Besides...

Matt interrupted her midrationale. "It'll only take a minute," he promised, rising to move toward the bus.

"Matt! You can't push the bus with Tommy on your back. He might get hurt."

"Oh. I'd sort of forgotten he was there." Matt glanced over his shoulder, noted that Tommy had fallen asleep, and slipped his arms carefully out of the padded straps. He lay Tommy gently on the ground, pulling the top flap of the backpack up to serve as a pillow.

"This really isn't necessary," Kate grumbled. "It won't be easy getting him on your back again. And Maria's going to start crying for her bottle again any minute."

"Mmm," Matt murmured, proving that he wasn't listening to a word she was saying as he ducked through the bus door to shift into neutral.

Kate grumbled about the sheer bullheaded stubbornness of the male gender, knowing that Matt couldn't hear and Charlie didn't understand. She watched broodingly as Matt set his shoulder to the back of the bus and strained to move it forward.

"You're going to throw out your back," she muttered. "Probably end up in traction."

Matt ignored her, if he heard her at all.

The bus creaked forward a few inches; Matt stumbled over a vine.

"You'll probably break your leg," Kate predicted even more crossly. "And I'm just going to leave you lying there. I can't carry all four of you back to the cabin."

He tossed a chiding look over his shoulder—at least he wasn't completely oblivious to her, she thought in faint satisfaction—and pushed again. The bus moved a foot forward. Matt pushed once more, then stepped back, breathing a bit heavily.

"I'll just check the front and then we can head back," he said, pushing a thick branch aside to duck into the brush.

Kate's frown deepened when she noticed that the right wheels of the bus—the side Matt was on—rested precariously close to a shallow rut that was just visible through the foliage. If the edge suddenly crumbled from the weight, the bus could conceivably overturn, she thought.

A sickening image of Matt crumpled beneath the heavy vehicle filled her mind just as a loud creaking noise made her realize that her prophecy was all too close to coming true. Dirt began to slide from beneath the wheels, and the bus rocked gently, beginning to lean in Matt's direction.

"*Matt!*" Kate yelled. "Move away from the bus!"

Startled by her shout, Charlie jumped and began to cry, as did Maria. Tommy awoke with a start, lifting his head from the makeshift pillow to add his cries to the others.

The bus settled without incident into the shallow ridge. Unharmed, Matt crashed out of the brush, his eyes wide. "What's wrong?"

Kate patted Charlie nervously, trying to calm him—and herself. Her heart was still pounding in double time, and she was furious with Matt for taking unnecessary risks. "I thought the bus was going to turn over on you!" she snapped. "Of all the stupid, reckless stunts, that was one of the worst you've pulled yet, Sullivan."

Matt spread his legs and planted his fists on his hips, staring at her in incredulity. "What the hell are you yelling about?"

"Look at the damned bus, Sullivan! Another few inches and it would have turned over on you."

Matt gave a snort of disbelief as he turned his head to look at the bus. Kate noted in satisfaction that he paled a bit when he realized how precariously the back wheels were perched on the edge of the ledge. "It probably wouldn't have rolled," he said, but without a great deal of conviction. "But it would have been tough to pull it out of there later."

"*Probably* wouldn't have rolled?" Kate repeated, her voice rising from renewed anger—and to be heard over the three-part harmony wailing of the babies. "Oh, that's reassuring! And what would I have done if it had rolled, and if you'd been trapped under it? Hmm? What if you'd been seriously injured—or even killed?"

He flushed. "Damn it, Hennessy. You're overreacting."

"I am not overreacting! I'm just making it clear that we can't afford to take stupid chances right now. These kids need us to take care of them. How are we going to do that if one of us gets hurt?"

He didn't have an answer for that. His jaw clenched, he picked up Tommy and tried to calm him before sliding into the backpack straps again.

Charlie quieted when Kate offered his pacifier. He nestled his head into her shoulder, making her feel like a jerk for startling him. She patted him apologetically.

Matt finally soothed Tommy back to sleep. Still scowling, he eased carefully into the pack, settling Tommy into the now-familiar position on his back. And then he efficiently unstrapped the still-crying Maria from the car seat and cradled her in the crook of one arm while he tossed the seat into the bus with his free hand.

"Okay," he said abruptly, turning in the direction of the cabin. "Let's go."

Kate followed sullenly. Fine, she thought. If he was going to be mad at her just because she'd tried to keep him from being hurt, so be it. Next time she'd stand back and watch him get flattened, she decided vindictively.

Her arms started to ache from Charlie's weight long before they reached the shack. What she wouldn't give for a baby stroller! She kept her mouth shut, of course. After all, she *had* insisted on coming on this walk, as Matt would be sure to point out if she dared complain. No way was she going to give him that satisfaction.

Matt broke the taut silence between them just then when he glanced at her and said, "So you were really worried about me, hmm?"

Something in his voice made her defensive again. It would be just like the conceited reporter to start reading too much into her behavior. Just because they'd managed to get along well enough during the past couple of days, just because she'd been forced to share a bed with him without putting up much of a fuss, he had probably convinced himself she was falling for that notorious Texas charm of his. She'd have to set him straight on that immediately.

She kept her voice cool, even faintly condescending. "I just didn't know how I was going to take care of you and the three *other* babies if you hurt yourself."

Suitably rebuffed, he snorted and returned his gaze to the path ahead.

By the time the babies were all fed and put down for afternoon naps, Kate and Matt were on reasonably civil terms again. Though she still thought he could have thanked her for her concern for his safety, Kate knew the cabin was too small and their responsibilities to the babies too pressing to permit a continuing rift between her and Matt. She did her part to put it behind them by pulling a battered deck of cards out of her pack and asking if he'd like to play gin rummy with her. That seemed like an innocuous, completely impersonal way to pass an hour or so.

Matt accepted civilly enough. He was even surprisingly good-natured when Kate won repeatedly—at rummy, at poker, even at a lighthearted game of Go Fish.

"I guess I'm just lucky when it comes to card games," Kate said, tossing her cards on the table.

"You know what they say about lucky at cards...."

Kate made a face. "Yeah. I've heard that one." And, in her case, "unlucky at love" had proven all too true.

She pushed a hand through her hair and rose abruptly to her feet. "I'm getting hungry. What canned delicacy do you want me to open for dinner?"

Matt shrugged his lack of enthusiasm. "Doesn't matter. Man, what I'd give for some real food. Steak. Fish. Chicken."

"Cheeseburger. Pizza. Chili dog." Kate grimaced at the selection of tins on the shelf. Soup, stew or pork and beans. Nothing resembling pizza.

"Can't you go out and bag a deer or something, Sullivan?" she complained. "We could roast it over an open fire like the pioneers did."

Matt scratched his chin and grinned. Kate glanced at him through her lashes, noticing—not for the first time, unfortunately—how rakish he looked with a beard. Rather appealing, actually. If one cared for the scruffy-adventurer look, she added quickly.

"I don't know if there are any deer out there or not. And I wouldn't know what to do with a deer if I bagged one," he admitted. "My dad was an enthusiastic fisherman, but he didn't like hunting. He and I bonded on the golf course rather than at a deer camp."

"A Texas boy playing golf instead of hunting? Guess you took some teasing over that."

"Not after I started making money in junior golf tournaments."

"Pretty good, were you?" Kate asked idly, deciding to open a can of chicken-and-rice soup for dinner.

"I thought about going pro at one time. Then I took a journalism class in high school."

"And you were hooked." Kate could identify all too clearly with that, since high school journalism had held the same appeal for her.

"Yeah."

"Me, too."

"I know. It's always been obvious that you love your work."

She cranked the handle on the manual can opener, struggling to hold it steady against the dented can. "So how come you're always criticizing the way I work?"

"I've never questioned your competence," Matt pointed out. "I just don't see why you always have to be so aggressive off the job. Why you have to wear that chip on your shoulder all the time."

"You'd know why if you'd ever been a woman trying to make it in a man's field," she muttered.

She lighted the stove and dumped the soup into the battered tin cooking pan. She would put a pan of wash water on to boil while they ate the soup. They'd learned to light the stove as rarely as possible, since the heat built up quickly in the small cabin.

"Still," Matt mused, moving to set the table with their limited supply of dinnerware, "we've worked together pretty well the last couple of days, not counting a few minor disagreements. Sort of surprising, isn't it?"

"The problem with us," Kate said, her gaze fixed on the soup she was stirring, "is that you've never been able to accept me the way I am. You've always thought I should be more feminine, less aggressive, more like your narrow idea of what a woman should be.''

"I think men should be men, and women should be women,'' Matt said flatly. "At least when it comes to some things. What's wrong with that?''

She shook her head. "You just don't get it. I'm not talking about women in general. I'm talking about *me*. This is the way I am, and I don't see any reason why I should try to change to suit you—or anyone else, for that matter,'' she added hastily, in case he got the idea that the conversation had any personal connotations. Which it didn't, of course.

"Everyone has to compromise sometimes, Hennessy. Especially in a, uh, personal relationship.''

Kate closed her hand around the handle of the pan, swore when the hot metal singed her skin and reached belatedly for a rag to use as a pot holder. She set the pan on the table with a thump.

"Well,'' she said. "Since there's not even the slightest possibility that you and I will ever be involved in a, uh, personal relationship, then there's no reason we can't learn to get along, is there? Just think of me as another one of the guys you work with. Another buddy. That's the way I work with the other male reporters and photographers.''

Matt's expression was hard to read, but he nodded. "Yeah, sure. If that's the way you want it.''

She spooned soup into her bowl to avoid his eyes. "Sure. Why not?''

"Fine.''

"Right.''

"Better eat fast,'' Matt advised, apparently bringing the conversation to an end. "Maria's starting to squirm over there. She's probably hungry again, and it's your turn to feed her.''

Kate sighed. "She's *always* hungry. Maybe she's ready to start some solid food."

"Maybe. I guess that will be up to her new parents to decide."

"Yeah," Kate agreed, trying to ignore a ripple of what might have been sadness. "I guess it will."

Tommy woke from his nap in an uncharacteristically cross mood. Though he was usually the most enthusiastic of the three babies, he spent that evening fussing and resisting all of Kate's and Matt's efforts to entertain him. They took turns talking to him, walking with him, even singing to him, though Matt's repertoire of songs was even more limited than Kate's.

"'Leaving on a Jet Plane'?" Kate said, looking around from the sink where she stood washing out clothing for the next day. Matt had been pacing the floor with the whining baby, doing everything he could think of to appease the kid. "Dating yourself, aren't you, Sullivan?"

"Wishful thinking," he said, grimacing as Tommy started to cry again. "What do you think is wrong with him?"

"Tummy ache, maybe? We probably haven't been feeding him the way the nuns did."

Matt looked down at the baby's flushed, unhappy face. "Does your stomach hurt, Tommy? Is that it?"

The child squirmed and rubbed his face against Matt's shoulder, whimpering softly. "Damn," Matt said, cradling the baby more closely and feeling frustratingly helpless. "I wish you could tell us what's hurting you."

What if it were something serious? A virus or infection. Appendicitis, maybe. What if the baby needed medical attention? What the hell were they supposed to do then? Matt bit his lip to keep from voicing his concerns aloud, but one glance at Kate's somber expression told him she shared his fears.

Long after Charlie and Maria had fallen asleep for the night, Tommy was still restless and fretful. Kate relieved Matt for a while, sitting on the edge of the bed and snuggling Tommy close as she rocked back and forth and softly sang a lullaby. Matt sat nearby and watched, torn between concern for the baby and his uncomfortably mixed feelings about Kate Hennessy.

He still thought she tended to be overly belligerent most of the time. But the glimpses of softness he'd seen in her during the past three days had made him reassess his earlier opinions of her.

She could still make him lose his temper faster than any woman he knew. But hearing her sing and watching her snuggle a baby against her small breasts elicited an odd, uncomfortable feeling deep inside him.

And had she really been worried about him earlier when she'd yelled at him to move away from the bus? Remembering the genuine note of fear in her voice, he wondered if he should take it personally—or if she'd have been just as concerned for . . . say, José. Or some total stranger.

Who could tell what Hennessy was really thinking or feeling? She masked it so well.

Both Matt and Kate were relieved when Tommy finally fell asleep. Kate tiptoed to the playpen and laid him carefully next to Charlie, letting out a soft breath when neither baby stirred.

She turned to Matt, her face looking tired in the yellow glare of the lantern light. "I think he'll sleep awhile now," she whispered. "He's worn himself out."

Matt had already kicked off his boots and stretched out on the bed. "Yeah. He's worn me out, too. Come to bed. Let's get some sleep."

Kate hesitated a minute, then blew out the lantern. Matt scooted to one side of the bed, protecting himself from awkwardly placed elbows as she settled beside him in the darkness. Oddly enough, he was growing accustomed to sharing a bed with Kate.

She squirmed restlessly on the hard cot, her leg brushing his with the movement. "I wish we had a real mattress," she murmured. "And a couple of pillows would be nice. I'm getting a crick in my neck."

"Probably tension," Matt suggested. "It's been a rough evening."

"You can say that again."

He shifted onto his back and reached out for her. She resisted when he tugged her toward him. "What are you doing?" she asked, sounding startled.

"Helping you work that crick out." He pushed her head down onto his right shoulder, wrapped his right arm around her to hold her in place and began to rub her neck with his left hand. He could feel the knotted muscles beneath her soft, slightly damp skin. The muscles tightened when she instinctively resisted the intimacy of their position, then loosened fractionally when she began to relax.

"You're tired, too," she murmured, sounding self-conscious. "You don't have to do this."

"I know. But you helped me out the other day when I had a headache. Now it's my turn."

"Oh." She subsided into silence, her face buried in his shoulder, her body very still as he continued to rub her neck.

She felt good against him, Matt thought idly, even with the thickness of their clothing between them. Her slight figure fit nicely into the curve of his arm, and her long legs lay against him, making him wonder how they'd feel wrapped around him. Merely idle speculation, of course, he reminded himself hastily. It was perfectly natural that he'd be curious, under the circumstances.

He ran his fingertips from the soft hair at her nape to dip beneath the rounded neckline of her T-shirt. Her shoulders were tight, and he felt more knots beneath the skin there. He squeezed, eliciting a low moan from her.

"Did that hurt?" he asked in concern, loosening his grip.

"No," she admitted a bit breathlessly. "It felt good."

"Oh." He started to knead her shoulder again, the movements made rather awkward by their positions. It would be much easier if she lay on her stomach, giving him better access to her neck, shoulders and back. And, of course, he could find the knotted muscles more easily if she were to remove her shirt. Which, of course, was out of the question for them.

He reached around to rub her other shoulder, the movement bringing his cheek against her hair. She wore her hair too short for his taste, but it was surprisingly soft and thick. Smelled good, too, despite the conditions they'd been living under. He wondered how she managed that. It had been all either of them could do to stay clean under such primitive constraints. He was much too aware of his own unshaven face and shaggy hair.

Kate shifted her weight and her breasts brushed his chest. Her knee rubbed against his thigh. And though Matt was sure she wasn't being consciously seductive, his body responded, anyway.

He set his teeth. "Your neck feeling better, Hennessy?" he asked, releasing his grip on her shoulder.

"Much," she agreed. "Thanks."

"You're welcome. Uh, I'd better retrieve my other arm. It's starting to fall asleep."

"Oh. Sorry." She shifted at the same time he did, bringing them accidentally into even closer contact.

Matt could feel her breath on his cheek. "G'night, Hennessy," he murmured and then, without stopping to think about it, brushed his mouth against hers.

He had the satisfaction of feeling her start to respond before she suddenly stiffened and jerked backward, almost falling off the bed with the force of her reaction. Matt caught her and steadied her, though she kept as much distance as possible between them.

"Uh, Sullivan?" she said, sounding even more breathless than before.

"Yeah?"

"When I said earlier that we should try to get along—be buddies—I didn't mean we should start... kissing or anything. Let's not get carried away, okay? I mean, we don't even particularly like each other half the time."

"True," Matt murmured, wondering what, exactly, he felt the other half of the time.

To be honest, he was as shaken by the kiss as Kate sounded. Why *had* he kissed her? He certainly didn't kiss his other casual buddies. Of course, none of his other buddies had Kate's eyes. Or Kate's mouth. Or Kate's long, luscious legs.

"We're just tired," Kate announced suddenly, firmly, as though the unquestionable explanation had just presented itself to her. "Yeah, that's it. We need sleep. Go to sleep, Matt," she said, her brusque command rather strained.

He scowled, turned his back to her and closed his eyes. Maybe she was right, he decided crossly. Maybe sleep deprivation was making him delirious. Why else would he be lying here like this, wondering what would have happened if she hadn't stopped the kiss when she had?

Chapter Seven

After a restless, frequently interrupted night, Kate woke the next morning to the sound of rain and the feel of water dripping steadily onto her cheek. She opened her eyes, then blinked when a huge drop splashed on her nose.

Great. The roof leaked. Now why didn't that surprise her?

She was alone in bed. She heard Matt moving around and talking quietly on the other side of the hanging blanket that provided an illusion of privacy. Still tired, she wished she could roll over and go back to sleep, but there were diapers to be changed, bottles and tiny T-shirts to be washed, three little mouths to be fed.

For once she rather hoped the babies would keep her busy for the next few hours. At least that way she wouldn't have a chance to dwell on what had happened between her and Matt last night. What in the world had he been thinking of when he'd kissed her? And why on earth hadn't she stopped him immediately, rather than allowing herself to respond for that one weak moment? Heaven only knew what Matt would make of that.

She dropped her feet to the floor, pushed a hand through her tousled hair and stood, shoving the blanket out of the way as she moved around it. "The roof leaks."

Matt was pacing the floor with Tommy, who lay against his chest, sucking two fingers and looking decidedly unhappy. "Yeah, I know." He nodded toward several wet spots on the floor. "I moved the playpen to a dry area."

Charlie lay in the playpen, kicking his feet as he drank from a bottle. Maria's pallet had been moved, too, and was now under the table to ensure that she stayed dry. Maria appeared to be asleep, which meant that Matt must have already fed her. Kate grudgingly admitted to herself that he was certainly taking his full share of responsibility with the babies.

"Have you had anything to eat?" she asked him.

He shook his head as he turned to take five steps in the opposite direction, all the pacing he could do in the limited space available to him. "No. There's another can of mixed fruit. I guess we could have that."

Without enthusiasm, she nodded and got out the can opener. "Is Tommy still fussy this morning?" she asked, worriedly eyeing the lethargic child in Matt's arms.

"Not exactly." There was an answering worry in Matt's voice. "He's just quiet and apathetic. It's not like him."

"No." Kate bit her lip. "God, I hope nothing's wrong."

"Me, too."

She dumped the fruit unceremoniously into the bowls. "What day is it?" she asked with a frown, realizing that she'd completely lost track of time.

"Friday."

José had left them on Tuesday. She wondered when they could reasonably expect to see him again. She hoped he'd reached help, that even now he was arranging for transportation for two stranded adults and three babies.

"What if he didn't make it at all?" she heard herself fretting aloud. "What if no one even knows we're here? How long should we stay here before we try to get help for ourselves?"

"It's too soon to worry about that yet," Matt answered sharply, following her line of thought without question. "José said it would take him at least three days to reach help. I think we should wait it out."

"But what if Tommy really is sick? What if he needs a doctor? How are we—"

"Kate," Matt interrupted firmly. "Chill out. It won't help any of us if you start overreacting again."

"I am *not* overreacting! I'm simply concerned."

"Well, so am I. So let's just stay calm and wait to see what happens before we start anticipating disaster, shall we?"

She resented his tone—as though he were dealing with a hysterical female, she thought petulantly. Just because she was worried about Tommy, and about José, did not make her hysterical.

She set the bowls on the table. "Breakfast."

He pulled up a chair. "Be careful not to kick Maria under the table."

"I'm not going to kick the baby. Would you please stop giving me unasked-for advice?"

"Stop being so sensitive. It was just a comment."

Kate opened her mouth to retort, but Tommy started to cry when Matt sat down. Matt had to eat while pacing, stopping by the table every few steps for another bite of the fruit, adjusting his path occasionally to avoid the various leaks from the ceiling.

Finishing her own portion, Kate reached for Tommy. "Here, I'll hold him for a while. Take a break."

"Thanks," Matt said, flexing his arm. "I've been walking him for over an hour."

Tommy didn't protest the switch but snuggled limply into Kate's arms. She pressed her lips to his forehead. "He feels warm," she fretted. "I think he's running a fever."

"I know," Matt admitted. "I thought so, too."

"You should have said something."

"It wouldn't have made any difference. We don't have anything to give him."

She thought of the acetaminophen capsules in her pack but rejected them instantly. They were for adults, not babies. "I wonder if there are baby aspirin in the supplies?"

"Not that I noticed. I guess I could go search the bus again."

Kate listened to the rain beating steadily against the roof. "Not now," she suggested. "He's only running a low fever, if any. If he starts feeling hotter, we may decide it's worth a look."

Matt nodded. "Whatever you think."

Now *that* was a novelty. Matt conceding to her opinion?

A thin, high-pitched sound came from beneath the table. Matt sighed. "I'll get her. She probably needs to be changed. Again."

Kate nodded and then tried to induce Tommy to take a bottle while Matt dealt with Maria. Tommy drank an ounce or so of the formula, then pushed the bottle away. He refused her offer of baby oatmeal, which he'd eaten so eagerly before. His chocolaty eyes were dull, his appetite gone. Kate grew more worried.

The rain continued most of the day. Matt moved the cot so that it wouldn't be soaked, then cursed when a leak developed in the new location. He finally set the cooking pan in the center of the bed to catch the worst of the drips.

Tommy alternately slept and fretted. As though sensing the tension between the adults, Charlie was fussy, needing extra reassurance from whomever was available at the time. Maria was no more trouble than usual, but her frequent bottle feedings and diaper changes, in addition to the demands of the boys, were difficult to keep up with. And then Tommy developed a mild case of diarrhea.

Kate began to worry about running out of supplies. They were conserving as much as possible, but the diapers and bottled water wouldn't last indefinitely. *Then* what would they do? Was the well water safe to mix with the formula? Would the babies get hepatitis—or something worse—if forced to drink it?

She didn't voice those concerns, of course. Matt would probably just accuse her again of being hysterical.

Matt's mood wasn't exactly sunny. Kate knew he was tired and probably worried about the same things she was, but there was no call for him to be so snappy and distant, she thought resentfully. This wasn't exactly a picnic for *her*, either, but she was making the best of it, wasn't she? She wasn't snarling and snapping like a caged animal, was she? And she needed to go to the bathroom, darn it, but she hated going out in the pouring rain to do so.

Feeling sanctimonious and unappreciated, she went about her chores in brooding silence for the most part.

The hours crawled by.

Forgetting that he'd moved the playpen closer to the stove, Matt lit the fire to heat well water so he could wash some clothes in the sink. He had turned to gather the soiled garments when a shriek from Charlie got his attention, as well as Kate's.

Charlie had been standing in the playpen, peering over the top, and had reached out to touch the stove. Fortunately, he'd snatched his hand away quickly enough so that his fingertips were only slightly reddened, but both Kate and Matt were painfully aware that it could have been much more serious.

"How could you be so careless?" Kate demanded of Matt, her heart still beating too rapidly in her chest.

"D'you think I did it on purpose?" Matt demanded, holding Charlie to comfort him. "It was an accident."

"You need to be more careful."

Matt clenched his jaw so tightly Kate could almost hear the bones grinding. He turned his back to her—pointedly.

Maria began to cry. Kate wondered almost absently how long it would be until she joined in.

The difficult day passed in a haze of diapers and bottles, mundane chores and bland canned food. Kate was so tired by nighttime that she could hardly walk upright to the bed. When all three babies were finally fed, dry and asleep at the same time, she practically crawled to the cot, threw herself facedown on the slightly damp blanket and lapsed into unconsciousness.

Her last fleeting thought was that at least she was too tired to be concerned about spending another night in bed with Matt.

Having fallen into bed as exhausted as Kate, Matt slept deeply for several hours. He wasn't sure what woke him, but he knew it was still several hours before dawn. The rain had stopped hours ago; the sound he'd heard had come from within the cabin.

Must have been one of the babies, he thought, resigned to feeding another bottle or changing another diaper. Maybe if he just lay still and pretended he was asleep, Hennessy would take care of it.

He heard a rhythmic creaking and then the sound that had awakened him, a forlorn sniffle he couldn't quite identify. Tommy? Charlie? Maria? He swallowed a weary moan and turned his head to see if Kate had heard anything.

She wasn't in bed.

Sighing, Matt yawned and rolled to sit up, deciding he'd better see if she needed any help. He knew he wouldn't be able to go back to sleep without making sure Tommy was okay.

The sight that met his eyes when he rounded the blanket brought a lump to his throat. Illuminated only by candlelight, Kate sat in one of the rickety chairs, rocking her body back and forth as she held a restlessly dozing Tommy. She wasn't aware that Matt was watching when she mopped with the back of her hand at the steady stream of tears running down her cheeks.

Unaccountably touched by Kate's tears, Matt stepped forward. She started at the movement, then quickly averted her face. He knew she was hoping he hadn't seen that she'd been silently crying.

"Go back to bed," she murmured, her voice husky. "Everything's okay."

"Everything is *not* okay," he disputed gently. "You're exhausted. You're the one who needs to be in bed."

Still looking away from him, she shook her head. "Tommy won't let me put him down. Every time I try, he wakes up and starts to cry again."

"I'll take him."

"No, I've got him."

Matt reached down and deftly lifted the drowsy baby into his arms. "Now *I've* got him. Go to bed, Hennessy. And don't get up again until daylight. I can handle things the rest of the night."

She swiped at her face again, then turned to him with her chin lifted proudly. "I'm as capable as you are at handling this."

"I know you are. But you need sleep. Just this once, don't argue with me, okay? Let me help."

She hesitated only a moment longer, so tired, she was weaving visibly. And then she nodded and turned toward the bed. "Let me know if you need me."

"I will. Good night, Kate," he said gruffly.

"G'night." She sounded half-asleep already as she climbed onto the cot.

Tommy whimpered and shifted in Matt's arms. Matt patted the baby's warm little back and sat in the chair Kate had been using, unconsciously taking up the rhythm of her rocking. Tommy settled back into sleep.

Matt couldn't stop thinking of how the sight of Kate's weary tears had affected him. Like a physical blow to the chest. She'd looked so tired, so dispirited, so worried. And yet she'd sat quietly comforting the baby, obviously taking care not to disturb Matt. Handling her problems herself, as was her usual stubborn, deeply ingrained habit.

It hadn't been fair of him to snap at her as he had during the day. Neither mounting cabin fever nor his secret worry about José's success in reaching help excused his behavior. And it wasn't Kate's fault that Matt had found himself battling his wayward hormones ever since she'd rested in his arms last night. Or that she couldn't walk around the cabin without Matt noticing how unconsciously gracefully she moved, or bend over to lift a baby without him focusing on her slender curves.

She'd made no attempt to call his attention to her long-lashed green eyes or the intriguing smattering of freckles across her nose; nor had she done anything to maximize the attractiveness of her soft, pouty mouth. But he'd noticed, anyway. And he'd remembered how good she'd tasted when he'd brushed his mouth so lightly, so briefly across hers.

Matt leaned over and blew out the sputtering candle to save the wax. And then he sat in the darkness, rocking the baby, listening to Charlie's soft snores and Maria's pacifier suckling, and wondering just how hard he was starting to fall for Kate Hennessy. And how much trouble he'd be in if he allowed himself to fall the rest of the way.

Sunlight poured through the dirty window when Kate awoke the next morning. She frowned, blinked, then sat up with a gasp. What time was it? How long had she slept? The babies must have awakened several times; why hadn't she heard them? Was Tommy better? Worse?

She all but jumped out of bed.

Matt had spread Maria's blanket on the floor, and he sat in the middle of it. Charlie and Tommy climbed happily over his lap while Maria lay on her back nearby, contentedly kicking her feet and sucking her fingers.

Matt looked up with a smile, though his eyes studied her intently. "Good morning. You look much better."

"Thanks. How's Tommy?"

Matt's smile deepened. "See for yourself."

Kate dropped to her knees on the blanket beside Matt. Tommy giggled and launched himself at her, crawling onto her lap. Kate anxiously searched his face. His eyes were bright, alert. She touched her hand to his cheek, finding the skin soft and cool.

"Thank God," she breathed, and then she snatched the baby close for a hug.

Cradling Charlie in one arm, Matt leaned close to place a finger against Tommy's lower lip. "Look at this," he said to Kate, pressing to reveal Tommy's lower gums.

Kate looked, and then her eyes widened. "Is that a tooth?" she asked, studying the tiny white nub just emerging from the reddened area.

"Yep. He's been teething. I should have realized. My mom and my sister once got into a heated debate because my sister's pediatrician said fever and diarrhea have nothing to do with teething, but Mom said he was wrong. She went into a long diatribe about old wives' tales being based on the knowledge of many generations of old wives."

Almost giddy with relief that Tommy was well, Kate laughed at Matt's wry story. "Did your mother ever convince your sister?"

"Oh, yeah. After my niece started teething and displaying all the symptoms the pediatrician said were only imaginary."

Tommy butted his head into Kate's chest and babbled, as though making up for the hours when he was uncharacteristically still and quiet. She laughed and tickled him under his chubby, drool-dampened chin, making him squeal and wriggle.

"Oh, Matt," Kate said with a slowly released breath. "I'm so glad he's all right. I was so worried about him."

As if by impulse, Matt threw his free arm around Kate's shoulders and squeezed. "You and me both," he confessed. "I was afraid he was really sick."

"Me, too." Her eyes met his, only inches away, and her smile faded. She was vividly aware of the weight of his arm around her. "Uh, thank you for letting me get a few hours of sleep. I really needed that."

"You're welcome," he said, and then they both fell silent.

Matt's gaze was still locked with hers. His arm tightened around her, drawing her closer. He leaned nearer, his lips only an inch from hers.

Kate caught her breath, and held it, her mouth already tingling in anticipation....

Tommy screeched playfully and threw himself between them, eager to reclaim their attention. Not wanting to be left out, Charlie grabbed Matt's nose and pulled himself to his feet, taking a tentative step or two on the blanket and using Matt's face as support. Maria spat out her pacifier and began to make the mewling sounds that meant she was starting to get hungry again.

Kate and Matt broke apart, instantly turning their attention to the babies, hiding their self-consciousness in a sudden flurry of activity.

That day passed much more peacefully than the previous one. Kate and Matt went about their chores with a mutual politeness that was almost humorous, had she been in the mood to laugh about it. But she was all too aware of the surreptitious looks that passed so frequently between them, and the tension that hovered just beneath their stilted conversation and perfunctory smiles.

Something was building between them, an explosion just waiting for the right catalyst. Kate didn't know whether to dread it—or look forward to it.

That night, Kate squirmed on the cot, trying to get comfortable, wishing for the hundredth time that she had a mattress, a soft pillow, a comfortable nightshirt. Her leg brushed Matt's, and her hip bumped against him. She stiffened and shifted immediately closer to her edge of the cot, foolishly tingling from that brief contact.

Matt rolled onto his side, accidentally touched her thigh with his hand, then snatched it away.

Kate winced, wondering if he could possibly be as painfully aware of their intimate proximity as she was. She almost wished one of the babies would awaken to give her something to do besides concentrate on Matt's nearness, but for once they were all sound asleep.

Matt muttered something inarticulate and climbed out of bed. Kate looked over her shoulder, squinting to see him through the darkness. "What's wrong?" she whispered.

"Nothing," he murmured. "Go back to sleep. I'm going outside. For a walk."

"A walk?" She listened to the sounds of the untamed jungle around the safe little haven of their shack and knew Matt was no more familiar with that primitive land than she was. "Have you lost your mind? It's the middle of the night. Heaven only knows what's prowling around out there looking for a midnight snack."

"I'll take the flashlight."

"And do what? Hit a lion over the head with it?"

"There aren't any lions out there, Hennessy," he said, but without a great deal of conviction.

As though mocking their ignorance, something screeched from the treetops.

"Come back to bed, Sullivan. You're delirious."

He ignored her. "Maybe I'll light a candle and read for a while. You got a book?"

She sighed in exasperation. "Yes. In my bag. In the bus."

"Oh. Well, then, I'll work on my notes. I'm sure there's a byline in this somewhere. I'm really not sleepy right now."

"Fine. Stay up, then. But don't blame me when you're exhausted tomorrow."

He muttered something else that she didn't catch. She didn't ask him to repeat it. Instead, she rolled onto her side, her back to him and determinedly closed her eyes.

It was much later when she finally managed to slip into a fitful sleep. Matt still hadn't returned to the bed.

What in the world was happening between them? she wondered with her last clear, conscious thought. Why did she suddenly find herself seeing Matt Sullivan in an all new—and oddly dangerous—way?

Sunday dawned clear and warm. Matt went through his usual morning routine of bemoaning the lack of coffee and real food, but was reasonably gracious afterward. Kate carefully avoided mentioning his strange behavior during the night. She was afraid that she knew all too well what had been bothering him.

After bathing the babies and feeding them breakfast, she sat on the blanket on the floor with them while Matt boiled water for their own bathing. Because it was Sunday, she sang "Jesus Loves Me" in Spanish, both to impress Matt and because that was the only song she knew in the language.

Matt pushed a drain plug into the sink and poured the hot water into it before refilling the pan with more cold water to be heated. "Did you ever sing professionally, Hennessy?" he asked idly when she'd finished the song.

"I sang in the church choir when I was growing up. Then in my college choir. But I'm really not that good, Sullivan. I never could have made it professionally."

"I wouldn't say that. You're better than you think. I like listening to you."

She averted her face to hide an unexpected flush. "Thanks. But I think I'll just stay behind the camera."

As though sensing her embarrassment, he changed the subject. "We're out of wood for the stove."

"Isn't there any more outside?"

"Nothing small enough to fit into the stove. There's a machete hanging outside. I'll try to chop some kindling with that this afternoon."

"Do you think we'll be here much longer?" Kate asked seriously, wondering just how long Matt thought they should stay on faith that the driver would return for them.

"Let's give José two more days," Matt suggested. "If he's not back then—well, we'll start considering other alternatives."

"Like what?"

He lifted his hands. "I don't know. I guess I'd go for help."

"You'd leave us here alone?" Kate demanded, looking from him to the babies. "No way, Sullivan. What if you disappeared, too? What would I do then?"

"No one's disappeared yet, Hennessy. Let's just give it another couple of days, okay?"

She bit her lip and nodded. He was right, of course. It wouldn't do any good to brood about it. But she'd be damned if she was letting him walk away and leave her stranded in the jungle with three babies!

Because they were all suffering from a touch of cabin fever, Kate and Matt carried the babies outside that afternoon. Kate spread blankets and sat in the center of them. Maria lay close to her side. The boys sat within easy reach, chewing on teething crackers that had been packed with the baby food.

Matt shed his T-shirt and started hacking at lengths of dead wood with the rusty machete, swearing creatively when the wood proved resistant to the dull blade. He quickly worked up a sweat with the unfamiliar exercise.

It was a gorgeous afternoon, the sky brilliantly blue in contrast to the deep green of the trees surrounding them. Kate couldn't resist shooting a roll of film of the babies and the surroundings, though Matt chided her for being unnaturally attached to her camera.

Colorful birds Kate had seen only in exotic aviaries at home flashed among the leaves, calling out and singing, making her think of old Tarzan movies.

Matt chuckled when she commented on that. "Wrong continent, Hennessy. Besides, I never would have figured you for the 'Me-Tarzan-you-Jane' fantasy. Although I'd be happy to play my part, if you like. Want me to swoop down on a vine, carry you off to a secluded tree house and make passionate, primitive love to you?"

She hated herself for blushing, though she managed to keep her voice light and mocking when she replied. "In your dreams, Sullivan. You aren't exactly the Tarzan type—you prefer golf to hunting, remember? And, anyway, we don't have a baby-sitter."

He chuckled. "Where's Cheetah when you need him, hmm?"

What might have been a monkey—or maybe a bird—chattered high above them. Kate couldn't help laughing at the timing before turning back to the babies.

She glanced down at Maria, who'd been lying so quietly on the blanket at Kate's side. The baby was watching her steadily, her dark gaze focused intently on Kate's face. When their eyes met, Maria broke into a sweet, trusting smile that brought Kate's heart straight into her throat.

She wondered why she'd never realized before that all these maternal instincts had been buried deeply within her. It felt oddly right sitting here with the children while Matt chopped wood nearby. Funny. She once would have turned up her nose at the very thought of such a primitively domestic scene.

Another colorful curse brought her attention back to Matt. She watched through her lashes as he bent to pick up another length of wood, arranged it in front of him and started hacking with the machete. Muscles rippled intriguingly in his glistening, tanned arms and lean back. His dark hair fell over his forehead, giving him a rakish appearance, and the short beard added a touch of pirate to the overall picture.

She couldn't resist framing him in the viewfinder and snapping his picture. She lowered the camera slowly, rather dazed at the realization that had just hit her like a blow to the stomach. For the first time in all the months she'd known him, she was seeing Matt Sullivan as a man she could want. Very badly.

As though sensing her watching him, Matt glanced over his shoulder. Whatever he saw in her expression made him stiffen, the hand holding the machete falling to his side. She saw her own awareness mirrored in his brown eyes.

They stared silently at each other—studying, assessing, acknowledging—until a sound from Charlie made Kate drag her gaze from Matt's.

The snake was coiled on the ground, only inches from Charlie's outstretched hand. Chubby little fingers wiggled in anticipation of playing with this interesting new toy as Charlie leaned closer, reaching, grasping.

"Charlie!" Kate lunged forward.

The baby's clutching fingertips had just brushed the snake's scaly body when Kate snatched his hand away. Her sudden movement startled the snake, which reacted by instinct.

Kate cried out in response to the sharp pain that lanced through her wrist and forearm when the snake sank its piercing fangs into her skin.

Chapter Eight

Matt was at Kate's side instantly, dispatching the snake in a few swift, savage slashes of the machete. He kicked the bloody carcass away before turning worriedly back to Kate.

Maria and Charlie, both unharmed but startled, had broken into noisy cries. Tommy whimpered, uncertain whether to join in.

Matt ignored the babies for the moment as he knelt by Kate's side. "Are you all right?"

She stared in disbelief at the bleeding punctures just above her right wrist. She was still too stunned to be frightened by what had happened. "It bit me," she said rather blankly.

"Oh, God." Matt grabbed her hand and turned her arm so that he could see the wounds. Tiny drops of blood dripped from the close-set lacerations. "Did you recognize the snake?'' he asked her urgently. ''Do you know if it's—''

She shook her head. ''No. I don't know anything about snakes, especially the ones around here.''

They looked at each other for a moment, and Kate saw the fear in Matt's eyes. And then he looked back down at her arm. He took a deep breath and lifted her wrist toward his mouth.

Realizing what he was about to do, she jerked her hand away from him. ''No!'' she said sharply. ''That won't help. It could only make you sick, as well, if it was, uh—''

Neither of them seemed able to voice the word poisonous.

''We have to do *something*.''

''We'll clean the wound and disinfect it.''

''With what?'' For the first time since they'd been stranded here, Matt looked scared, and rather helpless.

''Soap and water. And what about that bottle you found the first day we were here? It was alcohol, wasn't it?''

He nodded. ''Smelled like rot-gut whiskey.''

''Good. We'll use that as a disinfectant.''

All three babies were crying loudly now. Matt closed his eyes for a moment, took another deep breath, then opened them with a decisive nod. ''All right. Let's get inside. Can you walk?''

''Of course I can walk, Sullivan! Get the boys. I'll take Maria. Oh, and don't forget my camera.''

Matt growled something she didn't understand—which, she decided wryly, was probably just as well.

Kate scrubbed the wound with soap and water while Matt hastily prepared bottles for the babies. The boys lay in the playpen with theirs. He put Maria back onto her pallet and temporarily quieted her with her pacifier. "I'll feed her after I look at your arm," he told Kate.

She studied the two puncture marks. They looked clean. The skin surrounding them was reddened and a bit puffy, but not alarmingly so.

"I think it's going to be okay," she said, as much to reassure Matt as herself.

He ordered her to sit at the table, then joined her with the bottle of alcohol and one of his freshly washed T-shirts. "Hold out your arm."

She rested her arm on the table. A moment later, she flinched and hissed a curse as the whiskey burned into her wounds. "Damn it, Sullivan! That stings."

"Good. It's supposed to." He poured an inch of the liquor into one of the tin cups. "I want you to drink this."

She wrinkled her nose. "I think not. *You* drink it. You're the one who needs calming."

He held the cup to her mouth. "Drink it, Hennessy."

"Go to—"

He took advantage of her parted lips by placing the cup between them. She choked as the fiery liquid burned its way down her throat. "Oh, God," she managed in a croak. "That's horrible. It—"

He tilted the cup again, forcing more of the liquor into her mouth. She gagged, sputtered and swallowed about half of it. "You do that again, Sullivan, and I won't be the only one bleeding!" she said furiously.

"All right," he conceded in a mutter, setting the cup aside. "I guess that's enough."

She wiped her mouth with her left hand. "I can't believe José actually drinks that stuff. Are you sure it isn't lantern fuel? Maybe it came out of the carburetor of the bus."

Ignoring her complaints, he ripped a long, narrow strip from the bottom of his white T-shirt that he'd brought to the table.

"*Now* what are you doing? That was a perfectly good shirt."

"It's all I have to use as a bandage. We need to keep this wound clean." He wrapped her arm in the soft cotton, his touch so gentle that she felt herself softening at his obvious concern. And then he cupped her cheek with his hand, searching her eyes. "Do you feel dizzy? Nauseous? Weak?"

She was definitely feeling a little funny, but she didn't think it had anything to do with the snakebite—or the liquor. She moistened her lips. "I'm fine, Matt."

"Maybe you'd better lie down awhile."

"I don't think that's necessary."

"Just do it, will you, Hennessy? And let me know if you start feeling weird."

"I already feel weird," she muttered, grudgingly aware of how dangerously close she was to closing the short distance between them and soothing Matt's worried frown with a kiss.

His eyes widened. "What's wrong? What do you feel?"

She sighed in exasperation and shook her head. "Nothing. Just talking. You want me to lie down? I'll go lie down. Will that make you feel better?"

"Yeah. I'll feed Maria. You call me if you need me, all right?"

"I'll be three feet away from you, Sullivan. I don't think I'll have to call very loudly."

He managed a tight smile. "Anyone ever tell you you're a lousy patient, Hennessy?"

She had the grace to look sheepish. "Yeah."

"I figured." And then he leaned over to brush his mouth across hers. "Go to bed, Kate. I have babies to feed."

She walked to the cot in a daze, as unsettled by the look in Matt's eyes as she had been by the encounter with the snake.

She didn't start to tremble until she lay down and closed her eyes. Then all she could see was the snake, coiled and ready to strike at the helpless baby so innocently reaching for it. What if Charlie had been bitten? What would they have done?

What if—she gulped, hoping Matt didn't hear the sound—what if the snake *was* poisonous? How soon would the symptoms start to appear? And how would Matt manage with the babies if, heaven forbid, she became incapacitated—or worse?

She bit her lip and told herself to stop being such a wimp. But for one long, weak moment, she found herself wishing that Matt would just put his arms around her and hold her. Though she wouldn't admit it for anything, she could really use a bracing hug right now.

She hadn't expected to fall asleep, but she did, whether from genuine fatigue or the effects of the liquor or a combination of both. She woke to the feel of Matt's hand on her cheek. She opened her eyes and focused sleepily on his face, bent so close to her own.

"What are you doing?" she murmured.

"Checking for fever. You don't seem to have any. How do you feel?"

She thought about it a moment. "Hungry," she said. "I'd love a pizza. With everything."

"How about canned stew, instead?"

She shuddered, but said, "Yum yum. I can't wait."

"I'll heat some up and bring it to you."

"You will not. I'm getting up."

He started to protest, took one look at her face and prudently kept quiet.

Maria and Tommy were asleep. Charlie was standing in the playpen. He smiled at Kate and held up his arms entreatingly. She picked him up and kissed his cheek, deeply grateful that she'd been able to stop him before he picked up the snake. She couldn't bear to think of those wicked fangs piercing Charlie's tender skin.

"You shouldn't be lifting him," Matt said, fretting, looking up from the pan of glop he was stirring.

"Don't be silly. I'm fine. Obviously the snake wasn't poisonous, or I'd be feeling sick by now."

Matt didn't look particularly reassured. "It could still be too early to tell."

She pulled a face at him, which made Charlie laugh. "You could at least pretend to be optimistic, Sullivan."

He only muttered beneath his breath and dished grayish brown stew into the tin bowls.

Kate held Charlie on her knee while she ate. When he begged for a bite, she gave him a taste of the broth, then laughed when he twisted his face into an expression of extreme displeasure. "See, Matt? Even Charlie knows this stuff's awful. Makes baby food look pretty appealing, doesn't it, kid?"

Charlie gave her an affectionate look and rested his head on her shoulder. Kate looked across the table to find Matt watching her intently. "Eat your stew," she ordered him gruffly, self-consciously. "It's *really* repulsive when it gets cold."

Matt took another few bites, then pushed the rest away. "That's all I want."

She knew just how he felt, since she'd finished only half of her own portion.

Matt was quiet for several long minutes before he spoke again. "We've got to get out of here, Kate."

Trying to ignore her sore arm, Kate had been giving Charlie a "horsey ride" on her knee. She looked up in surprise when Matt spoke so firmly. "Now?" she asked rather stupidly, uncertain what he'd meant.

He shook his head impatiently. "Not now. Soon."

"You said we should give José another couple of days."

Matt's expression was grim, his eyes shuttered. "I've been deluding myself that we were safe here. That José would return with help and we'd go on our way."

"What suddenly changed your mind?" she asked, though she thought she knew.

"What changed my mind?" He looked incredulously from her face to the makeshift bandage, and then back again. "How can you even ask that?"

"Matt, it was an accident. It doesn't mean we're suddenly less safe than we were yesterday, or the day before."

He leaned slightly forward, his gaze locked with hers. "That's exactly my point. We *aren't* safe here. We never have been. God, we've been playing house with the babies while a war is waging all around us. We're stranded in a jungle neither of us knows, surrounded by heaven only knows what sort of predators and dangers. We have a limited supply of food and water, no medical supplies, no communication with civilization. Maybe the snake wasn't poisonous, but what if it *had* been? All I could have done was stand here and watch you—"

"Matt," she broke in gently, shaken that he, who'd been so calm from the beginning of their adventure, was suddenly the one in need of reassurance. "It's okay. We're handling it. We have families, friends, co-workers who will be looking for us. The babies have families who are waiting for them, who'll want to find them, make sure they're safe. Even if José . . . didn't make it . . . someone will find the bus, find us.''

"And if not?" he asked, repeating the very questions she'd asked only that morning.

"Then we'll figure something out," she said, quoting him. "We're a tough team, Matt Sullivan. Both of us are stubborn and strong and smart, and not the type to throw up our hands and admit defeat. If José hasn't shown up in a day or two, we'll walk out hauling the babies on our back, if necessary, but we *will* get them—and ourselves— to safety.''

He still wasn't smiling, but she could see that the muscles in his jaw had relaxed a bit. "You sound awfully sure of yourself.''

"I'm sure of *us*," she answered quietly.

Charlie prattled in her lap, as though to add his two cents' worth to the conversation.

Matt glanced down at the baby and managed a smile. "I think he just agreed with you.''

"Sure he did," Kate said, giving the child a squeeze. "He knows a couple of born survivors when he sees them, don't you, kid?''

Charlie snuggled his head trustingly into her shoulder.

Matt drew in a deep breath. "Thanks, Hennessy.''

She gave him a rather shaky smile across the table. "Anytime, Sullivan.''

After another moment, he gave a decisive nod and pushed his chair away from the table. "I'll wash the dishes.''

Tommy stirred in the playpen, opening heavy-lidded eyes. Kate knew another long evening of feedings and changes was about to begin. She peeked at Matt, found him glancing back at her and turned quickly toward the playpen, her cheeks suspiciously warm.

* * *

The babies were finally tucked in once again for the night, or until one or the other of them woke for a bottle, whichever came first. Kate and Matt had been lying on the cot only a few minutes in the mercifully quiet darkness when Matt spoke in a whisper. "How do you feel?"

She rolled her eyes, though she knew he couldn't see the wry gesture. "I'm fine."

"Does your arm hurt? Does it feel hot or swollen?"

"It's a little sore, but not disturbingly so. As if I'd punctured it with a nail or cut it with a piece of broken glass or something. I really think it's going to be fine, Matt."

"As long as it doesn't get infected."

"I hadn't even thought of that possibility. Thanks so much for calling it to my attention."

"Sorry."

"I'll keep it clean. And I'm current on all my shots, so there's probably nothing to worry about."

"Good." He lay quietly for another minute, then asked, "Still no nausea? Dizziness?"

This time she expressed her exasperation with a gusty sigh. "If I *were* nauseous—which I'm not—it would probably be from that revolting stew. Would you relax?"

"Sorry," he said again.

"Just give it a rest. I'm fine."

Another ten minutes or so passed. Kate lay on her back, staring at the dark ceiling and wishing she could sleep, aware that Matt was equally wakeful beside her. Again, it was Matt who broke the silence. "Kate?"

"Yes?"

"What you did this afternoon—deliberately putting your hand in front of that snake, not knowing whether it was poisonous or not—well, I just think you should know that was the bravest thing I've ever seen.''

She was particularly glad for the darkness when her face flooded with heat. "It, uh, I, er..."

Annoyed with her stammering incoherence, she began again. "I didn't know what else to do. There wasn't time to pull Charlie away. He already had his hand on the snake. I knew if he tried to pick it up the snake would bite to get away."

Matt shifted onto one elbow, looming over her, a darker silhouette against the shadows. "If anyone had told me a week ago that you'd be so good at taking care of three orphaned babies, I would have thought they were crazy. Looks like I was wrong about you."

Her fingers twisted into the blanket beneath her. "Matt—don't start turning me into something I'm not," she warned him thinly. "I've—*we've* been taking care of the kids because there wasn't any other choice, really. Anyone with any normal compassion at all would have done the same. They're so little and helpless and vulnerable. I certainly couldn't expect them to fend for themselves."

"They're very lucky you missed that press bus."

"That goes for you, too," she murmured, all too aware of how closely he was lying to her, his thigh brushing hers, his face so very close. "I couldn't have taken care of all three of them myself."

"Sure you could've. I'm beginning to think Kate Hennessy can do anything if she sets her mind to it."

His praise made her uncomfortable. He was wrong, of course. There were all too many things she couldn't do. Like cooking. Or playing a musical instrument. Or sustaining a relationship for more than a few awkward, painful months.

"Matt—"

He lowered his mouth to hers and she forgot what she'd intended to say.

The darkness, and the blanket hanging between the cot and the rest of the room gave them an illusion of privacy. They could have been alone in the cabin—in the forest—in the world, as far as Kate knew at that moment. She was aware only of Matt, of his mouth pressed against hers, his hands moving slowly down her body.

They shouldn't do this. It was foolish. Crazy. But she wanted him so badly, she ached with it. She parted her lips and he slipped his tongue inside her mouth with an eagerness that told her he shared her desire. How could she possibly resist him?

Though she couldn't see Matt, she could clearly picture him as her hands slid over his body. His strong, tanned arms. His broad, rippling back. His firm, sleek chest. Taut stomach, lean hips, impossibly long and lanky legs.

Matt Sullivan, hotshot reporter in a cowboy's body. A body she'd been wanting to get her hands on for longer than she could remember, no matter how furiously she would have denied it a week earlier.

His lips moved over her face, seeking, tasting, exploring. "Your skin is so soft," he whispered as he lowered his mouth to her throat. "So cool. Like satin."

His short, week-old beard was silkier than she would have expected, caressing her skin rather than abrading it. She shivered in pleasure.

"I wish I'd shaved," he murmured, as though sensing her thoughts.

"No," she whispered, sliding her fingers into his thick, shaggy hair. "I like it."

He groaned and kissed her mouth again, roughly, deeply. "Kate," he said hoarsely when he finally raised up for air. "I want you. God, I think I've wanted you forever."

She closed her eyes against a ripple of unease. "You don't even like me."

He laughed softly, his fingers moving in her short, tousled hair. "Where did you get that crazy idea?"

"You told me so."

She could feel him smile when he spoke against her lips. "I lied," he said, and then he kissed her again.

Her mind was spinning when that kiss ended, her breath coming in short, ragged gasps, her body trembling with the need to forget caution and common sense and simply attack him. "But you, uh, you said I don't know anything about being a woman. That I wasn't feminine enough for your tastes," she reminded him, her teeth clenched with the force of her self-restraint.

His hand closed gently over one of her quivering breasts, his palm warm through the fabric of her thin T-shirt. "You feel very much like a woman to me," he said simply. "You're the strongest, bravest woman I've ever known. And I want you, Kate. So much I'm shaking with it."

With a sense of awe, she felt the fine tremors running through him. She'd never made a man tremble before. She found the experience exciting—and somewhat frightening. "Matt—"

"This has been building between us for a long time, Kate. If I'm wrong about your feelings—if you want me to stop—say so now. I'll leave you alone, I swear."

There were so many reasons she should tell him to stop. Their history of antagonism. The surreal circumstances they'd been living under for the past five days. Her lousy history with relationships, and her deep-seated fear of being hurt by another failure.

"What about the babies?" was all she could think of to say.

"They're asleep."

The thought of babies reminded her of another good reason they should stop before this went any further. "I'm not protected, Matt."

He went still, and she thought she'd broached the one argument he couldn't counter. Instead of relief, she was aware of an overwhelming disappointment. She felt her arms tighten around him. Maybe if they were very careful, she found herself thinking recklessly.

"I don't know if you're going to thank me or hate me for this," Matt muttered.

She was confused. "For what?"

He climbed off the bed without answering. A moment later, she heard him fumbling beneath the cot, digging through the personal supplies he kept there. And then he pressed a small foil square into her hand. She recognized it by feel. "Oh," she said.

"I, uh, always carry a couple in my shaving kit," he explained, sounding oddly sheepish. "Not that I actually plan on using them or anything. It's just that it never hurts to be prepared—you know—especially these days—"

"Matt," she interrupted, knowing her smile was audible in her voice.

"What?"

"Come back to bed."

He hesitated. "You're sure?"

Nerves and impatience made her speak rather more acerbically than she intended. "If you're waiting for me to beg, Sullivan, you can just forget it."

He laughed softly. "I don't want you to beg, Hennessy. I just want you to be yourself."

And then he slid back onto the cot and took her into his arms, covering her mouth with his before she could think of a suitable reply.

Her decision made, Kate threw herself wholeheartedly into Matt's embrace. A small, practical part of her was still fully aware that she could be making a big mistake, setting herself up for another painful fall, but she ignored that quiet warning. For now, she could only bask in the pleasure of wanting and being wanted by Matt Sullivan.

There were no more words—perhaps because neither of them knew quite what to say. But Kate soon discovered that Matt could express himself very well with his lips, his hands, with subtle movements of his lean, strong body. He brought her very quickly to a point where she could not have spoken coherently had she tried.

He shed his clothing swiftly, dropping them carelessly on the floor beside the cot. Kate regretted the lack of light as she slid her palms over his sleek, warm body. She would have liked to have admired the strong lines she touched so savoringly. And then he slowly, carefully removed her clothes, stopping frequently to explore with his lips and fingertips the unseen areas he exposed.

Kate gasped and arched into his touch, distantly amazed that a man who'd so often made her feel awkward and inadequate could now make her feel so deeply appreciated. Attractive. Feminine.

He made it very clear that he wanted her. That he cared for her—at least for tonight. She told herself that was enough, that it was all she wanted. They were together now, and she would make the most of it, without worrying about tomorrow.

She wrapped her arms around him and kissed him until they were both gasping for breath. And when he finally moved forward to join them, she met him with a fervor that made him moan his approval.

Matt went still. Holding him tightly inside her, she locked her legs around his lean hips and strained upward. When he still didn't move, she whispered, "Matt? Is something wrong?"

"No," he murmured, his voice hoarse. "Something is very, very right. Nothing has ever felt this right. I'm savoring."

She drew a deep breath, taking a moment to savor, herself. Oh, he felt so good. So hard and warm and strong. His words echoed in her mind. *Nothing has ever felt this right.*

She knew exactly what he meant.

Growing impatient, she moved her hips again, slowly, testingly.

Matt groaned. "I'm not going to be able to savor much longer if you keep doing that."

She smiled in the darkness, pleased with the note of strain she'd heard in his voice. She liked knowing that she had him so close to the edge that it was within her power to push him the rest of the way over. She'd hate to think she was the only one hovering this close to insanity.

"Matt?" She slid her hand into his hair, pulling his face down to hers.

"Mmm?" He nibbled at her lower lip.

She whispered her request into his ear.

A moan ripped from his throat. "Kate, you're making it very difficult for me to hang on to my control," he warned her huskily.

Her laugh sounded wicked even to her. "Good," she murmured. "I want to see Matt Sullivan lose control. Just this once, Matt, lose control, okay?"

He crushed her mouth beneath his.

Matt wasn't the only one who lost control during those next few, wild minutes. For the first time in her life, Kate finally learned what all the fuss was about when it came to lovemaking. Always before, she'd found it overrated.

Now, she thought, as she lay dazed and winded in Matt's strong arms, she was in grave danger of finding herself addicted. Addicted to Matt Sullivan, a man who could only break her heart if she were foolish enough to let herself care too much.

Chapter Nine

Kate winced as the time-worn cliché crossed her mind. She hated clichés. But, damn it, she'd never felt like that before. It had been glorious. And she couldn't help wondering if she would ever know that feeling again.

"Kate?" Matt's voice was hushed, strained, almost as if he felt as awed as she did by what had happened between them. Was it possible that the experience had been as extraordinary for him?

She was suddenly embarrassed by her uninhibited response to him. What if it *hadn't* been as special to him? She assumed Matt had a great deal more experience with this sort of thing than she did—what if it had been just an ordinary, pleasant episode for him?

Typically, she hid her feelings behind a smart-mouthed comment. "Quiet, Sullivan, I'm basking in a sensual afterglow."

He chuckled. "Is that what you're doing?"

She was pleased by the casual amusement in his tone; it was exactly what she'd been hoping for to put her more at ease. "Of course," she said. "Aren't you?"

"Something like that." His arm tightened comfortably around her bare shoulders.

She rested her cheek on his shoulder, her hand on his chest, just over his still-pounding heart. The darkness covered them like a soft blanket. She could get used to this, she thought with a yearning ache somewhere deep inside her chest. Too bad it could only be temporary.

"Kate?" he asked again.

"What is it, Sullivan?"

"How's your arm?"

She'd forgotten all about it. It was with some surprise that she realized Matt's makeshift bandage was still neatly in place around her wrist. He'd taken such care that she hadn't even felt a twinge during their lovemaking. "It's fine."

"Not sore? Doesn't feel hot or anything?"

"No. It's fine, really. Feels almost back to normal."

"Good."

Something screeched loudly just outside the cabin. Kate flinched and burrowed more deeply into Matt's shoulder before she could stop herself.

"It was just a bird," he assured her. "Or something," he added, and she could tell by his tone that he had no idea what it had been.

"Yeah," she muttered, trying to restrain her overly active imagination. "Or something."

It had been nice to pretend for a while that they were somewhere safe and civilized—a fine hotel, a secluded resort. A place where they could forget about the real world and just concentrate on the pleasure they'd given each other. But that was only an illusion, of course. Reality was being stranded in a run-down shack in a forest, with what almost amounted to a civil war waging somewhere to the east of them, unidentified creatures roaming beyond the walls, three helpless babies needing to be fed and protected.

José would be back soon to collect them—God willing—and then Kate and Matt would be returning to their own lives. Lives that hadn't prepared them in any way for an involvement with each other.

Matt was quiet for so long that she thought he'd fallen asleep. She wished she could do the same. And then she became aware that his hand was stroking her thigh. Lightly. Lingeringly.

His skin was so warm beneath her cheek. So supple. She turned her head a fraction of an inch and pressed a fleeting kiss into his shoulder.

His hand moved higher, shaping the curve of her hip. A ripple of reaction raced through her. She wondered how she could possibly respond so intensely, so soon after making love with him.

"Kate?"

"Mmm?" Her murmur was noticeably breathless.

"I've got a couple more of those little foil packs in my kit." He slid his hand upward to cup her breast.

She shivered. "Do you?" Her voice sounded ridiculously shrill to her. She hoped he hadn't noticed.

His thumb rotated in a slow circle over her nipple. "Yes."

"Oh." She tilted her head back to give him better access when he began to nibble her throat. Her eyelids grew heavy. "It would be a real shame to let them go to waste, wouldn't it?" she murmured.

His lips left a damp, tingling trail from her throat to her right nipple. "Mmm-hmm."

She buried her fingers in his hair and held his head more tightly to her breasts. "What do you say we open another one *now?*"

She could feel his grin against her breast. "I was just about to suggest that myself."

Between their lovemaking and Maria's usual middle-of-the-night feeding, Matt and Kate didn't get a great deal of sleep. It was near dawn when Matt finally gave in to sheer exhaustion and fell asleep with Kate still clasped in his arms. Despite his weariness, he had no complaints, he thought with a faint smile on his lips as he slid into unconsciousness.

It was only a few hours later that the sound of a muffled explosion brought him back to full, heart-in-his-throat wakefulness.

Wearing nothing but his briefs, he jumped from the cot and bolted for the door. The sun was just starting to filter down through the treetops, the birds darting and chattering among the thick foliage. He saw nothing to alarm him, but that didn't particularly assure him.

"What was it?"

He turned to find Kate standing close behind him, clothes hastily donned, her hair still tousled from sleep. "I don't see anything unusual," he said.

Like him, she didn't look encouraged. "The violence is moving this way, isn't it?"

"I don't know," he admitted. "Maybe. It could have been another power plant or police post under attack. But whatever we heard, it was a long way off."

"What will we do if the sounds get closer? What if the soldiers push the guerillas in this direction? You know we'd be seen as political hostages if we were found here, don't you?"

"We're safe here, Kate," he said, trying to sound confident. "There's nothing of value to anyone around here. There's not even a real road, only that rutted old logging trail. And even that doesn't lead directly to this shack."

She nodded as though she understood his reasoning, but he saw that she was biting her lower lip. He gave her a minute to regain her composure after their abrupt awakening. And then he said, "Kate?"

"Mmm?"

"Are you afraid?"

She started to answer, stopped, cleared her throat and asked rather gruffly, "Afraid of what?"

"You know—the forest. Maybe worried that José won't come back for us."

"Oh." She looked out through the open door, and then slowly back to his face. "I'm a little worried," she admitted. "Mostly for the babies' sake. It wouldn't be so frightening if it were just the two of us."

He chuckled quietly. "Yeah. I think the two of us would recklessly take on the guerilla army if they got in our way."

"Right. But it's sort of hard to be tough and aggressive when you're holding a baby bottle and a dirty diaper."

"True."

He lifted a hand to stroke the soft line of her cheek with the backs of his fingers. "We'll get by, Hennessy. I don't know anyone more capable and self-sufficient than you. There's no one I'd rather be stuck with three babies in the middle of a war zone with," he added, trying to make her smile again.

He'd discovered that seeing Kate looking worried and vulnerable gave him a funny ache somewhere deep in his chest. Made him want to do something to comfort her.

Funny. The very things he'd criticized in Kate Hennessy before were the traits he now found himself complimenting. Her strength. Her courage. Her determination. Her refusal to give up, or stand back and let someone else take care of her.

He tried to imagine his sister faced with the situation he and Kate had found themselves in during the past week. And then he thought of the frilly, pretty-but-rather-useless women he'd tended to date in his past. Would any of them have taken charge as easily and as matter-of-factly as Kate had when the necessity had arisen?

Oh, maybe they'd have been more comfortable with the babies, more practiced in the little domestic chores Kate had struggled with. But how would they have handled the stubborn wood stove, the primitive outhouse, the absence of bathing facilities, the monotony of barely edible canned food, the awkward sleeping arrangements, the constant awareness of peril? The snake?

Kate had done her share of griping, as he had, but she'd never once whined or given in to self-pity. And as for last night—well, he still couldn't think of those intimate hours without breaking into a sweat. How could he ever have guessed it would be like that between them?

He still wasn't quite sure how he felt about a longtime involvement with Kate Hennessy, but he was damned glad she was here with him now.

Charlie had awakened and climbed to his feet in the playpen. He looked over the top at Matt and Kate. "Pybbixx," he said solemnly.

Kate smiled. "I think he said he'd like his breakfast now."

"Yeah," Matt answered, letting his hand drop from her face. "Sounded like that to me, too."

She turned away. "I'll dig out a jar of baby oatmeal. Why don't you see if there's any fruit or anything left for us? If you want to," she added with uncharacteristic courtesy.

He nodded. "Sure. I'll see what I can find."

He closed the door of the shack before he moved toward the kitchen, as though shutting out the dangers and uncertainties that lay beyond his field of vision.

After breakfast, Matt washed the dishes, then turned to Kate. "I want to look at your arm again."

She glanced at the bandage. "No need. It feels fine."

His face took on that stubborn set she'd come to know so well. "Nevertheless, I want to look at it."

She lifted a mocking eyebrow. "'Nevertheless'?" she repeated. "My, aren't we getting formal?"

"You're stalling, Hennessy. Sit down." He set the antibiotic cream on the table, along with the remains of the shirt he'd used for bandages.

She sighed loudly, but knew it was no use arguing any further with him. She sat in the chair and ungraciously offered him her arm. "All right, Dr. Sullivan. Get on with it."

The look he gave her was a reproving one. "I only want to make sure you're healing all right, Kate. Even if the snake wasn't venomous—and I guess we can assume by now that it was not—the wound could still get infected if we're not careful. Then what would we do?"

His gently reasoning tone had the effect of making her squirm with the awareness of how badly she was behaving. She didn't know why she was being so snappy. Maybe because Matt was so very hard to resist when he was being gentle and caring. Maybe because she was tired of reminding herself that she had to keep resisting in order to protect herself from the inevitable heartbreak if she let herself fall the rest of the way for him.

"I'm sorry, Matt. I guess I'm just tired," she said with unfamiliar meekness when he reached for her arm.

He looked startled by the apology. "That's okay," he assured her, though he eyed her a bit warily, as though expecting her to say something else more in character for her. When she remained silent, he smiled and unwrapped the makeshift bandage.

Matt looked relieved—as Kate was—to see that the punctures were still a bit reddened and swollen, but not alarmingly so. He spread more of the ointment on the area, wrapped it with a fresh bandage, then brought Kate's heart into her throat by placing a tender kiss in her palm before he released her and turned away.

They went about their chores very quietly that morning. Kate took care of the babies while Matt cut more wood for the stove, and he watched them while she did some housecleaning. They shared another can of pork and beans for lunch and then fed the babies and gave them bottles.

"I want to go to the bus this afternoon for the rest of the bottled water," Matt said when the babies had been fed and put down for naps. "We're getting low here."

Kate nodded. "You might bring the rest of the diapers, too, if you can carry them."

"You don't want to go with me?" He seemed surprised that she was willing to stay behind after kicking up such a fuss last time.

"You can't carry as much if you have to haul two babies," she pointed out logically. "I'll stay and baby-sit while you go."

At least she knew this time that Matt hadn't relegated her to child care simply because he didn't want the task himself. He had certainly proven during the past few days that he was willing to split all the chores evenly, without regard to frustrating, traditional gender expectations.

Matt glanced at the sleeping babies, then at Kate. "I might as well go now, while they're asleep. You'll be okay here by yourself, won't you?"

"Of course I will," she said with strained patience. "You're the one who'll be in the forest alone. You be careful, you hear? And don't try moving the bus again. It's fine where it is."

"Worried about me, Hennessy?" he asked, as he had after he'd frightened her by moving the bus before.

This time she didn't bother with bravado. "Yes," she said simply.

His gaze was warm on her face. He leaned over and brushed his mouth across hers. "I'll be careful," he promised.

"Good," she said with a forced smile. She watched him until he closed the cabin door behind him, and she hoped she was successful at keeping her raw feelings hidden. She was afraid they were all too visible in her eyes.

During the short time that Matt was gone, Kate bathed herself as well as she could and changed into clothes that were as clean as she'd been able to get them by washing by hand in well water with no detergent.

Peering into the small mirror she carried in her pack, she combed her hair and found herself thinking of the small cosmetics bag tucked into her bag on the bus. She wished she had a few of those things now—her favorite eye shadow, a touch of blusher, a little mascara and lip gloss, maybe.

And then she shook her head in self-disgust. "Don't be an idiot, Hennessy," she said aloud. "You aren't on vacation."

She wasn't acting like herself, hadn't been all day. Neither had Matt, for that matter. Both of them had been so polite and judicious that their best friends wouldn't have known them.

And then there was this sudden domesticity they were both displaying. Kate puttering around the kitchen, while Matt chopped wood and hauled supplies...it was just too bizarre. Unreal.

When he'd asked her earlier if she was afraid, she'd almost blurted out that she was terrified. She'd thought for one fleeting moment that he'd been talking about what was happening between them, rather than whatever might be going on outside the cabin.

Sure, she worried about the possible dangers and the growing likelihood that something had happened to José. That it would be up to her and Matt to get themselves and the babies to safety. But the way she was beginning to feel about Matt—now *that* really frightened her.

She bit her lip, thinking about the night before. And found herself haunted by those same troubling questions. Had it meant as much to Matt as it had to her? Had it been as special, as phenomenal for him? Did he know how deeply it had affected her?

Would they make love again tonight?

Maria started to fuss. Kate sighed, put the mirror away and moved to the baby's pallet. "What's the matter, sweetie?" she asked, lifting the disgruntled infant into her arms. "Surely you aren't hungry or wet again. It hasn't even been an hour since you were fed and changed!"

But it seemed that Maria had only wanted attention. She quieted immediately when Kate picked her up and started talking to her. Because the babies seemed to like it when she sang to them, Kate sat in one of the rickety chairs and began the opening verse of "Mockingbird." Maria lay contentedly in her arms, the ever-present pacifier in her tiny mouth. Charlie stood in the playpen, chin propped on his chubby hands as he listened. Tommy sat at Charlie's feet with his battered teddy bear, making noises as though he were trying to sing along.

It was a very tranquil, very domestic scene. As Matt walked back into the cabin and smiled at the sight, Kate was painfully aware that it was also very illusionary.

Could what they'd discovered together last night possibly survive the return of harsh reality? And would she be able to pick up the pieces of her heart if this budding relationship ended as painfully as those few, half-forgotten others in her past?

Later, Kate tried to wash socks and underwear in the rusty sink while Matt boiled another pan of water in which to wash bottles and nipples. "We're really running low on bottled water," he said, a worried crease wrinkling his brow. "The case I brought from the bus was the last of it. I wish I felt safer using the well water."

"We have enough bottled water for another couple of days. Surely José will be back by then. If not..." Kate left the sentence dangling. Both of them knew some sort of action would become necessary if José wasn't back in another two days. They simply hadn't enough supplies to last any longer than that.

There was barely enough room for the two of them to move around in the cramped corner that served as a kitchen. Matt bent to put another stick in the stove, and his elbow bumped Kate's leg with the action. "Sorry," he apologized. "Did I hurt you?"

"No, of course not." She pulled a pair of his socks out of the wash water and began to wring them as dry as possible.

Matt reached over to remove them from her hands and finish the task himself. "I'd better wring out the rest of these things," he said. "You don't want to overwork that wrist."

"That's okay. I can handle it. Go back to whatever you were doing."

"I was just heating water. Why don't you sit down and rest a few minutes while I finish this up? You've been on your feet all day."

"So have you," she pointed out, frustrated by the unnatural solicitousness between them. "I'm hardly going to exhaust myself by washing a few socks and underwear."

"I really think—"

"Sullivan," she snapped, losing patience. "Stop treating me like an invalid. Move your butt and let me get back to what I was doing before I drop-kick you out of my way!"

He blinked, frowned, then looked at her with a dawning smile. If he laughed at her...

The smile broke into a full-fledged grin. "Anyone ever tell you you're cute when you're mad, Hennessy?"

Her reply should have singed his ears. Instead, he laughed and snatched her into his arms for a long, thorough kiss.

He released her as suddenly as he'd grabbed her. "I'll get out of your way and let you finish your washing. Don't put any starch in my shorts, okay?"

She bit her lip against an unexpected urge to smile and regally turned her back on him. She didn't want him to get the idea that he could melt her spine with nothing more than a kiss. Even if it was all too true.

For some reason Kate and Matt were both in a much better mood after that brief contretemps. Having no other chores to keep them busy, they spread the blankets on the splintery floor and sat down with the babies, giving the boys the freedom to crawl around and get some exercise. Both boys loved playing with Matt, who tickled them and wrestled with them while Kate watched with a grin and Maria with wide-eyed fascination.

As though he worried she might be feeling left out, Tommy crawled to Kate and climbed clumsily onto her lap. She hugged him, then spent a few minutes balancing him on his bare feet, trying to encourage him to stand without assistance. Each time she released him, he plopped onto his diapered bottom with an expression of surprise, followed by a peal of giggles.

"You aren't even trying," she accused him fondly, ruffling his thick brown curls.

"He's a little young to walk, isn't he?" Matt asked. "I don't think my niece walked until she was a year old, and Tommy's not but—what?—eight months, maybe?"

"Beats me," Kate answered, tugging the baby upright again and supporting him with a hand on either side of his chubby belly. He bounced happily between her hands, enjoying the play, but making no effort to support his own weight. "I don't think he's any older than that," she said cautiously. "Probably somewhere between six and nine months."

Matt glanced at Charlie, who'd pulled up on one of the rickety chairs and was pounding the worn-smooth seat with one little hand. "Charlie's going to be walking soon," he commented.

"Yes. He's probably closer to a year old."

"They grow a lot in that first year, don't they?" he asked, looking from tiny, totally helpless Maria to Charlie.

"My friends who are parents are always talking about how quickly their children grow," Kate replied. "It seems as though they progress from birth to drivers' licenses in the blink of an eye."

"That's what my mom says. She's been hinting very strongly lately that I should start having some of my own before I'm too old to keep up with them."

Kate cocked her head, suddenly curious. "How old are you, Matt?"

"Thirty-one. How about you?"

"I'll be twenty-seven next month."

"Your parents pushing you to get married?"

"They've dropped a few hints."

"And . . . ?"

"And what?"

"You think you'll ever tie the knot? Settle down with a couple of little rug rats of your own?" His tone was rather conspicuously offhanded.

She answered in the same studiously casual manner. "I don't know. Maybe." She stroked Tommy's soft cheek. "I suppose I have the usual instincts, but—"

Matt bent his head over Maria, tucking her pacifier back into her seeking mouth. "But?" he asked, sounding as though he were giving only half his attention to the conversation.

Kate knew full well that he was more interested than he pretended, though she wasn't exactly sure where he was leading with these uncomfortable questions.

"I'd have to be absolutely sure that it would work out," she said slowly, gravely. "I don't like starting something I can't finish. I take my commitments very seriously—too seriously, maybe. I give them all I have, all I am. It's the way I approach my work, and it's probably the way I'd go into a marriage. All or nothing. And anytime I invest that much of myself in something and it doesn't work out—well—"

"You get hurt."

She nodded in response to his quiet observation. "Yeah. I get hurt. And I hate that."

"No one likes being hurt, Kate."

"No, of course not. Some people just seem to shrug it off more easily than others."

She was very careful not to meet his gaze. "And there's always that LWS thing," she said, deliberately lightening her tone.

Matt groaned, not needing a reminder of what the letters stood for in her vocabulary. "There you go again. Always blaming the men."

"I speak from bitter experience, Sullivan."

"Maybe you've just used lousy judgment with the men you've known before, Hennessy. Ever considered that?"

"Of course I have. Which means I'm going to be damned careful in the—Matt! Look at Charlie!"

Blinking at the sudden change of topic, Matt looked—then grinned. "How about that?"

A frown of intense concentration on his face, Charlie swayed on his feet several inches away from the chair, his hands spread at his sides for balance. While Kate and Matt watched, he lifted one fat little bare foot, wobbled a bit, then set it down carefully on the blanketed floor, moving himself a step farther.

"He's walking," Kate whispered, as though a loud noise would cause him to fall. "Matt, he's walking!"

Seeing that they were watching him, Charlie grinned, proudly displaying both his teeth, spread his arms as though to welcome applause and fell smack down on his bottom. Apparently content with the progress he'd made, he didn't try to get back up, but sat there smiling and coo-ing with satisfaction at his accomplishment.

Kate and Matt laughed and hugged him—and then hugged each other. A warm glow began somewhere inside her, a glow of pride, of affection, of a deep, unexplain-able contentment. Her eyes met Matt's and they smiled in one quiet, heart-stopping moment of absolute under-standing.

Matt slipped a hand behind her head and pulled her mouth to his for a quick, urgent kiss—a promise of more kisses to come at the first opportunity. Kate kissed him back with every intention of seeing that he followed through on that promise.

The babies broke them apart, clamoring for attention. It was time for a change of diapers, and then dinner. Kate welcomed the activity, which precluded further conversa-tion until she had time to pull her rampaging emotions firmly back under control.

After the babies were changed and fed, Kate and Matt sat down for an early dinner. Kate picked at the unidenti-fiable canned meat without enthusiasm. She was hungry, but heartily tired of the bland, preservative-laden meals they'd been forced to eat for the past week.

Matt was watching her sympathetically across the ta-ble. "It's not very good, is it?"

She shrugged. "It's keeping us alive. We shouldn't complain."

"Doesn't mean we have to like it."

"True." She took another bite and repressed a shudder. "Actually, this stuff makes me long for my mother's cooking."

"Your mom's a great cook, is she?"

"Can't boil water without burning it," Kate replied cheerfully. "Came up with some of the most horrendous concoctions you could ever imagine when I was growing up. But even those culinary disasters tasted pretty good in comparison to this."

"My mom's a terrific cook," Matt said with audible wistfulness. "She could take this can of goo and turn it into a gourmet delight with a pinch of basil and a little flour. As for her baking—man, I can almost smell her kitchen now!"

Kate was painfully aware that her own cooking skills left a great deal to be desired—even in comparison to her own mother. Of *course* Matt's mom would be a cross between June Cleaver and Julia Child.

She pushed away the remainder of the food, even though her stomach still felt empty. There was no way this thing between them was going to work out, she thought glumly. She might as well start preparing herself now, before she let herself get hurt any more than the inevitable pain she already faced.

She was still sitting at the table, feeding Maria a bottle while Matt rinsed their dinner bowls, when the door to the cabin burst open without warning and a man stepped inside.

Chapter Ten

Startled by the unexpected intrusion, Kate gasped and tightened her arms around Maria's tiny body. A tin bowl dropped from Matt's hand, clattering loudly on the floor as he threw himself protectively in front of Kate and the babies. He braced himself between them and the door.

Kate recognized the small, dark man who'd entered the cabin at the same time Matt spoke. "José," he said in relief. "Damn it, you scared us."

The driver lifted an eyebrow in mild surprise. "You were expecting me, no?"

"We've been expecting you for days," Matt replied wryly. "But you startled us anyway."

Kate could almost see the tension leaving Matt's body. She thought of the moment he'd thrown himself in front of her, unarmed, vulnerable to attack, but prepared to fight, if necessary. A strange little thrill ran through her.

Odd. She had never wanted a man's protection, had always preferred to fight her own battles. So why was she reacting with such primitive exhilaration to Matt's ridiculously macho behavior?

José looked at the babies in approval and spoke in rapid Spanish to Matt. Matt turned to Kate to translate. "He thanks us for taking such good care of the kids, and he says their adoptive families are very concerned about them."

"He reached the orphanage safely?" Kate asked, then almost blushed at the stupid question. Obviously José had reached safety, or he wouldn't be here now!

Matt didn't seem to notice her momentary confusion. He nodded. "He's brought a van to take us to San Arturo. We'll be able to arrange transportation home from there."

Kate nodded, wondering at the lump that had suddenly formed in her throat. "That's . . . that's good."

"Yeah," Matt agreed without smiling.

José said something else.

Matt looked surprised. "He contacted our associates to let them know what happened to us, and why we've been delayed. He also asked them to notify our families that we're safe."

A bit startled herself, Kate looked at José, who showed no expression on his dark, lean face. "It seems he thought of everything. Thank you," she added for his benefit. "*Gracias.*"

José only nodded.

Matt turned back to the driver. "Should we leave tonight or wait until morning?"

"We go," José answered in his careful English. "I help you carry," he said with a swing of his arm to indicate the babies and anything else they would take with them.

As though the movement had reminded him that he was holding a paper bag, he set it on the table and motioned toward it. "Food," he said briefly. "From the seesters. Eat now. Then we go."

Kate looked quickly at the bag. "Food?" she repeated, her mouth beginning to water. "*Real* food?"

Matt had already opened the bag. He looked at her with a smile. "Wait until you see it."

And then he started pulling out neatly wrapped little packages. Fried chicken. Long, crisp-looking carrot sticks. Bread. Fresh fruit. Even flaky pastries oozing with nuts and honey.

Kate moaned. "Oh, God, that looks good."

For the first time in her presence, José smiled. He reached for Maria. "You eat," he urged Kate.

She hardly hesitated before giving him the child and reaching for the plump chicken leg Matt was holding out to her.

There wasn't a scrap of food left by the time Kate and Matt finished. They'd offered to share with José, but he'd refused, explaining that he'd already eaten. He was visibly impatient to be on the way, so they didn't linger at the table.

Kate noticed that José was walking with a marked limp that was more pronounced at times than others. She tried to remember whether he'd limped before but was almost convinced that he had not.

"Did you hurt yourself while you were walking for help?" she asked him, knowing Matt would translate if José didn't understand her question.

The man looked self-conscious. He murmured something to Matt, who frowned and asked several questions. Matt turned to Kate with a look of wonder in his eyes. "He fell off a bluff the day after he left us. Sprained his ankle.

He said he had to use a walking stick for support during the next couple of days, and he apologizes because the injury slowed him down a great deal. He would have been back sooner had he been able to move faster.''

Kate's eyes rounded. The man had walked alone through uncleared, predator-inhabited forest, injured, foraging for food and water along the way—and he was apologizing to *them* for taking a few days more than he'd expected? She felt very guilty for any complaints she might have made during the past week.

José brushed off her praise, and her concern, assuring them that his ankle was nearly healed, hardly even sore now. Kate didn't believe it, but she allowed him his dignity by accepting him at his word.

Matt told José about the snake that had bitten Kate and frightened them so badly the day before. José examined her arm, listened to Matt's description of the snake and reassured them that it wasn't poisonous, though its bite was painful and had been known to cause dangerous allergic reactions. Kate was relieved that she was apparently not allergic, and Matt looked equally grateful.

Kate glanced at Charlie in his playpen, receiving a sleepy smile from him. She knew she would have done the same thing even if she'd known the snake had been deadly, rather than let anything happen to that sweet baby. When it came right down to it, there hadn't really been a choice.

In a remarkably short time, they'd straightened the cabin and packed their belongings. José explained that there were fresh diapers, bottles and formula in the orphanage van and told them to leave everything nonessential behind. He would come back to clean his cabin, he said optimistically, when the fighting had ceased.

Since Kate's backpack had been sacrificed to make a baby carrier, she and Matt shared his, leaving out everything that wasn't particularly valuable to them. Kate, of course, made sure that her camera was safely packed. The photos contained in it now were precious—to her, not to her employer.

Matt zipped the pack and glanced around the cabin. "That everything?"

Kate nodded. "I think so." She gathered Maria into her arms, making sure the baby's pacifier was securely fastened to her tiny shirt. They would need it during the long trip to the orphanage.

Matt carried Tommy in the backpack-carrier, and held the flashlight in his right hand, since it was rapidly getting dark outside. José balanced Charlie on his hip, looking completely at ease with the child. Kate wondered again if the man had ever had a family of his own.

She looked slowly around the ramshackle hut before stepping outside behind Matt. This was the rescue she'd been waiting for, she reminded herself, but now she was beginning to wonder exactly what she had been rescued from. Being here with Matt and the babies hadn't been all bad.

In fact, she thought, her gaze lingering on the narrow cot, some parts of the past few days had been very nice, indeed.

"Let's go, Kate," Matt urged. She turned to look at him and thought she saw a reflection of her own feelings in his expression.

She managed a smile. "Just making sure I haven't forgotten anything."

He nodded and turned away. After all, there was really nothing more to say, Kate thought sadly.

When all of them were outside, José closed the door to the cabin behind them. It shut with a very final-sounding snap.

Kate didn't look back as they walked away.

The trek to the logging road seemed to take much longer in the dark than it had in daylight. They were forced to walk slowly, placing their steps carefully as they balanced babies and baggage.

Kate couldn't help jumping at every rustle, every strange noise—and there were many of them—but José didn't seem at all perturbed. If Matt was uncomfortable about strolling through a forest in the dark, he didn't allow it to show, though a time or two Kate thought she noticed the flashlight beam wavering a bit.

The orphanage van was parked at the side of the rutted road, close to the abandoned bus. While Kate made sure all the babies were securely strapped into car seats, Matt and José retrieved the rest of their personal things from the bus and stowed them in the back of the van. Again, anything that wasn't important was left behind.

The men talked quietly in Spanish as they worked, speaking so rapidly that Kate caught only a few words. Apparently, José was updating Matt on the military events that had occurred during the week since the press evacuation. As Kate and Matt had surmised by the noises they'd heard that morning, the uprising was far from over.

Matt asked José if there was any danger to them on the way to San Arturo. José replied that they were safe—for now. The nervous looks he cast around them let them know that he didn't want to waste any time leaving the area.

It was a long, exhausting trip. The babies quickly grew restless in their car seats. They slept in snatches, waking to fuss and strain against the bindings. José had to stop the van several times for diaper changes and bottle feedings.

Kate and Matt napped when they could and did their best to keep the babies entertained. Matt convinced José to let him drive for a couple of hours, but José seemed to find the trip less arduous than either Kate or Matt did. Maybe because he was more accustomed to such hardship, Kate reflected.

At 7:00 a.m., José pulled the van to the side of the road and announced that he was hungry. They were still several hours away from the orphanage, he added. Pulling out a picnic basket provided by the nuns at San Arturo, he assured Kate and Matt that there was plenty for all of them and that they could eat outside on the grass.

Kate was almost too tired to be hungry, but she knew the fresh air and the short break from traveling would be refreshing.   Maria in her arms, she climbed heavily out of the van, then stopped with an exclamation of unexpected delight.

The spot José had chosen for his impromptu picnic was a cleared overlook on the side of a mountain. Twenty feet from the road, the ground dropped into a high bluff. The rising sun, beaming from behind thin, pink clouds, illuminated tiny villages and sprawling forestland scattered through the mountains spreading across the horizon.

"What a beautiful place to have breakfast," she said with a smile for José.

He didn't return the smile, but his eyes gleamed with pleasure at her approval. Ducking his head in apparent shyness, he spread a blanket and began to unpack the food.

Freed from the confining car seats, the boys were bundles of suppressed energy. Kate, Matt and José somehow managed to eat while preventing the curious babies from tumbling off the side of the mountain. Maria lay on the blanket on her back, kicking her legs as though she, too, would have liked to crawl around and explore.

"It's so nice to eat something that didn't come out of a can," Kate said with a blissful sigh, then sank her teeth into a tortilla-wrapped mixture of seasoned meat and vegetables. She couldn't remember anything tasting so good in a very long time, except maybe the chicken she'd eaten before they'd left the shack. She was already growing very fond of the sisters of San Arturo.

Matt opened a disposable container of orange juice and emptied it with several thirsty swallows. "Wow," he said, wiping his mouth unselfconsciously with the back of his hand. "I'd forgotten how good real juice could taste. Now if only we had some fresh, hot coffee. . . ."

Fending off Tommy, who was trying to grab her carton of juice, Kate made a teasing face at Matt. "Always complaining about something," she accused him mildly.

He looked back at her with exaggerated affront. "I think I've handled the past week quite well."

She gave him a smile over Tommy's curly head. "You've done okay, Sullivan."

"High praise, coming from you," he said, his eyes locking with hers. She thought she read a great deal in them, none of which had anything to do with their casual conversation.

Aware that José was watching them with interest, Kate dragged her gaze away and gave Tommy a sip of her orange juice. She hoped neither of the men would notice the heightened color in her cheeks.

Kate was greatly relieved when José announced that the outskirts of San Arturo were coming into view. Not only was the long trip almost over—it had taken over twelve hours—but the babies were safe. The danger was now behind them, a problem to be resolved by the local authorities. Having done their job and recorded the onset of the hostilities, Kate and Matt were free to return home, to pursue their next assignments. Wherever those assignments might take them.

There was little opportunity for personal conversation during the remainder of the trip, and Kate made no effort to initiate any. But she found a great deal of time to think, and her thoughts were disturbing. She couldn't help wondering what would happen once the babies had been delivered to the orphanage and she and Matt were freed from their responsibility.

She had to go home, of course. She had an apartment in L.A., and a career there. Matt's job was in Washington, D.C., the entire width of a continent away from her. She knew about the difficulties of long-distance relationships, even if she and Matt didn't have so many strikes against them in addition to geography.

The real problem was that once this interlude ended, they'd go back to the lives they'd led before, to being the way they'd been before. People who hadn't even particularly liked each other, much less . . .

She thought of their lovemaking and shivered, knowing she would never forget one heart-stopping moment of it. It had been like something out of a romantic fantasy. Which, of course, was the problem. It hadn't been real. None of it had been.

It had all been make-believe, she thought bleakly, staring blindly out the van window beside her and seeing nothing of the passing landscape. They'd been playing house—Mommy, Daddy, three sweet little babies—and while it hadn't all been nice, it had still been enough of an illusion to make them start believing in fairy tales. And

Kate was no fairy-tale princess, even if Matt *had* been a dashing prince.

Maybe it was best for the affair to end now, before it went any further. Before it ended the way the others had.

Something deep inside her flinched at the thought of Matt's leaving her in disgust when he inevitably realized that she hadn't really changed during the past week. That she was still the same stubborn, temperamental, independent, unfeminine woman he'd disdained before they'd been stranded together.

They could part now with few regrets, she tried to assure herself bravely. Maybe—eventually—she'd look back on this escapade with amusement, and a few fond memories. Maybe she and Matt could be relatively friendly if their paths ever crossed again. Just a couple of fellow journalists who'd once shared an interesting adventure.

And maybe her heart wouldn't really break when they said goodbye. Just crack a little. Maybe.

She was sprawled wearily in her seat, drifting somewhere between unhappy reality and gray unconsciousness, when Matt touched her shoulder. "You awake?"

She forced her eyelids open, squinting against the sunlight streaming through the front windshield. "Yeah. I think so. What time is it?"

"Nearly 10:00 a.m. José says we're about five minutes from the orphanage. I thought you'd want to know."

"Yeah." She sat straighter and pushed a hand through her hair, knowing it was hopelessly tousled. "Thanks."

"Kate, I—"

Kate was relieved when Maria whimpered, giving her an excuse to busy herself with the baby. She didn't know what Matt had been about to say, but the gravity in his eyes had warned her that it was something personal. And she wasn't ready for that. Not yet.

As though realizing that this wasn't the time, or the place, to talk, Matt sat back and lapsed into silence. Kate was intensely aware that he didn't take his eyes off her until José turned the van into the long gravel driveway of the orphanage. She only hoped Matt wasn't able to read her gloomy thoughts behind her deliberately bland expression.

Kate carried Maria into the orphanage, while Matt and José held Tommy and Charlie. They were greeted by a middle-aged American nun who introduced herself as Sister Beatrice. "You must be exhausted from your ordeal," she said, smiling sympathetically at Kate.

Aware of how tired and disheveled she must look, Kate managed a smile in return. "It wasn't too bad," she fibbed.

Sister Beatrice gestured slightly with one hand and three other nuns came forward. "We will call the babies' adoptive families and let them know they have arrived. They are all so grateful to you for taking care of the children—as we are," she added kindly.

Kate's arms tightened instinctively around Maria when a tiny, dark-eyed nun reached for the baby. "They're going to good homes?" she couldn't help asking, just to reassure herself.

Sister Beatrice seemed to understand Kate's concern. "Very good homes," she promised. "The little girl has two parents and a three-year-old brother anxiously waiting to meet her. The boys are being placed with two couples who have prayed to God for children to love and raise as their own. You have helped to answer their prayers, Miss Hennessy. Your unselfish efforts will not be forgotten."

Kate looked down at Maria, who gazed so trustingly back up at her with her huge, dark eyes. "She's very attached to her pacifier," she said to the petite nun, "but she has trouble keeping it in her mouth."

The sister smiled and carefully took the baby. "We will take very good care of her, Señorita Hennessy," she assured her in precise, yet heavily accented English.

Still holding Tommy, Matt reached out one hand to touch Maria's cheek. "She's a good baby," he said, and Kate thought his voice was a bit huskier than usual.

Kate ruffled Tommy's curls. Clutching his battered teddy bear, the boy smiled at her, his tiny tooth shining. "I hope your new mom sings for you, Tommy," she murmured. "And I hope she has a lot of energy. She's going to need it, to keep up with you."

Tommy gurgled, as if in agreement.

While Matt said his own goodbyes to Tommy before handing him over to a waiting nun, Kate turned to Charlie. She held out her hands and the child fell happily into her arms. José stepped back.

"Well, Charlie," Kate said, finding it rather difficult to speak around the lump in her throat. "You keep practicing that walking, okay? Before long, you'll be playing soccer with the big boys."

His straight, silky hair tumbling over his forehead, Charlie gave her one of his sweet smiles and patted her cheek with one chubby little hand. Almost, Kate thought fancifully, as though he were thanking her for taking care of him. His dark eyes gleamed with such intelligence and awareness that she could almost imagine he knew they were saying goodbye.

"He's a bit more sensitive than the other two," Kate explained to the patiently waiting nun. "He'll probably be a little fussy until he adjusts to his new surroundings."

The woman smiled vaguely, and Kate suspected that she spoke little or no English. She probably hadn't understood a word Kate had said.

Kate turned her attention back to the baby, who was looking at her now with a bit of a frown, as if sensing her mixed emotions. "You'll be okay, Charlie," she promised him softly. "You'll have a real home, with a mommy and a daddy and shoes and everything. It'll be great."

Charlie babbled something and tugged at her nose. Kate caught his hand and planted a kiss in the palm. "Take care of yourself, kid," she whispered. And then she handed him over to the waiting arms.

Matt leaned over to pat Charlie's head and say a few words to him. He watched the nuns leave the room with the babies and then turned to Kate, slipping a supporting arm around her shoulders.

"They'll be fine, Kate," he said, as though he'd seen her worry in her eyes.

She knew she had to mask her feelings or she'd burst into weary, confused tears—and she had no intention of doing that in front of Matt and the others. So she swallowed hard, lifted her chin and stepped smoothly out of the curve of Matt's arm.

"Is there a place where I can shower and change?" she asked Sister Beatrice. "I feel very grubby."

"Yes, of course. Sister Angelita will escort you. I'm sure you would also like to make some telephone calls."

"Yes, thank you. I'd like to let my parents know I'm all right. And I'll need to make some arrangements for transportation home, of course."

"Of course. There is a telephone available for you to use. Lunch will be served at noon. I would be honored if you and Mr. Sullivan would join me at my table—unless you would like to rest for a while before eating?"

"No. I'll rest later. Lunch would be very nice, thank you," Kate accepted without looking at Matt. Her first priority now was a hot shower and a change of clothing. After that—well, she would just play it by ear.

In the meantime, she wanted to delay that serious, inevitable talk with Matt for as long as possible. She'd said all the goodbyes she could handle for now.

Chapter Eleven

The first available flight out wasn't until early the next morning, so Kate and Matt were forced to stay overnight in San Arturo. Politely declining Sister Beatrice's gracious invitation to stay at the orphanage, they chose, instead, to find a hotel close to the airport. José drove them to the hotel.

Matt took the driver's hand and spoke to him seriously and at length in Spanish. From the uncomfortable way José shifted his feet, Kate could tell that Matt was thanking him for what he'd done for them. José kept protesting that it had been Matt and Kate who'd been of assistance, by staying behind to care for the babies when the bus had broken down.

"*Gracias,* Señorita Hennessy," he said, ceremoniously taking her hand. "The families weel not forget you."

"It is you to whom they owe their gratitude," Kate replied, equally formal. "You were the one who was willing to travel alone with three babies through a forest. And you're the one who rescued Matt and me along the way. Our contribution was very little in comparison to what you did.''

Just to make sure José understood, Matt repeated Kate's words in Spanish. José actually flushed a bit, then gave a stiff little bow and released Kate's hand.

"Vaya con Dios," he bade them, then turned and with a dignified limp climbed back into the orphanage van.

Kate's eyes felt hot and moist as she watched him drive away. She blinked furiously, blaming the incipient tears on weariness.

Though it was still only late afternoon, Kate was so tired, she could hardly move. All she could think of now was falling into bed—a real bed, with pillows—and lapsing into merciful unconsciousness.

Matt didn't look to be in much better shape. "You wait here with the bags," he instructed, motioning her into a quiet corner of the hotel lobby. "I'll get us a room."

That brought her eyes fully open. "*A* room?" she repeated.

He met her gaze steadily. "Are you making an objection?"

She hesitated. She knew she should insist on two rooms, knew they would be saying goodbye the next morning and flying to different coasts. But they had one more night together, and it was so tempting to take advantage of it. Would it hurt any less to say goodbye now than it would tomorrow?

"Kate?" Matt was frowning now, searching her eyes with an intensity that made her uncomfortable.

She forced a weak smile. "One room's fine, if you want. I just can't promise that I won't fall asleep the minute I touch a real bed."

"Trust me, honey, sleep is all I have in mind right now," he assured her with a wry smile. "But I've kinda gotten used to sleeping with you beside me."

He'd have to get accustomed to sleeping without her again, she almost reminded him. But something held the words inside her. "Get us a room, Sullivan," she said wearily. "Before I curl up right here on the carpet."

He chuckled tiredly and touched her cheek before moving toward the registration desk. All but swaying on her feet, Kate lifted a hand automatically to the spot he'd touched. Then, realizing what she was doing, she dropped her arm.

Had he really called her 'honey'? She'd have to talk to him about that. Later. Much later.

Kate hadn't been exaggerating much when she'd predicted she'd fall asleep as soon as she saw the bed. She walked into the room, dropped her few possessions on the floor, kicked off her shoes and disappeared into the bathroom for maybe fifteen minutes. She reappeared wearing an oversize knit sleepshirt, her hair wet, skin glowing from a quick shower. Less than ten minutes later, she snuggled beneath the covers of the queen-size bed, sound asleep.

Propped on one elbow beside her in the bed, Matt watched her sleeping, wishing he could escape so easily into unconsciousness. Heaven only knew he was tired. In fact, he felt as though he'd been run over by a van rather than having ridden in one for too many hours. So why couldn't he sleep?

Something was bothering him. And it had everything to do with the way Kate had been looking at him since they'd left the shack.

He couldn't figure out what had gone wrong. Was she regretting that they'd made love? If so, why? He certainly wasn't.

Those brief, intimate hours he and Kate had spent together had been the most special time of his life. He'd never felt more attuned, more connected to anyone. They'd been through so much together, had learned so many things about each other. For that one night, he thought he'd grown to know Kate Hennessy as he'd never understood another woman, and he'd thought she felt the same way about him.

And then morning had come, and with it, an invisible, but very real, wall between them. A wall that Kate had carefully, deliberately, and almost visibly erected. Why?

Even now, when she was sleeping so deeply and he was so tired he could hardly move, he wanted to reach out to her, to take her in his arms and make her admit that what they'd had was special. But even now he could feel that barrier between them. Kate had pulled back. She was going to tell him goodbye. And he didn't for the life of him know how he would respond when she did.

The sheet had slipped from her shoulder. Matt gently tucked it back into place. She didn't stir. He knew she'd hate having him watching her as she slept, knew exactly how she'd feel about being seen defenseless and vulnerable—but he couldn't seem to tear his gaze away from her softly flushed face.

Her lashes looked long and dark against her fair skin. Her full mouth was slightly parted, making him remember how sweet it had tasted, how eagerly she'd returned his kisses. The smattering of golden freckles across her nose made her look young, fresh, completely natural. Utterly desirable.

He remembered watching her sleep on the bus, soon after José had rescued them after they'd missed the press evacuation. He'd been annoyed with Kate then, mistakenly believing that she'd be no help with the babies, that she'd only be another annoyance he'd have to bear until he could get back to his real life. How wrong he'd been—about a lot of things.

He'd always found her attractive, even when he hadn't thought he'd liked her. Now he realized that he must have wanted her even then, that he'd spent a great deal of time and effort futilely denying a pull he'd recognized from the first time they'd met.

She'd handled the past week so well, so admirably. She'd worked hard, taken charge at times, taken suggestions when necessary. She had given excellent care to the three orphaned babies, even risking her life to save Charlie pain or harm.

He'd thought she'd grown quite attached to the babies. He'd been rather surprised when she'd said goodbye to them with very little visible emotion. She hadn't even mentioned them since. Hell, he'd been on the verge of bursting into tears himself, but Kate had only patted the kids, made sure they'd be well cared for and then walked away.

Would she walk away from him as easily? Would he let her if she tried? Was there anything he could do to stop her if she'd made up her mind that they weren't meant to be together?

It was dark when Kate finally stirred. She opened her eyes with a frown, wondering if it was time to check diapers or give bottles. When was the last time she'd fed Maria or checked Tommy's diaper? She couldn't remember.

And then her memory returned, along with an accompanying hollow ache. Someone else was responsible for the babies now. Kate was no longer a part of their young lives.

She turned her head on the pillow, sensing Matt's presence beside her. They weren't touching, but she heard his even breathing, felt the warmth that radiated from him as he lay so close beside her. One more night, she found herself thinking despondently, and then she would wake in the dark to find herself truly alone again.

She was still tired, but not yet ready to go back to sleep. She was hungry, and she needed to go to the bathroom. She slid her feet to the floor, deciding to take care of the latter problem before worrying about the first.

Matt's hand closed around her arm. "Where are you going?" His voice was still rough from sleep.

"To the bathroom," she answered with some asperity. "Should I have asked permission first?"

"Sorry. I'm not quite awake yet." He yawned noisily as if to confirm his words.

"So go back to sleep."

"I'm hungry. What time is is?"

She glanced at the luminous dial of the bedside clock. "After ten. Sort of late to get dressed and go out to dinner, isn't it?"

"Let's order room service. They serve until midnight, don't they?"

"I don't know. I wasn't interested in the hotel services when we arrived."

"It's a chain hotel. Should have basic services available." He sat up and snapped on the bedside lamp. Both he and Kate blinked against the resulting bright light.

Suddenly conscious of how rumpled she looked after her nap, Kate slid her hand from beneath Matt's. "I'm going to the bathroom. You look for a room-service menu."

"What do you want me to order for you?"

She gave him a quick smile over her shoulder as she disappeared into the other room. "I don't care," she replied, "as long as it doesn't come out of a can!"

It was midnight by the time they'd eaten and finished the desserts Matt had ordered. They watched television cable news as they ate, both curious about what had been going on in the real world while they'd been stranded in limbo. "Doesn't sound like we missed much," Kate commented.

"That situation in Central Africa bears watching," Matt said absently, sprawled against the headboard of the bed with an after-dinner cup of coffee in his hand. "Probably where I'll end up next."

A sharp pain shot through Kate's stomach. She pressed her hand against it, wondering if the rich food had been too much for her after a week of bland canned fare, knowing all the time that food had nothing to do with it.

"Ever been to Africa?" she asked, trying to sound casual.

"Once. You?"

"No. I've been to Europe and Moscow, and I spent a month in Australia two years ago. Most of my assignments have been in North and South America."

"I've spent a lot of time in the Middle East."

"I know."

He nodded, not surprised that she knew his work. Journalists tended to keep track of their associates—print or broadcast. The competition was fierce, yet there was a camaraderie that developed through common goals and interests.

"Where do you think you'll go next?" he asked.

She shrugged. "Wherever I'm sent."

He nodded. Neither of them was smiling.

She plucked at the hem of her sleep shirt. She hadn't bothered to change for dinner—for one thing, she didn't have that many clothes to choose from and wanted to save her one reasonably clean outfit for traveling the next day. The heavy knit fabric of the knee-length green sleep shirt made it as concealing as a loose dress. Matt had on a pair of jeans and a denim shirt, though he hadn't tucked in the shirt, nor fastened the top three buttons.

She glanced at him from beneath her lashes. Still lounging on the bed, he looked lean and dark and distant, and so good her mouth all but watered in response. He'd shaved that morning after showering at the orphanage. At first she'd been startled at seeing him without the short beard. She'd liked it on him; but she found him just as appealing clean shaven.

The fact was, she simply found Matt Sullivan appealing—and wasn't *that* a joke on her? She, who'd so often scoffed at all the other women who flocked around the sexy reporter like paper clips exposed to a powerful magnet, had learned to her great dismay that she was no more immune to the pull.

"You're staring at me," Matt said without taking his gaze away from the television screen.

She flushed. "No, I'm not."

He gave her a look that made his disbelief clear. "Oh. I thought you were."

She tossed her head. "You always have been terribly conceited, Sullivan."

He shrugged and a grin tugged at the corner of his firm mouth. "When you've got it..."

"Pig."

Matt laughed. "I like you, too, Hennessy."

Like? Oh, how she wished that was all it was!

"You seem awfully far away in that chair. Why don't you come over here and talk to me?" he suggested, patting the bed beside him.

Talking was the last thing she wanted to do. They would inevitably begin to discuss their relationship, and what direction it should take, if any, after this night. And Kate simply couldn't handle that discussion right now.

"If I come over there, it won't be to talk," she said, steadily meeting his gaze.

His eyes widened, then narrowed. He pushed a button on the remote control, silencing the television set, then set his soft drink on the nightstand. His voice had gone a shade deeper when he said, "Then come over here and don't talk to me."

Clinging shakily to her courage, she rose and moved toward him. She snapped off the overhead light on the way, so that the bedside lamp was the only illumination. She reached for the lamp switch, but Matt caught her hand in his. "Leave it on," he said huskily. "I want to see you."

She looked wryly down at her slender figure, her gaze lingering on her slight chest. "There isn't a lot to see."

He gave a tug on her arm and she tumbled onto the bed, right into his arms. "Once again, you don't know as much as you think you do, Hennessy."

She would have retorted, but his mouth covered hers, effectively cutting off whatever she might have said.

Sparring was abruptly abandoned. Kate had no desire now to antagonize him—her present desire was much more basic. She parted her lips, inviting him to deepen the kiss, and Matt did so with gratifying alacrity. His arms were tight around her, his legs tangled with hers, their mouths tightly meshed. The pleasure of being so close to him was enough to tighten her chest, almost as intense as the fear of never being this close to him again.

Taking her by surprise, Matt shifted his weight, rolling Kate onto her back as he loomed over her. Draped halfway over her, he cupped her face in his hands. "Have I ever told you that I think you're an extremely attractive woman, Kate Hennessy?" he asked almost whimsically, making a leisurely study of her flushed face.

"No," she murmured. "We both know I'm not beautiful, Sullivan, so don't bother with flattery tonight, okay?"

"I didn't say you were beautiful," he corrected her, his thumb slowly stroking across her lower lip. "I said that I find you attractive—extremely attractive. Your sparkling green eyes— "He kissed her eyelids, one at a time.

"The little freckles on your nose—" He touched the tip of his tongue to her skin, as though sampling those golden sprinkles.

"The sexiest lower lip I've ever seen—or tasted," he murmured, brushing his mouth over hers.

The words were typically Matt. Candid—yet devastating. She didn't quite know how to respond, especially since her mouth had gone so dry, she wasn't sure she could speak coherently. Fortunately, Matt didn't give her an opportunity to speak. He kissed her again, slowly, deeply, then reached for the hem of her nightshirt.

Her face warmed even more when he swept the shirt over her head, leaving her in nothing but tiny bikini panties. It was the first time he'd actually seen her unclothed, since they'd made love in darkness before. She'd never been more aware of her slight size—and she'd heard through the gossip lines that Matt's tastes usually ran to exotic and voluptuous. Kate was neither.

He looked at her for so long, so quietly, that she grew even more uncomfortable. She squirmed against the sheets. "What are you staring at, Sullivan?"

He met her eyes and his expression was so tender it made her ache. "Perfection," he murmured, cupping his hand over one small, firm breast.

Though she knew full well she was far from perfect, she found that she was no longer inclined to argue. Matt slid his hand slowly down her side, tracing the slender curve of her waist, the slim flare of her hip, the long line of her thigh. The appreciation in his eyes made her almost believe she *was* perfect—and no other man had ever given her that. Whatever happened, she would always be grateful to Matt for letting her feel beautiful, at least for this one night.

His fingers slipped beneath the elastic band of her panties. He stroked the cinnamon curls until she was writhing against the pillows. Her legs brushed his jeans, making her intensely aware that he was still fully clothed while she was nearly nude.

She tugged at his shirt. "Take this off," she demanded, too impatient to trust herself with the buttons.

He laughed softly. "Was that an order?"

"Yes. But I want you badly enough to beg, if you want," she said simply.

His smile faded. "No. That's not what I want from you, Kate. I want you just the way you are."

At least for tonight, she almost said. But she kept the words to herself. She refused to think about tomorrow. She had the rest of this night to enjoy.

It was a long time later when Matt spoke. "Kate? You asleep?"

She lay limply against his shoulder. They'd long since turned out the light, and had been lying in the shadows recuperating. Kate had been very quiet, but something told him she was still awake. She confirmed his suspicion when she spoke. "No, I'm not asleep."

"Good. We'll be in a hurry in the morning to make it to the airport." Their flights left within an hour of each other early the next morning, so they would share a cab to the airport and part there. He thought of that parting with a hollow pang of regret. "We really should talk now."

He felt her tense against him. "Talk about what?" she asked guardedly.

Was she being obtuse, or deliberately evasive? He suspected the latter. "You know what I mean," he chided. "We should talk about us. About what we're going to do after tonight."

"I would think that's obvious," Kate said, her tone so bland she could have been talking about the weather. "You go back to Washington and I return to L.A. Within a week or two, we'll probably both be out of the country again pursuing other stories." She rolled onto her back on her side of the bed, breaking the contact between them.

He couldn't believe she could sound so blasé about it, especially after the lovemaking they'd just shared. "I'm sure you don't mean that the way it sounded."

"How did I make it sound?"

"As though we'll be saying goodbye at the airport tomorrow. As though we'll be taking up our lives just where we left off last week."

"We *will* be saying goodbye at the airport tomorrow," she said matter-of-factly. He wished he could be sure that he wasn't imagining the pain underlying the brusque words. "And we will be taking up our lives again," she added. "I assume we both still have jobs to return to, even though we took a week's unscheduled leave."

"Are you trying to tell me you don't want us to stay in touch after we leave in the morning? That you don't want to see me or talk to me again?"

"I'm sure we'll be seeing each other again, Matt. We do seem to be assigned to the same stories quite often."

Shoving himself upright, Matt reached over and snapped on the bedside lamp. Kate blinked at the light, and pulled the sheet to her chin. That gesture only made him angrier. She hadn't been trying to hide from him earlier—either physically or emotionally. Why now?

"We really should get some sleep," she said, not quite meeting his eyes. "Our planes leave early in the morning."

"I'm not going to let this go that easily," he told her bluntly. "Damn it, Kate, I refuse to believe the past week hasn't meant something to you. That what we found together wasn't important."

"Of course it meant something to me, Matt," she said in a soothing tone she might have used with one of the fretful babies. "It was very special. But now—well, it's over. Or it will be when we get on those planes tomorrow."

"Why?" he demanded, fiercely holding her gaze with his own. "Why does it have to be over?"

She plucked at the hem of the sheet. "We both know it would be a mistake to make more out of what happened than it really was."

"And just what *was* it?" he asked, his voice low and furious.

Her gaze slid away from his. She frowned at her hands as though wondering what to do with them. "Proximity," she replied in a murmur. "Propinquity. Certainly a healthy dash of hormones. We both know better than to start reading more into it than that."

He was so angry, he could hardly speak. Somehow he managed to form the words and was pleased that he could sound cool. "Do we?"

She nodded. "We got along well enough when it was necessary, but we both know we'd probably kill each other if we had to spend any more time alone. We're both stubborn and temperamental and determined to have our own way. And we're both workaholics. Neither of us is willing to compromise when it comes to our work or our freedom."

"You're making a lot of sweeping assumptions."

"Have I said anything that isn't true?"

"I still haven't heard any good reason why we shouldn't try to have a relationship. We've been a great team during the past week, Kate. We're good together, despite the problems. How can you just be willing to walk away from it without even making an effort to see if it can last?"

"How do you think we can be together when we don't even live on the same coast?" she countered, finally meeting his eyes. "Are you willing to leave *your* job on the gamble that you and I can have a relationship without being at each other's throats in a month? Or are you proposing that we stay in touch through letters and phone calls and the occasional weekend when neither of us is assigned God-knows-where?"

He had to acknowledge the validity of her concerns. Yes, their jobs were on separate coasts—and no, he wasn't willing to walk away from his just yet. He'd worked too hard to get where he was to give it up without some guarantee that there'd be another, comparable position open to him. And he knew exactly how hard Kate had struggled in her career, knew how important her job and professional reputation were to her. She wouldn't easily leave that niche for him—nor would he ask her to.

"Okay, so it won't be easy," he admitted. "But we can try, damn it. Other couples manage to be together and still have demanding careers."

"Other couples do," she agreed, the first trace of sadness appearing in her shadowed green eyes. "I just don't think it's possible for us."

He remembered her claim that she would go into a relationship with everything she had and that she feared being devastated if it didn't work out. Was she so deeply afraid of being hurt by him? And, if so, didn't that mean that her feelings for him were much more than casual?

"What is it you want, Kate? What do you want me to do now?" he asked, watching closely for her reaction to the puzzled question.

She seemed to struggle with her answer, as if she really didn't know what she wanted. As if she didn't really like any of the possibilities open to them.

Finally she met his eyes with a beseeching look and whispered, "I guess what I want is for you to give me time. Give us both time. This happened so fast, and the circumstances were so bizarre—don't you understand that I can't just change my life on the basis of the past week?"

"I understand that you're afraid," he said gently.

For a moment, denial flashed in her face. He knew how hard it was for Kate Hennessy to admit to fear. But then she seemed to acknowledge the futility of denials he wouldn't believe, anyway. "Yes," she said so softly he could hardly hear her. "I'm afraid. I really don't want to get hurt again, Matt."

God, he hated being compared to the men in her past. Hated being forced to pay for their mistakes, their stupidity. Yet he knew that pushing her would have the effect of driving her away for good. She was too wary, too ready to bolt. And as much as he hated to admit it, the only way he was going to have any chance with her would be to let her go. At least temporarily.

It was quite a risk he was taking. Saying goodbye tomorrow, letting Kate go back to L.A. without him, leaving her alone for a few weeks—or months—could make her realize how much they'd come to mean to each other. How senseless it was for them to be apart when they were so very good together. How foolish it was to give up without even giving it a try.

Or it could backfire on him. Being alone just might give Kate time to reinforce her defenses, to convince herself that she was, indeed, better off without him. That she was perfectly content with the unfettered, uncomplicated single life she'd led before they'd been stranded in the forest together.

The thing was, he really had no choice. She was scared, and exhausted—physically and emotionally—and she'd made up her mind that it was best for them to end it now. He could only go along with her for now with hopes of changing her mind later, after she'd had time to miss him. And, oh, how he hoped she would miss him. God knew he was going to miss her. Her fire, her spirit, her courage, her companionship. Her kisses.

She was watching him warily, obviously wondering what he'd been thinking for so long. He saw the smudges of weariness beneath her eyes, the pallor of her delicate skin, the evidence of frayed nerves in the way she chewed her full lower lip. And his heart twisted for her.

This was no time to push her, he told himself. She'd given all she had to give during the past week. She needed time to rest, time to recover. And if she would accept nothing else from him now, at least he could give her that time.

"You're tired," he said, reaching to turn off the light. "You need some rest. You have a long flight home tomorrow."

"So do you," she said, and he heard the suspicion in her tone. She was obviously wondering if he was really going to concede so easily to her request.

"Yeah. Guess we'd better get some sleep." He reached over and pulled her onto his shoulder again, settling her firmly against him when she instinctively resisted for a moment. He brushed his lips across her forehead, forcing himself to speak lightly when so many more heartfelt words trembled on his lips. "Good night, Kate. Sleep well."

"G'night, Matt," she whispered. "See you in the morning."

But he didn't want to think about the morning. Not now, when he had her in his arms for the last time in what might be a very long time.

He refused to accept that it could be the last time ever.

Chapter Twelve

They rose and dressed the next morning with little conversation. Matt was unusually quiet and Kate couldn't think of anything to say that hadn't been said last night.

She still wasn't sure exactly why he'd made it so easy for her to veto any future relationship with him. Had he seen her determination, realized the futility of arguing with her? Or had he secretly agreed with her?

Had he only been looking for a graceful excuse to break it off now? If so, he must have been relieved that she'd done so first, without making him look churlish.

They reached the airport with just enough time for Kate to check her terribly battered bags. Struggling with the language barrier, she claimed her ticket and checked in at the gate. Matt trailed behind her. He still had some time before his own plane departed, and he seemed in no hurry to separate from her, though he said little as he followed her. Nor could Kate think of much to say to him.

She hated the awkwardness between them, when they'd learned to talk so easily in the shack.

She clutched the tote bag that held her camera equipment and a few other personal belongings, holding it in a white-knuckled grip. Matt stood so closely beside her that their shoulders brushed, and yet she felt a gulf widening between them as the time for her flight drew nearer.

Almost as though they were already apart, she thought sadly. As though an entire continent already lay between them.

A tinny voice came over the loudspeaker, making an announcement in Spanish, then in English. Kate swallowed hard and turned to Matt, making an effort to smile. "That's my flight."

He nodded. "You have everything?"

"Yes."

"You must be getting hungry. I wish we'd had time to eat breakfast."

She shrugged. "They'll serve breakfast on the plane."

He smiled. "It'll probably come out of a can."

She just managed not to wince at the memories his words evoked—memories that should have been grim, but somehow weren't. "Probably," she agreed. "But I'm really not very hungry, anyway."

He touched her cheek. "We had ourselves quite an adventure, didn't we, Hennessy?"

She nodded, her throat tight. "Yes, we did. I'm just glad we managed to come out of it unharmed. And as pals."

"Pals?" Matt repeated, a slight frown appearing between his dark eyebrows.

"Sure," she said breezily. "Pals."

His frown deepened.

Kate cleared her throat. "I'd better go."

He dropped his hand and stepped back. "All right. See you around, Kate."

"See you around, Sullivan."

She forced herself to turn away.

She'd taken only a step when Matt's hand fell on her shoulder, spinning her back around. The kiss all but melted her kneecaps, leaving her dazed, shaken and rather bruised when he finally released her.

"Goodbye, *pal*," he said.

And then he turned and walked away, without looking back.

Kate all but bolted onto her plane, leaving Matt alone to await his own flight to the opposite coast from her.

Kate stared blankly out the tiny window beside her, watching the banks of clouds passing below her without really seeing them. She didn't know how long she'd been flying. Breakfast had been served; she hadn't eaten more than a few bites of it.

Passengers around her slept, or talked quietly or listened to music. She ignored them, lost in her own pain.

"Excuse me, but are you all right?" a British-accented voice asked from beside her.

She turned her attention with some effort to the passenger in the seat next to her. The silver-haired, middle-aged man was watching her in visible concern.

"Yes, I'm fine," she assured him with distant courtesy. "Why do you ask?"

"Well—you're crying," he pointed out, looking uncomfortable.

Her eyebrow rose. "I never cry."

"Oh." He cleared his throat and rustled the newspaper he'd been reading. "Sorry. I thought you were."

Kate nodded and turned back to the window. Only then did she realize that her face was wet, and that a steady stream of tears was still running down her cheeks.

Annoyed with herself, and afraid of what she might do if she really let her emotions go, she fumbled in her bag for a tissue and resolutely dried her eyes.

Her first day home was difficult. Fatigued and disoriented, she returned to find a long list of messages and a stack of unopened mail to be dealt with. She first called her parents and listened patiently to their fear-inspired lectures about being more responsible in her pursuit of award-winning photographs.

She heard the same lecture from her employers and her closest friends. By that time, her patience was wearing thin. Had it not been for the praise she received over the dramatic photos that she'd transmitted while on assignment, she might well have lost her frayed temper.

She woke several times during the night with the vague feeling that she should check the babies. Each time, she remembered almost immediately where she was, but each time it was harder to fall back asleep. She was much too aware of the silence in her apartment, of the emptiness of her big, soft bed.

She was almost relieved when another out-of-town assignment came her way a few weeks after her return from South America. Covering a civil riot in Miami wasn't her idea of a good time, but at least it kept her too busy to think about Matt—more than a few times an hour, anyway.

Several of the national journalists covering the riot were staying at the same hotel. Kate saw a few she knew—some quite well, others only in passing—when she entered the hotel bar late one evening to rest and escape from her unhappy thoughts.

"Kate. Over here." The woman who motioned to her was a tall, thirtyish African-American TV reporter who'd once worked in Los Angeles before taking a position with a station in Chicago. She and Kate had known each other for several years.

"Hi, Jeri. I thought I saw you across the lobby this morning." At the other woman's gestured invitation, Kate slid into the opposite side of the tiny booth. "How have you been?"

"Fine. Though I had a close call this morning. Someone started throwing rocks at my cameraman and me when we were filming a report. Cliff, the cameraman, had to have three stitches at his right temple."

"You weren't hit, were you?" Kate asked in quick concern.

Jeri shook her head. "Just shaken. Police appeared very quickly to help us. Of course, the rock throwers didn't stop then, but they started aiming at the cops instead of us."

"It's the cops they're really angry with," Kate said with a slight shrug. The rioting had started because of alleged violence against a black man who'd been arrested by three white police officers.

"Yeah, well, I sure was glad to see those uniforms this afternoon," Jeri said with heartfelt sincerity. "Of course, the suits back at the station were delighted with the footage Cliff shot as he was being hit by the rocks."

"Exploitive pigs," Kate muttered, but without a great deal of heat. They both knew how things went in this business. Sensationalism attracted viewers, and viewers were measured by advertising dollar signs. It made Kate sick sometimes, but she'd long since stopped hoping to change things single-handedly, figuring the best contribution she could make would be to shoot dramatic, revealing, illuminating photos of human tragedies without lowering herself to exploitation any more than necessary.

"What's this I hear about you and Matt Sullivan smuggling a busload of orphans out of Colombia a few weeks ago?" Jeri asked with avid curiosity, abruptly changing the subject.

Kate wasn't surprised that Jeri had heard the story. The gossip network among journalists was an amazingly efficient one. "A month ago," she replied. "And it was only three babies. Club soda, please," she added to the waitress who'd approached with an order pad.

"White wine," Jeri ordered, then turned immediately back to Kate. "So tell me all about it. This sounds like a fascinating story."

Kate's job kept her on the go so much that it was difficult for her to maintain close friendships. Her friends tended to be journalists who, like her, moved around a great deal. Jeri had been one of her closest friends in L.A., though they hadn't kept in touch very well after Jeri moved.

Since her return from South America, Kate had said little about her experiences, other than a carefully edited version for her parents, and a somewhat more detailed explanation for her employers. She'd declined two requests for interviews by feature writers who thought her adventure would make a good human interest piece; she'd heard from one of the reporters that Matt was also refusing interviews about his role in the evacuation.

Now she found herself talking, starting from the beginning and leaving out only the personal relationship that had developed so unexpectedly between her and Matt. Maybe it was because she genuinely liked Jeri and had missed her during the ten months or so since she'd moved away from L.A. Or maybe it was because she just needed to tell someone what had happened to her and how it had affected her.

Not that she could expect Jeri to understand exactly how the experience had changed her without hearing the parts of the story she was so carefully leaving out.

But Jeri was an excellent reporter, with a journalist's instincts and abilities to read between the lines. "You and Matt got personally involved, didn't you?" was the only question she asked when Kate concluded her tale.

Kate almost choked on the sip of club soda she'd just taken. She decided to play dumb. "With the babies? Yes, I guess we did. They were so sweet and so cute—it would have been hard not to get involved with them."

Jeri rolled her eyes expressively. "I know you fell for the babies, Kate. I could hear that in your voice. But what about Sullivan? You fell for him, too, didn't you?"

"Don't be ridiculous. You know how I feel about Matt Sullivan," Kate bluffed, avoiding her friend's eyes.

"Uh-huh. I know how you used to feel about him. So why do I get the feeling that something has definitely changed? Was a week of the Sullivan charm more than even *you* could resist?"

Kate neatly broke a pretzel into three even pieces. "I'll admit that it wasn't as bad as I would have expected. I mean, he annoyed the hell out of me at times, but he certainly pulled his weight with the housework and taking care of the babies. He had to, of course. God knows *I* didn't know anything about babies when we first—"

"Kate," Jeri interrupted firmly. "You're evading the question."

Kate finally met her friend's eyes. "Let's just say I found I wasn't as immune as I'd always thought I was."

Jeri grew serious. "You got hurt."

"No," Kate assured her. "I didn't. I had enough sense to get out before it went that far." Which wasn't exactly true, of course. She had been hurt by having to tell Matt goodbye. She hadn't stopped hurting since.

There were times when she even wondered if it could have been any worse if they *had* tried and failed to carry on the intimate relationship that had developed in that forest cabin.

Jeri didn't look convinced. "Have you heard from him since?"

Kate shook her head. "No. Last I heard through the grapevine, he was on his way to Somalia."

She hadn't expected to hear from him, of course. After all, she had been the one who'd broken it off between them. She'd known at the time that Matt hadn't liked it. She attributed most of his displeasure to bruised ego. She was quite sure that being rejected by a woman wasn't a common occurrence for Matt Sullivan. Not that she'd rejected him . . . exactly.

"Well, did you—"

"Jeri," Kate interrupted with an attempt at a smile. "We've talked enough about me for now. Tell me what's been happening with you during the past year. How do you like Chicago? Are you dating anyone special? How's it going at the station? You still hoping to get that anchor spot?"

To Kate's gratitude, Jeri took the less-than-subtle hint and allowed her to change the subject. Kate thought that was the true measure of friendship. She knew Jeri would be happy to listen if Kate wanted to talk; but she was equally willing to avoid a topic that had to be obviously painful for Kate.

* * *

Ten weeks after his return from South America, and two weeks after returning from Somalia, Matt went out on his first date in months. The woman he'd asked out was a member of the White House press corps. Tall, blonde, classically beautiful, intelligent and articulate, she was a far cry from the "walking, talking Barbie doll" Kate had accused him of admiring.

Still, Damaris was Kate's opposite in many ways. She was completely comfortable with her femininity, which she emphasized with skillfully applied makeup, artfully styled long hair, a daringly cut dress and a deliberately seductive smile. She obviously loved her job, yet during their discussion of federal policies on family leave and child care, she made it clear that marriage and family were definitely part of her planned future.

Matt had asked Damaris out primarily because she didn't remind him of Kate. And yet he still found himself thinking about Kate all too often during the otherwise pleasant evening. In fact, he hadn't really stopped thinking about Kate since he'd parted from her at the airport two and a half months ago.

Damaris lifted her wineglass to her lips and Matt couldn't help noticing her long, perfectly polished fingernails. How could she do any work and keep them looking so nice? he wondered absently. They wouldn't last two hours in the jungle. And she'd never be able to change diapers with them—she'd probably stab the kid in a very sensitive place. As for scrubbing clothes and baby bottles by hand in water she'd pumped from a well and then boiled on a wood-burning stove... forget it.

This was not a woman he would want to be stranded in the jungle with. Funny, he'd never realized that was one of his criteria.

"How do you feel about snakes?" he heard himself asking out of the blue—then could have kicked himself for being so stupid.

Damaris lifted an arched brow. "Any particular reason you're asking?" she inquired in her soft, throaty voice. "Is there one on my shoulder or something?"

He managed a smile. "Sorry. I was just kidding around."

"Oh." She looked a bit confused, but matched his smile. "Well, in answer to your question, I hate snakes. Just the sight of one sends me screaming in the opposite direction. Even if it's only a photograph of a snake."

"I don't much like them myself," Matt said, remembering the sick, horrifying feeling he'd had when he'd seen the snake sink its fangs into Kate's arm.

He changed the subject abruptly, asking another question about Damaris's job. It wasn't fair of him to be so obsessed with one woman while he was out with another, he reproved himself sternly. Unfortunately, there didn't seem to be much he could do about it.

Mostly because she seemed to expect it, he kissed Damaris when he took her home. It was a nice kiss. She was certainly well skilled in that physical exercise. Yet there was just no staggering explosion of sensation, as there had been with Kate. The embrace didn't leave him shaken and confused and intrigued and more than a little nervous, as his first kiss with Kate had.

The simple fact was that Damaris just wasn't Kate. And it was Kate he wanted. Still.

Hands deep in the pockets of his jacket, shoulders slumped in discouragement, he stepped out of the elevator in the lobby of Damaris's apartment building. A man and woman of about his age waited to board. The man carried a sleeping toddler on his shoulder, and his free hand rested possessively at his wife's waist. Matt nodded to them, then walked away.

He loosened the knot of his tie and wondered why his throat had suddenly gone so tight. And then he remembered how it had felt to have little Tommy sleeping on his own shoulder.

He pressed a hand to his stomach, feeling as if there was a gaping, painful hole inside him. He wondered what it was going to take to fill it.

The image of Kate's face was firmly locked in his mind as he started his car and drove away from Damaris's building without a backward glance.

Kate sat in front of the computer in her home study, trying hard to concentrate on an outline for a photo assignment she had once wanted very badly to be given. Now she found herself having to struggle to find any enthusiasm for the project.

Her telephone rang. She picked up the cordless handset beside her with held breath and racing pulse—the way she'd reacted each time she'd received a call during the past three months. It was never Matt, of course. She was quite sure it wouldn't be this time. But still she found herself hoping—and hating herself for doing so. "Hello?"

"Kate? It's so nice to hear your voice, instead of your answering machine, for a change."

Kate tried to ignore the sinking feeling in her chest. "Hi, Mom," she said. "How are you?"

"Just fine, thank you. And your dad's doing very well. He shot a 76 today. You'd think he negotiated world peace, from the way he's carried on."

"Tell him congratulations for me," Kate said with a smile, shaking her head at her father's long-time addiction to golfing. She herself had never understood the at-

traction of the game. The few times her father had
managed to drag her onto a golf course had been less than
successful.

"So, how are *you?*"

"Great," Kate lied without blinking. "I was just doing
some work on a proposal for a new photo assignment."

"Not something dangerous, I hope," her mother fretted.

"Not at all," Kate replied airily. She wasn't exactly lying that time. Just stretching the truth a bit.

"Well, I won't keep you away from your work. I just
wanted to make sure you're all right. You've seemed a bit
down the last couple of times we've talked."

Kate should have known her overly cheerful manner the
past few times they'd spoken wouldn't have fooled her all-
too-perceptive mother. She swallowed a sigh and carried
on with the bluff. "I'm fine, Mom. Really. I guess I've just
been tired when we've talked."

"You don't get enough sleep. And you work too hard."

"Yes, Mom," Kate agreed patiently. "I'll try to do better."

"Nothing's bothering you, dear?"

Kate's gaze drifted to the large corkboard hung on the
wall nearest her. On it were pinned scraps of memos, notes
she'd written to herself, yellowed assignment sheets. Three
candid photographs were fastened directly in front of her
where she could easily see them each time she turned in
that direction. One was of Matt, standing with the forest
behind him, his hair wind tossed, his unshaven chin jutted
forward as if in defiance of circumstances. The second shot
was also of Matt, holding Tommy in his arms and pointing to a bird in a tree overhead. The third photo was of the
three babies, Maria lying in the center of the blanket,

Tommy and Charlie sitting on either side of her, both smiling at the camera.

"No, Mom. Nothing's bothering me." This, of course, was the biggest lie of all. Kate couldn't talk to her mother about this—not yet, anyway. She hadn't cried since that moment of weakness on the airplane headed home. She was afraid that if she started now, she wouldn't be able to stop.

"I'm fine," she repeated mechanically. "Really."

"I don't believe you," her mother replied with an audible sigh. "But I know you'll tell me about it only when you're ready. You call me when you need to talk, Kate. Promise me."

"I will. I promise." Kate's voice was little more than a husky whisper, but she knew her mother had heard her.

"I love you."

"I love you, too. Give Dad a kiss for me."

"Yes, I will. Don't work too late tonight, dear. You need your rest."

"I know. 'Bye, Mom. Thanks for calling."

Her gaze was still focused on those three photographs as she turned off the telephone and set it aside. She'd been telling herself for weeks that she should take them down, put them away where she wouldn't see them every time she was in her office. She'd left them up mostly because she knew that even if the photos were out of her sight, the memories wouldn't be as easily wiped from her mind. Her thoughts—and her dreams—were always filled with the images. And it hurt.

She'd thought of calling him. Maybe dropping him a note. She'd even started a letter once, in a weak moment when she should have been working on her proposal. "Dear Matt," it had begun. "How are you? I am fine."

She'd erased the inane words from the computer screen with a furious slap of her hand and a string of curses that would have singed her poor mother's ears.

She looked at her watch. It was only 7:00 p.m. on a Friday evening. Any single woman with a normal social life would probably be out on a date right now. Or at least out with friends, at the mall, taking in a movie, maybe having dinner and drinks and gossiping about mutual acquaintances.

Kate couldn't get enthusiastic about calling any of her friends, none of whom could possibly understand her pain. As for dating—the very thought of going out to dinner with some guy and working to be charming and interesting only depressed her further.

She sighed and turned off her computer. Maybe she *would* go out, she decided. It would certainly beat sitting here moping, feeling sorry for herself, bitterly regretting a decision she'd made for what had seemed the very best of reasons at the time.

There was a new Harrison Ford film she'd been wanting to see. Maybe she'd go. Maybe concentrating on that cute little scar on Harrison's chin would help her forget how sexy Matt had looked with his shirt off as he'd chopped wood for the stove. Her mouth twisted as she acknowledged the slim possibility that anything—even Harrison Ford—could make her forget about Matt Sullivan.

Her doorbell rang as she turned out the light to her office, which had been intended as a second bedroom in her small, moderately priced apartment. She ran a hand through her hair and frowned, wondering who'd be calling without an invitation or announcement. Probably someone had the wrong apartment, she decided, and considered not answering the door. But then the bell rang again and she shrugged. What the heck. She could at least see who it was.

Trained by years of living in the city, she automatically checked the peephole before she opened the door. Her breath caught hard in her throat. It looked like...but it couldn't be....

"Who is it?" she called out, her voice shaky, her hands trembling as she anticipated the answer.

"It's Matt."

It was definitely his voice. Odd that she'd remember it so clearly after three months. She bit her lip and stared at the door as though she could see through it. Or as though she'd find some answers on its unrevealing surface. Why was Matt here? What did he want from her? What would he do if she snatched open the door and threw herself at him?

"Come on, Hennessy, open the door," Matt said impatiently, rapping against the wood. "Don't keep me standing out here in the hallway."

Typical Sullivan, she thought. Didn't stop to think that she might have company. Or just might not want to see him. He couldn't possibly know that she was aching to see him.

Taking a deep breath for courage, she wiped her damp palms on her baggy knit shorts and reached for the doorknob.

He stood in the hallway, scowling a bit, looking as cowboy lean and roguishly handsome as she'd remembered. She gripped her hands behind her back to keep herself from reaching out to him. It was with some effort that she spoke brusquely. "What are you doing here, Sullivan?"

Chapter Thirteen

Matt didn't bother to answer Kate's question immediately, but stood still for several long moments, staring at her. She'd been running her hands through her cinnamon-colored hair again, leaving it rumpled and standing in spikes around her face. She wasn't wearing any makeup, and he could clearly see the dusting of golden freckles across her nose. She was wearing an oversize Raiders T-shirt and a pair of baggy knit shorts that hung almost to her knees, which sported a couple of smudgy bruises. Her feet were bare.

He couldn't help comparing her to elegant, perfectly groomed Damaris. He almost laughed at the contrast. His amusement faded with the acknowledgment that the very sight of Kate aroused him as the exquisite woman in the slinky, sexy dress could not.

"Hello, Hennessy," he said at last.

He saw her throat tighten with her swallow. "Hi," she said, and he wondered why she looked and sounded so nervous.

She didn't move from her position in the doorway. Matt motioned past her. "Mind if I come in?"

Her cheeks pinkened and she stepped quickly backward to let him pass. She was still looking intently at him when she closed the door behind him. "What are you doing in L.A.?" she asked again. "Are you on assignment?"

"No. I've taken a couple of weeks off from work," he answered, watching for her reaction. "I had some vacation time coming."

"So, uh, what are you doing here?"

"I came to see you, of course."

The slightest frown creased her forehead. "You should have let me know you were coming. What if I'd been out of town? Or what if I'd had other plans for tonight? Company, maybe."

Company, as in male? He refused to even consider the possibility that she'd seen anyone else since they'd parted. "I knew you were in town," he answered, instead. "I called around."

"You couldn't call *me*?"

He shrugged. "Let's just say I wanted to surprise you." And to make sure that she didn't conveniently disappear rather than face him.

She didn't seem to know what to say. She stood silently in front of him, shifting her bare feet against the carpet, twisting her hands at her waist.

He glanced away from her and looked around the room, not at all surprised to learn that her decor was eclectic, to say the least. Furniture styles were mixed—an Adams table, a contemporary sofa, a Mission Oak chair. Awards and framed photographs were grouped with surprisingly mainstream collectibles—a small cluster of David Winter cottages, a Lladró porcelain clown, two Norman Rockwell plates and three Royal Doulton figurines.

His attention was caught by several intriguingly shaped pottery pieces scattered around the room. In one corner, a pink porcelain flamingo stood beside a green neon cactus in a red clay pot. Those oddities were more in line with what he would have expected. Yet, if there was one particular thing he'd learned about Kate during that week in the forest, it was that she wasn't entirely predictable.

"Interesting place you have here, Hennessy," he said, keeping his voice light as he turned back to her, hoping to put her more at ease.

She darted a suspicious look at him, as though wondering whether he was complimenting or mocking her. "Thanks," she said after a moment.

He abruptly abandoned evasion. "I've missed you."

The huskily spoken words brought her gaze back to his. Her lips trembled, as though she would have responded in kind had she not bitten back the words—or was he deluding himself about her feelings? *Had* she missed him? Why was she being so distant? So unreadable? "Kate?"

"What?" she whispered.

"You want to help me out a little? You're not saying anything."

"I don't know what to say," she admitted, twining her fingers more tightly together. She looked so defenseless and uncertain that some of her own best friends would probably have found it hard to believe this was the Give-'em-hell Hennessy they'd all grown to know.

"You could start by saying you missed me, too," he prompted, hoping it was true.

"I, uh—" She shuffled her feet again. "I thought about you often, of course. Wondered how you were doing. I heard you were in Somalia for a couple of weeks. You'll have to tell me about it."

"I will—later. You still haven't answered my question."

A small spark of rebellion flashed into her green eyes, and Matt was relieved to recognize it. He could deal with her temper; it was her vulnerability that shook him so badly.

She dropped her hands to her sides and stood just perceptibly straighter. "Would you like a cup of coffee, Sullivan? I have a fresh pot in the kitchen."

"Yeah, that sounds good. Thanks." She was still evading the issue, but at least she wasn't throwing him out. He'd be content with that—for the moment.

Kate disappeared through a doorway on one side of the living room. Matt glanced across the room to another opening, which must lead to her bedroom. Without the slightest compunction, he moved toward it. He wanted to see where Kate lived, slept, worked, relaxed. He needed to learn everything there was to know about her.

Her bedroom was the first door on the left of a short hallway. The bed was large, made of wood and iron and covered with a colorful, handmade quilt in lieu of a bedspread. Several throw pillows had been tossed against the headboard, and a tattered old doll, also handmade, lay in a position of honor in the center. Kate's doll from her childhood? He smiled at the thought.

The dresser was also old, built of sturdy distressed oak, its top decorated with framed portraits and snapshots. A matching, mirrored vanity was cluttered with more makeup and perfume bottles than he would have expected, given Kate's general disregard for cosmetic enhancements. An oversize wooden rocking chair sat in one corner of the room, holding more throw pillows and a stuffed cat. Framed floral prints hung on the walls.

The room was comfortable, welcoming and intimate. His gaze lingered for a moment on the bed. It was with some effort that he forced himself to turn and cross the hallway to the bedroom on the other side. That one, he discovered, had been converted to a home office. She had invested in an expensive computer system, a good laser printer and a small copying machine. He had the same computer sitting in his own apartment. Interesting.

He looked at the corkboard hanging near her desk. His eyes widened at the sight of his own face. Without looking away from those three revealing photographs, he took an automatic step closer to them.

"What are you doing in here?" Kate demanded from behind him.

He spun to face her, suddenly confident again. "You *did* miss me!"

Her fists were on her hips—she must have left the coffee in the living room, he thought inconsequentially. Her eyes sparked with temper and her cheeks blazed. "Didn't anyone ever tell you that it's rude to snoop through other people's things, Sullivan?"

He advanced purposefully toward her. "Say it, Kate. You missed me."

She stood her ground, her stubborn chin lifted in defiance. "Go drink your coffee before it gets cold."

"*Dammit,* Kate!" Frustrated, he clutched her shoulders. It was with some effort that he kept himself from shaking her. "Why can't you just admit the truth?"

"Because I'm scared!" she snapped, the hot color draining from her cheeks to leave her unnaturally pale. "There. Are you satisfied?"

Taken aback, he frowned. "Scared? Of what?"

"It hurt to have to tell you goodbye before," she murmured, her green eyes huge and gleaming with what might have been unshed tears. "I don't know if I can bear to do it again."

His heart twisted. "What makes you think we'll have to say goodbye again?" he asked quietly.

"Because you don't really want me," she muttered, her eyelashes falling to conceal her misery from him.

He pulled her slowly, deliberately against him, making no effort to hide the state of arousal he'd been in ever since she'd opened her door to him. "I want you, Kate. Badly."

He heard her gulp, felt her tremble. But then she shook her head and pushed her hands against his chest to put several inches between them. "That—that's just sex. I'm talking long-term reality. You'll end up wanting someone feminine and frilly and domestic. Someone entirely opposite from me."

He refused to release her entirely, though he loosened his hold. "No," he assured her, thinking fleetingly of Damaris. "I want someone strong and loyal and brave. Someone who'd risk her life for a defenseless child—a stranger, or her own. Someone who'd risk her life for me, if necessary. Just as I would be willing to risk my life...for you."

She darted a glance upward, and he saw that one tear had escaped to trail down her cheek. He continued without pausing, "I want someone who pitched in without whining or complaining in a difficult situation that called for quick thinking and personal discomfort. I want an equal—not a dependent. I want you, Kate. I have wanted you for a very long time."

She sniffed inelegantly, looking disconsolate. "It won't last. You'll change your mind."

"You're wrong."

"That's what they all say at first," she replied glumly. "And then they start trying to change me. Make me into something I'm not. They start resenting my job and the demands it makes and the time it keeps me away from home. And the—"

"You're comparing me to those men from your past," Matt cut in roughly. "Don't. I hate it."

"I'm sorry. But I learn from my experiences."

"I can't accept that. If I'm going to be dumped, it's going to be because of my own shortcomings, not someone else's. Give me a chance, Kate. Let me prove to you that I don't suffer from your stupid LWS. That I know what— and who—I want."

She bit her lower lip, indecision written on her worried face.

"Two weeks, Kate," he said, encouraged by her silence. "Give me the next two weeks."

Her eyes widened. "You want to stay here for the next two weeks? With me?"

"Yes. Just us. No babies to distract us this time. And no snakes," he added, hoping to make her smile.

He was pleased when she did, if only faintly. "No outhouse," she said.

"No suspicious well water."

"No wood-burning stove."

"No canned stew. Or pork and beans."

Her smile deepened. "Sounds nice."

"Is that an invitation?" He held his breath.

She hesitated, still chewing her lower lip. And then she nodded, slowly. "All right. We'll give it two weeks. But—" she added hastily, when he eagerly pulled her closer "—I can't just drop everything to entertain you, Sullivan. I have other obligations, other plans. I won't change them all just because you're here."

"I didn't ask you to," he pointed out. "I know you have a life, Kate. I only want to be a part of it."

She sighed. "I guess you'll just have to see for yourself that it won't work."

Matt frowned at the fatalism in her words. Despite his preliminary victory, he was fully aware that he had a long way to go in convincing her that they were meant to be together.

But that could wait. He had the next two weeks to show her what a well-matched couple they were. In the meantime...

He pulled her closer again. "I haven't even kissed you yet," he murmured. "It's been much too long since I've kissed you, Kate."

Kate slid her arms around his neck and lifted her face invitingly to his. The pessimism was still there, in her eyes, but he could also see the stirrings of desire. She wanted him, he thought with a surge of relief, just as he wanted her.

All he had to do was convince her that there was no reason they shouldn't have each other. For a lifetime, if they were lucky.

Kate threw herself into the kiss with a desperation born of apprehension and long-suppressed hunger. Matt's arms closed more tightly around her. His mouth moved eagerly with hers. She hadn't forgotten how good it had felt to touch him like this; she just hadn't allowed herself to remember.

She was trembling by the time the kiss ended. And when Matt reached up to cup her face between his unsteady hands, she realized to her amazement that he was, too.

"Do you know how badly I want you right now?" he asked, his smile looking forced. "How much I need you?"

She moistened her lips. "I want you, too."

"I've been going crazy during the past three months. I don't know how I stayed away from you as long as I did."

She couldn't help wondering if he'd really been completely abstinent during those long weeks past, as she had. She wouldn't ask, of course. It was none of her business; she was the one who'd sent him away. But, oh, how she hated the thought of Matt touching anyone else!

"Let me give you a tour of the rest of my apartment," she said huskily. "We'll start with my bedroom."

His smile deepened. "I've already seen it," he confessed. "But I'd very much like to get a closer look."

She took his hand in hers and turned toward the doorway.

Items of clothing lay scattered across the formerly neat bedroom. The handmade doll had been tossed onto the rocker with the stuffed cat. Mounds of throw pillows lay on the floor beside the bed, and the bedclothes were already damp and twisted.

Matt pulled his mouth away from Kate's with a gasp for air. Their limbs were intimately tangled, their arms wrapped tightly around each other, their breathing ragged, pulses rapid. He looked down at her, lying flushed and damp against the pillows, and a groan rumbled from his chest.

"Oh, hell, Kate. I don't think I can last much longer," he warned, his voice raspy. "Three months is a long time to live like a damned monk."

Her eyes widened, then suddenly gleamed with satisfaction. He wondered if she'd honestly thought there'd been anyone else, if he could really have wanted any other woman after what they'd shared in that rickety cot back in the forest. She really had underestimated his feelings for her, even more than he'd realized.

She slid her hands into his hair and lifted her face enticingly close to his, her kiss-darkened lips only a breath away from his own. "You don't have to wait any longer on my account," she whispered. "Three months was a long time for me, too."

A wave of possessiveness coursed fiercely through him. She was his, damn it. She'd better not even have thought of being with anyone else since they'd parted!

A fleeting memory of his dinner date with Damaris crossed his mind, but he shoved it away. That had been nothing more than a meal, their kiss no more than a touching of lips. Even then, before he'd convinced Kate to give them a chance at building a relationship, he'd have felt disloyal if he'd taken it any further.

"Matt?" Kate swiftly reclaimed his attention when she brushed her lips against his and subtly shifted beneath him. "What are you waiting for?"

"Nothing," he growled, surging forward. "Absolutely nothing."

Kate clung tightly to Matt long after the passion of their lovemaking had faded to deep satisfaction. It was almost as if she were afraid to release him for fear that he'd slip away from her if she did. Yet she knew too well that sometime she would have to let go.

"Kate?" His voice was a low, contented rumble beneath her cheek, which rested on his chest.

It was the first time he'd spoken since they'd cried out in the throes of climax. What would he say now? Would he tell her how special it had been for him? How earthmoving? Would he tell her again that he cared enough about her to come all the way across the country just to convince her to give him a chance? Would he force her to admit her true feelings for him, despite her fear of making herself that vulnerable to him?

"Yes, Matt?" she asked warily.

"Have you had dinner?"

She blinked. "Um, no, I haven't," she said, after a moment of trying to remember what she'd been doing before he'd arrived so unexpectedly at her door.

"Me, either. I'm starving."

Her relief at the emotional safety of the conversation he'd initiated made her light-headed. "I guess I could open a can of pork and beans," she said, lifting her head to watch his reaction.

He exaggerated a look of dismay. "Please, not that. Anything but that," he begged comically.

"Mystery stew?"

He growled and bared his teeth. "Not if you value your life," he said with feigned menace. "Why don't we just order out?"

"A luxury we didn't have in the forest," she reminded him.

"One of many," he agreed. "But it still wasn't all bad, was it, Hennessy?" he asked whimsically, toying with a strand of her hair.

"No," she said, her throat growing tight. "It wasn't all bad at all."

"They're doing fine, you know."

She didn't follow him for a moment. "Who're doing fine?" she asked blankly.

"The kids. I called Sister Beatrice. Maria's in a home with a very nice couple and their three-year-old son. They've named her Carmelita. Charlie's being adopted by a doctor and his wife. They rather liked the name we gave him, so they're calling him Carlos. Tommy's new parents are already nuts about him. They named him after his new father, Julian. Sister Beatrice said she has checked on them several times and they're all healthy and happy and safe.''

Kate was touched by Matt's lingering concern for the babies who'd been their responsibility for such a short time. She touched his cheek. "I'm glad you called her."

"I thought you'd want to know," he said, looking a bit sheepish.

"I already knew. I called her, too."

Matt's eyes widened. "You did?"

She smiled and nodded. "I take it she didn't tell you."

"No, she didn't mention it."

"Well, I did. And she said all the families wanted her to tell us that if we're ever back in the neighborhood, they'd love to meet us and thank us in person for taking care of the babies."

"Hey, that was nice of them."

"I thought so, too."

Matt suddenly broke into a grin and pulled her into a bruising bear hug.

"What was that for?" she gasped, when she could breathe again. She pressed one hand experimentally against her rib cage, just to make sure it was still intact.

"In San Arturo, you acted like you were almost relieved to turn the babies over to the nuns. I couldn't figure it out, because you'd seemed so fond of them. But you were faking it, weren't you? You've missed them. You keep their picture on your bulletin board, and you've called to check on them. You're not nearly as tough as you want everyone to think, are you, Hennessy?"

Embarrassed, she squirmed out of his arms and reached for her clothes. "Don't be ridiculous, Sullivan. I was just making sure the kids were okay. After all the trouble we went through to get them safely transported, I'd have been damned mad if they weren't properly taken care of by the people we trusted them to."

"Right. And the pictures on your wall?"

"They're good shots. Nice examples of my work. I've been meaning to put them away, but I kept forgetting."

"Yeah. Sure." He was still grinning, clearly not believing a word of her airy explanation.

She lifted her chin. "I thought you said you were hungry."

"Yeah. Starved."

"I'll call in an order. What do you want? Chinese? Pizza?"

"Chinese. Lots of it," Matt decided with little hesitation.

She nodded and turned toward the doorway.

He reached out and caught her wrist in his big, work-roughened hand, detaining her when she would have walked away. "Kate?"

"Yes?"

"I'm glad you're not so tough."

She pulled her lower lip between her teeth, worried by his admission. "Don't start trying to romanticize me, Sullivan, or you're only going to be disappointed. I'm exactly the way you always accused me of being. Nothing's changed just because we've become, uh—"

"Lovers?"

"Involved," she said firmly, even more uncomfortable with the term *lovers*. Somehow that word seemed to imply the condition of being in love. And she wasn't at all sure that was what they were. Even the thought of the *L* word had her breaking into a cold sweat beneath her T-shirt and shorts. "Now let go of my hand so I can order some food, or I really will have to feed you canned pork and beans."

He brushed a kiss across her knuckles before releasing her. He wasn't notably worried about her thinly veiled warnings. Did this stubborn, thick-skulled cowboy *ever* listen to anyone else? she wondered in exasperation. He certainly hadn't paid any attention to her feeble attempts at making him see reason.

She couldn't decide whether she was more pleased or terrified by his persistence.

Chapter Fourteen

Matt spent the entire weekend trying to convince Kate that they were a perfect couple. They hardly left her apartment on Saturday—in fact, they hardly left her bed, except to eat and shower. On Sunday, they dressed in jeans and T-shirts and went out.

Matt had been to L.A. many times, but Kate took him to some of her favorite places he'd never seen. They strolled hand in hand along the sidewalks, peered into shop windows, laughed at their own silly jokes, argued good-naturedly—but heatedly—over politics, spent too much money on frivolous impulse items and generally had a wonderful time.

Kate couldn't remember ever having as much fun on a date. Which only depressed her more when she thought of what her life would be like when Matt left it again.

Matt managed to hang on to his temper in the face of her determined pessimism, but it wasn't always easy. Every time he tried to discuss their future, she skillfully evaded the issue or changed the subject. It was glaringly obvious to him that she still didn't believe they *had* a future.

They were sitting in an old-fashioned soda shop, scarfing down banana splits and cherry sodas, discussing the president's wife's role in national policy decisions when one such incident occurred.

"All I'm saying, Kate, is that if the First Ladies are going to continue to be influential in the making of public policy, they shouldn't complain when their background and character becomes a point of discussion during the election process. The voters have a right to know exactly who they're putting in power when they cast their votes."

"Of all the—" She stopped and took a deep breath, set her ice-cream spoon down and crossed her arms over her chest. "First," she said sharply, "you're assuming that the president's spouse will always necessarily be a woman."

He sighed. "I did *not* say—"

"You said 'First Ladies,'" she cut in to remind him. "Not 'first spouse.'"

He shuddered. "What a stupid term."

"No stupider—and a lot less sexist—than 'First Lady,'" she insisted. "Second, we both know that the media tends to get carried away looking into every intimate detail of a politician's life. If you claim that their spouses deserve no right to privacy, simply by reason of *being* a spouse, then you could well be exposing innocent bystanders to—"

"Innocent bystanders?" Matt interrupted. "Not if they're going to hold official positions! Not if they're going to actually take part in forming national policy."

"I suppose you think they should stay meekly in the background and bake cookies?" she demanded. "That's a perfect example of LWS, if I ever heard one!"

"Who's being sexist now?" Matt snapped. "Now *you're* the one assuming we're talking about women. Gender has nothing to do with this, anyway. I'm talking politics, Hennessy, not women's rights. Stop looking for excuses to get rid of me, will you?"

Her eyes widened almost comically. "I am *not*—" she began, but again he interrupted.

"Yes, you are. You're looking for evidence to justify your gloomy predictions about us. Well, just to show you what a patient and understanding man I am, I refuse to let you draw me into an argument right now. Finish your ice cream and we'll take in a movie. A comedy would be best, I think."

Kate hesitated a minute, as if trying to decide whether to keep the argument going, and then apparently thought better of it. "I was thinking of seeing the new Harrison Ford film," she said, picking up her spoon.

"Okay. It's not a comedy, but I think we can handle that one without coming to blows in the theater."

She muttered something around a mouthful of ice cream and strawberry topping. Matt prudently decided not to ask her to repeat it.

They slept late Monday morning—probably because neither of them had gotten much sleep the night before. Neither had complained, however.

It was after ten when Matt woke. He rubbed the sleep out of his eyes and looked at the clock, then frowned and nudged Kate's bare shoulder. "Kate? Hey, Kate, wake up."

"Hmm? What?" She yawned and burrowed more deeply into the pillow.

"It's ten o'clock. Monday," he reminded her, in case she was still too out of it to remember. "Isn't there someplace you should be?"

"I'm there," she muttered, pulling the covers to her chin. "Give me another half hour."

He shook her again. "Kate. Wake up."

She sighed loudly without opening her eyes. "Go read the morning paper, Sullivan. Let me know if anything world-shaking happened during the night."

"Kate, don't you have to work today? It's Monday."

She opened one glazed eye. "I know it's Monday. Yesterday was Sunday, tomorrow's Tuesday, so I'm bright enough to figure out the rest. Now go away. Let me sleep thirty more minutes, okay?"

"I just don't want to be accused of keeping you away from your work."

"Hmm." She closed her eyes again and hugged her pillow a bit tighter. "I formally absolve you of all responsibility for my actions. Now be a good boy and belt up, will you?"

He looked at her in exasperation, shook his head, started to say something else, then realized he was wasting his time. Kate had already gone back to sleep.

"She's going to blame me for this, I just know it," he muttered, climbing out of the bed. "No matter what she said, she'll still find a way to blame me if she misses something important at work."

He was still muttering dire predictions when he stepped into the shower.

Matt was sitting at the kitchen table, reading the newspaper and drinking a cup of coffee, when Kate finally joined him at ten forty-five. She yawned as she walked, her bare legs flashing beneath the short hem of a satin kimono. She'd taken a quick shower, and her hair was still wet. Scrubbed clean of any makeup, her face glowed from the heat of the shower.

Matt thought with utter sincerity that she looked great. He wanted very badly to see her every morning when she got out of bed. "Good morning."

"Morning. Please tell me there's more of that coffee."

"Plenty. Want me to pour you a cup?"

She shook her damp head. "Keep your seat. I'll get it. What did you have for breakfast?"

"Coffee."

"Oh. Want me to fix you something?"

It always pleased—and surprised—him when she offered. "No, thanks. I'll wait a few more minutes and then we can have brunch."

"Sounds good to me," she said, stirring sweetener into her coffee. "Anything interesting in the paper?"

"No. I didn't write any of it." He smiled and set the newspaper aside.

"Conceit."

"Hey, it's hard to be humble when you're this good."

Kate snorted and rolled her eyes, but her answer was swallowed along with a sip of her coffee.

Matt rested his elbows on the table and looked at her, growing serious. "You're sure you don't have to work this morning? You don't feel like you have to baby-sit me or anything while I'm here, do you?"

"I'm not baby-sitting you, Sullivan. But I called my boss yesterday. I'm taking some time off—a week, ten days maybe."

Matt narrowed his eyes at her. "Why?"

"I had some vacation time accrued. Quite a bit, actually. Now seemed like as good a time as any to take advantage of it."

"Why?"

She frowned. "Because you're here, and I want to spend more time with you. What's the big deal?"

"Why didn't you tell me yesterday that you'd arranged for time off?"

"Maybe because I knew you'd make an issue of it, or even try to talk me out of it just to prove you won't get in the way of my work. Well, I've got the time coming and I want to take it, Sullivan, so just leave it alone, okay? Don't you *want* to spend more time with me?" she asked, suddenly turning the questioning to him.

"Well, sure, but—"

"Okay, then," she cut in with satisfaction. "Subject closed."

"I really wouldn't have minded if you'd gone to work this morning," he couldn't resist saying. "I'm perfectly capable of entertaining myself for a few hours."

She shrugged, picked up the front section of the paper and started scanning headlines, having said all she intended to say about it.

Matt wasn't entirely satisfied. Her action still bothered him, for some reason. For one thing, he wished she would have at least discussed it with him. She had a right to take time off from work if she wanted, but arranging it so secretly implied a lack of trust in him that he couldn't help resenting. And, though of course he would enjoy having the extra time to spend with her, how could he prove to her that he wouldn't interfere with her job if she wouldn't let him demonstrate?

"It's not like these two weeks are really going to prove anything," Kate said suddenly, as though she'd been reading his mind.

Matt looked up to find her watching him over the top of the newspaper. "I beg your pardon?"

"We're both taking vacation time to spend together— and even if I'd worked today, you've already taken off to be here. What about when you have to go back to work?

We live on opposite coasts, Matt. How do you think we can carry on a relationship when we're always so far apart? How many times are you willing to go for three months—or more—without, uh—''

"Sex?" he supplied bluntly.

She looked a little disconcerted, but nodded. "Well, yeah. Among other things.''

"I'm perfectly capable of controlling my desires, Kate. If it were only sex that I wanted, I wouldn't have to fly all the way across the country to get it. I want you. I care very deeply for you. I—''

He stumbled, catching himself on the verge of saying something that would probably scare the freckles off her. "I think we can manage this," he said, instead, then instantly regretted the inanity of his words.

"Yeah? How? Cards? Letters? Phone calls?"

"Seems like we had this same argument in San Arturo.''

"Yes. And we never resolved it then. Now you act like it's all taken care of. But it's not. Next week you're going to have to go back to Washington. All I'm asking is—then what?''

"This is exactly what I've been trying to talk to you about," he said, spreading his hands on the table. "The future. Options we can take that will let us be together, at least most of the time, when one or the other of us isn't out of the country on assignment. We can work it out, Kate, if we just put our minds to it. Other couples have.''

She suddenly seemed to regret bringing the subject up. "I can't concentrate on arranging my future on an empty stomach," she said brusquely, pushing the newspaper aside and rising to her feet. "How about an omelet for brunch? With fresh fruit on the side. Or blueberry waffles. You like waffles, Matt? I use my grandma's recipe. It's great.''

He tried to tell himself that every little step forward was progress. He only wished Kate would stop taking two steps back after every slight advance.

"I want to take you someplace nice this evening," Matt announced Wednesday afternoon. It had occurred to him that he'd never dined by candlelight with Kate—José's lantern didn't count. Or danced with her. Or walked hand in hand at night on a romantic beach.

In fact, he'd given her very little romance thus far in their unusual relationship. He wanted to give her romance tonight.

"Nice?" Kate repeated. "You mean a place where the food's really good?"

"That—and the atmosphere," he clarified. "I thought we could go dancing or something after dinner."

"Dancing?" She shook her head in quick self-disgust, and he guessed that she was annoyed with herself for parroting him again.

"Yeah. How about it, Hennessy? Want to dress up and go out on the town with me?"

She looked hesitant and then intrigued. "It sounds nice," she admitted.

"Great. You know the area better than I do. Tell me where to make reservations."

Matt showered and dressed first that evening. He was glad he'd thought to bring a couple of suits. He selected the dark blue one, with a lighter blue shirt and his favorite designer silk tie.

Kate's eyes widened when she saw him. "You look... great," she said, studying him from the top of his neatly combed head to the toes of his shined and polished black leather shoes. "I'm used to seeing you in jeans and boots.

Now you look more like a business executive than a cowboy on his day off.''

Matt faked a frown. ''I'm trying to decide if that was a
compliment.''

She smiled. ''It was,'' she assured him, and reached up
to kiss him.

Matt hid his immense pleasure at her action. Kate rarely
took the initiative on her own to kiss him. He figured she
was still holding back, still protecting herself from the
painful breakup she was so certain lay ahead for them.

He stayed in the living room to watch the early news
while Kate disappeared into her bedroom to prepare for the
evening. He couldn't seem to concentrate on the words
being spoken by the well-coiffed talking heads on screen.
He was too busy thinking about Kate, and about that
stubborn pessimism of hers.

He'd tried several times since Monday morning to talk
again about the future. Each time, she'd listened and
nodded and then politely—for her—changed the subject.
She was still wary, still scared, and Matt was rapidly running out of ways to convince her that he had no intention
of hurting her.

He wanted tonight to be perfect. He wanted Kate to be
so thoroughly enthralled, so completely enchanted that she
couldn't even imagine trying to live without him.

He tugged carefully at his tie, wondering if he'd knotted it a bit too tightly. It suddenly felt as though it were
strangling him.

And then Kate said his name from the doorway, and he
forgot the tie. Nearly forgot his own name.

''Wow,'' he said, hoping his mouth hadn't dropped
open at the sight of her. ''You look—''

Beautiful. *Really* beautiful. She was wearing something
black and slinky that bared her arms and shoulders and

emphasized her slender waist and long, luscious legs. She'd poufed up her hair, somehow. The red highlights gleamed like smoldering fires when she moved her head. And she was wearing makeup, so skillfully applied that he was startled. When had Kate learned to make her eyes look so smoky and mysterious, her mouth so dark and enticing?

He'd always been drawn to Kate, more so after he'd stopped fighting that attraction, but tonight she was quite simply the most beautiful woman he'd ever known. How much of that beauty was in the eye of this beholder? How much did his feelings for her influence the way he saw her? But no—he couldn't imagine any man seeing Kate Hennessy and not wanting her for his own.

He'd have to keep a close eye on her tonight, he decided with a surge of primitive possession that would have infuriated her had she known about it.

"I look . . . ?" Kate prompted, watching him curiously.

He actually flushed as he realized he'd been standing there staring at her for an awkwardly long time. "Sorry. You look beautiful," he said after silently clearing his throat. "I didn't know you could, uh—"

He almost winced at the clumsy way he was acting. Honestly, he thought in disgust. One would have thought he was a teenager on his first real date!

She frowned. "I do know how to dress for a nice evening out, Sullivan. You've always seen me relaxing, or on assignment, wearing my working clothes. I could hardly pursue news photos in dresses and heels."

"No, of course not," he said apologetically. And then he began to smile. "Besides, I think you look as sexy as hell in your working clothes. And even sexier out of them."

This time Kate was the one who blushed. Her color hadn't completely returned to normal by the time Matt swept her out of the apartment.

Candlelight flickered from the midst of fresh flowers arranged in the center of the snowy tablecloth. The intimate table for two was elegantly set—delicate china, fine crystal, heavy silver utensils and chargers. Impeccably dressed servers moved silently and efficiently, taking care of every need of the restaurant's patrons.

Matt sipped his wine, then glanced down at the plate that had just been slipped in front of him. The veal was paper thin, perfectly cooked, the side dishes exquisitely prepared and artfully arranged. He sighed. "Now *this* is eating," he murmured and looked up at Kate with a smile.

She was looking wide-eyed around the room. "This is the first time I've been here," she whispered. "I'd always heard it was nice, but I had no idea . . . The prices must be exorbitant."

"Don't worry about prices," Matt told her expansively. "Just enjoy it."

She smiled and picked up her fork. "I fully intend to."

Matt watched her take her first bite. Her eyes closed in ecstasy. "Oh, God, that's good," she crooned.

He loved watching her enjoying herself. "Better than the food we shared in José's cabin?" he teased.

She made a face. "Don't even remind me of that stuff while I'm enjoying this meal. I don't care if I never see another can of soup."

"I know how you feel. I could get used to this."

A distinguished gentleman in an expensively tailored suit escorted a tall, thin blonde past their table. Matt noted with a glare that the man looked with interest at Kate as he passed her. "Forget it, old man. Stick to your bimbo," Matt muttered, fully aware that no one heard him.

Kate looked up in inquiry. "Did you say something, Matt?"

He smiled and shook his head, ignoring the jealousy that had temporarily gripped him. "I just said I'm looking forward to dancing with you after dinner."

"Oh." Her answering smile looked almost shy. Amazing, he thought. Who'd have thought Hennessy could look sweet and shy?

"I hope you aren't disappointed," she said, toying with a tiny carrot on her plate. "I'm not that great a dancer."

"Neither am I," he replied with a shrug. "But something tells me you and I are going to dance very nicely together."

She didn't look entirely convinced but turned back to her food without further argument.

Matt insisted that Kate order dessert. "Something really rich and sinful," he urged as the waiter hovered helpfully beside the table. "Something you don't get to have very often."

"Might I suggest the chocolate ganache cake with fresh raspberries?" asked the waiter. "It's quite the favorite with the ladies," the man added, discreetly checking out the low neckline of Kate's dress as he spoke.

Matt frowned at the waiter, who immediately straightened and focused his attention on the flower centerpiece.

Kate hadn't noticed the silent, masculine exchange. "Okay, I'll have that," she said, looking up from the dessert menu with an eager smile. "It sounds heavenly. What about you, Matt?"

"Make it two," Matt told the waiter, who nodded and moved swiftly away.

"Lecher," Matt muttered.

"You're certainly mumbling a lot tonight," Kate said with a shake of her head that made her glittery earrings sparkle in the candlelight. "What did you say?"

Matt gave her a winning grin. "Sorry. I guess I'm a bit intimidated by these elegant surroundings. Not exactly what I'm accustomed to, you know?"

"Me, either. But it's nice, at least for a little while."

"Yeah," he said, holding her gaze across the table. "It's very nice."

The lounge was even more blatantly romantic than the restaurant had been. The lighting was dim, the music low and bluesy. Couples swayed on the dance floor and murmured over drinks at tiny, shadowed tables. Matt had never seen a setting more ripe for seduction. It was exactly what he'd hoped it would be.

He turned to Kate and held out his hand, gesturing toward the dance floor. "Shall we?"

She set her hand in his, and he noted that her smile was still sweet and shy. And he knew that this was a part of Kate as real and as natural as her feisty, temperamental side. He felt privileged to have this glimpse of a side of her that she usually kept well camouflaged.

She fit beautifully in his arms. The high heels on her evening shoes brought the top of her head to his jaw. He leaned his cheek against her hair and savored the feel of her so close to him.

"I thought you said you weren't a good dancer," he murmured when the first song ended and another began with barely a pause. Matt hadn't even bothered to release her between numbers.

"I'm not."

He smiled and guided her into a tight turn that she followed effortlessly. "You could have fooled me."

She draped an arm around his neck and laughed softly, obviously enjoying herself. "It must be that you're a very good leader," she told him.

Her eyes were wide and gleaming in the soft lighting, her hair glowing with hidden fires. Her fair skin glistened softly in contrast to her dark dress. Matt wanted her so badly, he hurt. He was tempted to rush her out of the lounge, bundle her in the car and take her straight home to bed. But he was reluctant for the magic of this evening to end.

He touched his mouth to hers. Kate responded with a soft kiss that weakened his knees. He drew back with a sharp breath, clasping her closer so that she had to know that their dancing was arousing him. "Much more of that," he warned, "and we'll be lucky to make it out of here without getting arrested."

Her laugh was sultry. Utterly feminine. He was bewitched by her, and she knew it. He could see it in the pleased expression in her eyes.

"Would you like a drink?" he asked her when they'd finally had enough of dancing—at least for a few minutes.

"Yes," Kate agreed, willingly turning with him toward the cluster of tiny tables.

Someone bumped into Matt's shoulder. "Oh, sorry," a man's voice said. "I wasn't—Kate? Is that you?"

Matt glanced at Kate, who was looking at the other man without expression. "Hello, Richard," she said.

Richard? Matt looked back at the guy who'd bumped him. The man was an inch or so shorter than Matt, a couple of years older. His gold-streaked hair was styled so perfectly that he must have spent a lot of time working with it. His suit was expensive and trendy, probably hand tailored for him. The woman beside him was dark-haired and slender, striking, but not as pretty as Kate, in Matt's opinion.

"Kate, you look fabulous," the man said, his gaze sweeping Kate's slender figure with an overly familiar thoroughness that made Matt's fingers twitch. "How have you been?"

"Fine, thank you." Reluctantly conceding to good manners, Kate nodded toward Matt. "Richard, this is Matt Sullivan. Matt, Richard Hancock. He's an account executive for Smithers, Layton and Caruthers Advertising Agency."

The two men shook hands. Briefly. Hancock introduced his companion. Matt didn't quite catch the name. Mitzi? Missy? Mimi? It didn't matter.

"I saw your byline on some damned striking photographs of that riot in Miami a few weeks ago," Hancock then said to Kate. "You really got into the middle of the violence, didn't you?"

She inclined her head. "That's my job, Richard."

He sighed gustily. "How well I know that." He turned to Matt, lowering his voice conspiratorially. "It's tough being involved with a woman who would rather hug a camera than a man, you know, Sullivan? A woman who's just as likely to slug you as kiss you."

Matt hated the guy. He felt Kate flinch at his side, and tightened his arm around her waist in warning. "Oh, I don't know," he said coolly to Hancock. "I've always preferred to be with a woman who's capable of looking out for herself. And I admire Kate's accomplishments—she's a talented photojournalist who has rightfully earned quite a reputation for her work. A man would be a real fool not to recognize professional brilliance—or to try to stifle it in any way."

"Richard, I thought we were going to dance," the other woman said in a tone that hovered just a bit too close to a whine.

Hancock shot her a repressive look. "Yeah, all right. See you around, Kate. Don't say I didn't warn you, Sullivan."

Matt led Kate silently to a corner table.

She waited until they were seated and then, when Matt didn't say anything, cleared her throat and murmured, "I'm afraid Richard's still stinging at a few things I said to him. He and I dated a couple of times, you see, and we didn't part under the best of terms. He made me mad. I lost my temper and chewed him out. He never fails to get in a few digs in retaliation whenever we run into each other now."

"He's a jerk," Matt said simply, feigning disinterest. "I'm surprised you ever dated him in the first place."

"He caught me at a weak moment," Kate admitted. "I didn't realize he had a terminal case of LWS until our third date. By then, I'd already grown tired of pandering to his enormous ego."

"He still wants you."

Kate's eyes went wide in response to Matt's growl. "That's ridiculous. He can't stand me."

Matt stubbornly shook his head. "He wants you. He just knows he's not man enough for you. And that galls him."

"You're crazy," Kate muttered, her cheeks suspiciously dark.

Matt only shrugged. He knew what he'd seen in the other guy's eyes. He'd recognized the desire all too well.

He pushed his chair away from the table so abruptly that Kate stared at him in surprise. He held out his hand to her. "I don't think I want a drink, after all," he said.

"You want to dance again?"

"No. I want to go home. I want to make love to you. Soon."

She blinked, then looked thoughtfully from Matt to the direction in which Hancock and his lady friend had disappeared. "Why, Matt Sullivan. If I didn't know better, I would swear you were jealous," she accused him.

He took her hand and hauled her to her feet. "Why should I be jealous?" he asked roughly, sliding an arm around her waist to bring her against him. "I'm the man who's going home with you tonight. I'm the man you'll be waking up with in the morning."

She smiled. "Yes," she said simply. "You are."

"Let's go home, Kate." His tone was urgent now, his need too great to be denied any longer.

She touched her fingertips to his rigid jaw and stepped away from him. "All right, Sullivan. Take me home," she murmured.

He wasted no more time.

Chapter Fifteen

The next few days were idyllic—*too* idyllic, Kate was afraid. She found herself going out of her way to please Matt, and she was sure he was doing the same for her. Though the setting was entirely different, the situation reminded her of their time in José's shack. Unreal.

She knew it was only a matter of time before Matt insisted that she commit herself fully to their relationship. He wanted to talk about the future, make plans for them, while she was still afraid to face the next morning in case she awoke to find him gone.

She knew he was getting frustrated with her; she was growing frustrated with herself, for that matter. But she couldn't help being scared. Her feelings for him were so deep, so consuming, that she was afraid she would be devastated when she lost him. *When*, she thought sadly. Not if. She was still afraid to even think about the possibility that it might not happen after all.

"We have to talk about it, Kate," Matt said on Friday evening, after they'd eaten and moved into her living room on the pretext of watching television. "We can't keep pretending we can freeze time, or make the problems go away by ignoring them."

"We have almost another week before you have to leave L.A.," she reminded him. "Maybe we should wait and talk about the future when it gets closer to time for you to leave."

"Why wait? Why not talk about it now?"

"Because—"

"Because?" he prompted when she hesitated.

"You may not *want* to talk about it after spending another week here," she murmured.

"Damn it. You're still predicting disaster, aren't you? Haven't you realized during the past week that we get along great? That another week won't change the way I feel about you? My feelings will only grow stronger the more time we spend together, Kate. They won't go away."

"You can't know that."

"I *do* know that. I want to marry you, Kate. Does that sound like I'm expecting my feelings to change anytime soon?"

Her breath caught so hard in her throat that she choked on it. "Ma—ma—"

Marry? Had she really heard him correctly? Surely not!

A taut silence grew between them, disturbed only by the low noise of the television and the muted, familiar sound of sirens wailing down the street outside the building. Kate could almost hear her own heart beating—much too rapidly.

"Marry," Matt repeated, eyeing her grimly. He was obviously not at all pleased by her stunned reaction to his announcement. "You've heard the word before, I'm sure.

It means making a commitment. Being together forever, starting a family, maybe. I told you I've always intended to do so someday."

"Yes, but—with *me?*"

"So it took me a while to figure out who I wanted," he said with a trace of sheepishness.

He was obviously remembering some of his early, blatantly outspoken criticisms of her. And she wasn't the one who'd changed, she thought despondently. All the things he'd said about her were still true. Could she really believe his taste in women had changed so drastically solely on the basis of one week stranded with her?

She shook her head. "We can't talk about getting married. It's too soon. There are still too many other problems we have to face first."

"Such as?" he asked rather coolly. She could tell he was annoyed, maybe even a little hurt, by her reaction to his words.

She was achingly aware that he hadn't said anything about loving her. She couldn't bring herself to point that out just yet. She chose a less painful conflict for her example. "Our jobs."

"What about them?"

"Do I have to keep reminding you that yours is in Washington and mine is here? How do you plan to work around that? I really don't think either of us earns enough to commute from one coast to the other on alternate weekends. Do you?"

"Okay, that's a legitimate point for concern," he acknowledged. "We both like our jobs. I would never ask you to consider changing your profession—you're too damned good at it, and I know how much you love it. But it's not an either/or situation, Kate. We're flexible, and we've both built solid professional reputations. Either of us could find a new job tomorrow, if we wanted to. I could look into opportunities here in California, or you could check out D.C., or we could both look somewhere else, for that matter. New York, Atlanta, Chicago—there must be a dozen possibilities.''

He cupped her face in one hand, as if hoping that physical contact would make communication easier between them. "It's not a matter of either of us giving up everything or making sacrifices for the other," he insisted. "Of course there will be compromises—there are always compromises—but we'll both make them. Equally.''

He made it sound so easy. So damned tempting. But Kate still wasn't convinced he knew exactly what he was getting himself into. He knew she was dedicated to her career, but did he really understand how thoroughly it possessed her? Did he realize how many days and nights she spent in single-minded pursuit of a photograph that would show people something they'd never seen, or illustrate life with a new slant that subtly changed the way they'd perceived the world before?

What would happen when she got caught up in her work at a time when he wanted her free to do something else—something *he* wanted to do?

And what about his own career? Matt was a highly respected foreign correspondent, out of his own country as much as he was in it. Would he expect her to be waiting at the doorstep for him when he returned? And who did he think was going to take care of that family he wanted if both of them were off God-knows-where chasing a story? Had he never thought of that?

Not to mention their inevitable clashes of temper. Kate was honest enough to admit that she was stubborn and impatient and sometimes selfish, that she'd grown accustomed to her independence and wouldn't learn to compromise without making a lot of mistakes along the way.

Could Matt live with those mistakes? Did he understand that she'd been on her best behavior during most of the past week, but that she didn't know how much longer she could keep it up? She was sure to lose her temper eventually, and it wouldn't be pretty when she did. How would he feel about that?

Matt's gaze was focused intently on her face, as though he were trying to read the emotions that must be reflected in her eyes. "I swear, Kate, if you say one word about your stupid LWS, I'm liable to do something violent," he warned.

"You're the one who brought up family," she reminded him spiritedly. "Who's going to have those kids, hmm? Who'll have to take off work to give birth?"

"Well, I hardly think I can handle that part," he answered with some asperity. "Give me a break, Hennessy. I had nothing to do with the assignment of ovaries and uteruses. Or is it uteri? Whatever. When—and if—the time comes that we're ready to start a family, I would hardly expect you to be solely responsible. Didn't I change my share of diapers in José's cabin? Didn't I get up for two o'clock feedings and walk the floor with Tommy when he was teething, and scrub the baby puke out of Maria's shirts?"

The mention of the babies made her ache to hold them again. Those recently discovered maternal instincts hadn't receded completely into obscurity during the past three months. Kate wanted a family someday, and she wanted her career. Like so many modern women, she wanted it all—and she wasn't at all sure that it was possible.

She opened her mouth to tell Matt so, but was interrupted when the telephone rang.

She considered letting it ring. She'd neglected to turn on the answering machine, but she was sure that whoever it was would call back if it was urgent.

The phone rang again. "You'd better get that," Matt said, motioning toward the demanding instrument. "It could be important."

"All right," she said. "Don't forget where we were."

"Trust me," Matt muttered. "I won't forget."

Five minutes later, Kate replaced the receiver in its cradle and turned to Matt. "That was one of the reporters from the magazine," she said. "He said there's a huge apartment building on fire only a few blocks from here. There are people trapped inside. He's on his way to cover the story and thought I might want to bring my camera and join him."

How would Matt feel, she wondered, about having her job interfere when they were discussing something as important to them as marriage? Would he be annoyed? Would he point out that she was on vacation and that their relationship was more important than her quest for a dramatic rescue photo?

"I'm going," she said. And she knew that she wasn't testing his reaction as much as she was responding to a need of her own to pursue the career she loved.

He nodded. "I'll come with you. I'm a reporter, too," he added when she looked surprised. "Maybe there's a prizewinning story there for me, too."

There were so many questions still to be answered, but there was no time to pursue them now. Kate nodded acceptance of his company and raced after her camera equipment.

Kate went to work the moment they arrived at the burning building. She pushed past the boundaries of the fire and police barricades and disappeared into the chaos beyond.

Matt stayed back out of her way, making no effort to keep her in sight. Kate knew her job, he thought. She'd probably infuriate whoever called himself in charge around here, but she'd get some damned good shots of an unfolding real-life drama.

Crowds of spectators were already gathering, most of them reflecting concern for the people trapped in the building and a rather guilty fascination with the suspense and excitement. Others made no pretense of being there for any reason other than their own rather morbid entertainment.

The noise level was deafening—screaming sirens, excited chatter, hoarse yells, the clatter of rescue equipment, the rush of highly pressurized water, the roaring of hungry flames, an occasional scream. Smoke poured from broken windows of the glass-and-metal high-rise, rising in a dark, ominous cloud above the scene, drifting on the breeze to set off occasional coughing spells among the crowds, who only moved closer rather than being driven back.

Police and rescue workers raced through the pandemonium, shouting orders, cursing mishaps, their faces grim, yet eyes bright with the intensity of their dedication to their work. Matt knew that somewhere in the mass, Kate was doing her job with much the same expression.

"Matt? Matt Sullivan? What the hell are you doing here?"

Matt turned and was jostled by a spectator pushing to get a better look at someone being loaded onto an ambulance. Matt stubbornly pushed back, clearing a way for him to move to his right.

"Oh, hi, Phil," he said, recognizing a reporter of about his own age whom he'd met a few times at national meetings of the journalism society in which they were both active. "You covering this mess?"

"Trying to," Phil answered with a shrug. "I've been trying to get some details, but everyone's too busy now to answer many questions."

"What have you got so far?"

Phil eyed Matt warily. "You covering?" Friendship was one thing—professional rivalry something else entirely.

Matt shook his head. "I'm only a spectator."

"Oh. Well, the fire broke out in one of the fifth-floor apartments over an hour ago, then spread rapidly to the neighboring apartments. I'm hearing rumors that we may have some violations of fire safety regulations in evidence here. There are questions about the fire walls and sprinkler systems."

Matt winced. "Someone's head is going to roll."

"A lot of heads," Phil agreed in satisfaction, tapping the notebook in his left hand. "I'm taking names."

"How many residents are still inside?"

The paunchy, slightly balding reporter shrugged. "Don't know yet. They've got the lower floors mostly evacuated, but there are still people stuck on the top three floors. Fire chief says the flames are controlled at the moment, and no one up there's in imminent danger—but, of course, that could change at any minute if things go wrong."

Someone beside them pointed upward and shouted to call attention to a hovering rescue helicopter. Searchlights swept the outside of the building, illuminating pale, frightened faces in upstairs windows, the yellow-clad bodies of fire fighters perched on ladders, the gaping stares of spectators.

"I wonder where Kate is," Matt murmured, more to himself than to Phil.

Phil looked curious. "Kate?"

"Kate Hennessy—you know her, don't you?"

"Yeah, sure. She taking pictures?"

"Somewhere," Matt said with a nod, still searching the crowds. "I was at her place when she got a call about the fire. She thought there might be some opportunities for some interesting shots, so she hurried over here. I came along to watch."

"You were at her place?" Phil repeated, turning to look at Matt in surprise. "I didn't think you two even liked each other. I still remember that shouting match you got into in Chicago. I think you were, uh, discussing the Clarence Thomas hearings."

Matt grimaced at the memory. He and Kate had almost gotten themselves thrown out of a hotel bar over that one. Fortunately, several of their co-workers had interceded, whisking them in opposite directions for the remainder of the evening. Even then, had the fireworks between them been prompted by the smoldering attraction they'd been fighting so furiously?

"Yeah, I remember," he said, realizing Phil was still waiting for a response. "But we've, uh, agreed to disagree on some topics."

"Hey, wait a minute. You and Hennessy were the ones stuck in South America with a bunch of babies during that leftist uprising a few months back, weren't you? Everyone in the business was talking about it. No one could believe those poor tots survived being looked after by you and Hennessy."

Matt cleared his throat. "Yeah. That was us."

"So, you've been seeing each other since?"

"We're, er, we've, umm—"

"You're an item now, huh?"

Matt lifted both hands and made a wry face. "We're in the middle of negotiations for a permanent truce."

Phil's eyes widened. "Sounds serious."

"Yeah. The *M* word has even been mentioned. I'll let you know how it works out."

"Whoa. The *M* word." Phil shook his head in amazement, then paused as though to consider the development for a moment. "You know," he said slowly, "I guess I'm really not so surprised by this, after all. You and Hennessy always have had strong feelings about each other. Maybe you were just misreading them before, hmm?"

"I guess we were," Matt said, rather pleased that Phil had reached the same conclusion he'd arrived at.

"Good luck, Sullivan. Hope everything works out for you."

Matt nodded. "Thanks. I'm quite sure we're both going to need all the luck we can get."

"That's what people said when I married a brilliant research scientist," Phil confided, surprising Matt, who hadn't known what Phil's wife did for a living. "Glenda and I don't have a damned thing in common, but it's been working somehow for nearly ten years," Phil added, looking quite satisfied.

Matt could almost feel his optimism swelling again. At least he and Kate had plenty in common. Maybe he'd persuade Phil to talk to Kate, he thought.

"Oh, hell. Speaking of Kate..." Phil said suddenly, roughly nudging Matt's arm and pointing toward the building.

Matt turned, muttered a curse from between clenched teeth and broke into a run.

Kate had been standing beyond the safety barricades, her camera trained upward at a fireman who was helping a young woman climb down a very long, very thin ladder. Her concentration on framing the shot was so intense that she hadn't seen the large piece of flaming debris falling from directly above her.

Matt took her down in a flying tackle left over from his high school football days. They hit the pavement with a teeth-jarring, lung-emptying thud. The debris crashed onto the sidewalk behind them. Matt felt the resulting sparks sting his exposed skin as they showered otherwise harmlessly over him.

"What the—" Kate gasped when she was capable of speech, of sorts. She shoved herself upright and stared at him. "What the hell do you think you're doing?"

Matt pushed himself experimentally to his feet, a bit bruised and shaken but otherwise in full working order, he was relieved to discover. And then he reached down and jerked Kate upright. "Are you all right?"

"All right? You threw me to the ground, knocked the breath out of me, probably left me covered in bruises and you've very likely broken my camera! No, I'm not all right. Have you lost your mind?"

"Get back out of the way," a soot-covered, irritated-looking woman in a fire fighter's uniform yelled at them. "Behind the barricades! Now!"

Matt jerked on Kate's arm, pulling her in the direction of the barricades.

She resisted. "My camera."

Cursing steadily beneath his breath, Matt knelt and scooped up the camera, not bothering to check to see if it was broken. And then he half led, half dragged Kate to a relatively secluded spot in the shadows beyond the blazing rescue lights.

"Of all the— Let me tell you, Matthew Sullivan, I do *not* appreciate having you tell me how to do my job. Is that clear? Now get out of my way and let me get back to work or—"

Matt reached out with both hands, grabbed the lapels of her short-sleeved jacket and hauled her so close their noses almost touched when he bent into her face. "I am *not* telling you how to do your job," he yelled, just to make sure she heard him correctly. "I'm telling you it's possible to get your award-winning pictures without taking stupid chances with your life!"

Obviously startled by his burst of temper, she gasped, then gaped at him in openmouthed astonishment.

Matt was on a roll, too angry to care whether he was making her madder at him. "Keep your eyes open when you're working, damn it! Make sure nothing is aimed at you, speeding toward you or falling on you when you choose your shot. If you're going to ignore safety barriers to get better angles, use enough common sense to mini-mize the risks."

He took a deep breath and continued before she could break in. "You're damned good at what you do, Hen-nessy, and I know you've got brains in that stubborn head of yours, so use them next time, will you? If I *ever* see you pull another stupid, reckless stunt like standing under falling debris just to get a shot, I'll clobber you, I swear to—"

Kate threw herself at him, her mouth covering his to smother anything he might have added for good measure.

Staggering with the impact of her enthusiastic embrace, Matt steadied them, then returned the kiss, his mind spin-ning with questions. Why was she kissing him? He'd just yelled at her in front of half of L.A.—*and* threatened to clobber her. She should be yelling back at him, or swing-ing at him or something. Instead, she was kissing him so thoroughly and so heatedly that his ears were probably steaming!

He really shouldn't question his luck, but . . .

"What the hell was that for?" he asked, when she finally drew back for air.

She was grinning from ear to ear. "You love me!" Her tone was jubilant.

Matt blinked. "Of course I love you," he said rather crossly, still trying to figure out what her game was now. "What has that got to do with anything?"

"Don't you see?" She caught his shirt in her hands as though to shake the answer into him. "You're mad at me, but you aren't treating me like a helpless little woman. You're yelling at me, and you're not pulling any punches. You thought I was being reckless, but you didn't try to tell me not to take any more chances. You just, umm, advised me to approach the risks a little differently in the future. Because you love me!"

Slowly shaking his head, Matt looked at her in frank bewilderment. "I love you," he repeated, "but I still don't quite understand—"

"It's like when I yelled at you about pushing that bus deeper into the forest by yourself. I thought you would be hurt and I was furious at you for taking unnecessary risks. That's what you were mad about just now, right?"

"Right. But—"

"It's only natural for two people to worry about each other when they love each other, right? I mean—"

Matt gripped her forearms. "When they *what?*"

Her gaze locked with his. She smiled. "When they love each other," she said again, more solemnly this time.

He started to pull her closer.

"Kate! Matt! Are you okay?" Phil joined them with a harried look on his broad, pleasant face. "I've been looking for you two everywhere. Man, when I saw that stuff falling at you, I thought you were a goner, Hennessy. Matt saved your life with that tackle!''

"I know," Kate acknowledged happily. "I was really hacked off with him about it at first, but I've gotten over it. We're getting married—did he tell you?"

Phil frowned, looking as bewildered as Matt had been only a moment before.

Matt was finally starting to understand. "Is that a yes?" he asked Kate, catching her chin in his hand to force her to look up at him.

"That's a yes," she said gruffly. "We'll work out the details later."

Matt leaned over and kissed her, oblivious to the noisy pandemonium still going on around them.

"Well, I'm glad to see you're both okay," Phil said with amusement edging his voice. "Oh, and congratulations on the wedding plans. It should be a very, umm, interesting marriage."

Phil had blended back into the crowds by the time Matt lifted his mouth from Kate's. They'd already forgotten the other reporter.

"You have the most convoluted thought processes of anyone I've ever known," Matt said with a grin. "But I love you, anyway, God help me. And you'd better get used to the idea that I'm going to be around to yell at you for a long time—the rest of our lives, to be specific."

Kate grinned. "I love you, too. And you'd better be prepared that I'm going to be yelling back at you."

"Our relationship is going to be very noisy—but spectacular," Matt predicted with a smile. "Like fireworks," he added, thinking of all the excitement they'd already faced together.

"Well," Kate said contentedly. "That's the way it goes sometimes in real life."

She reached up to kiss his cheek, then drew away. "Now about my camera—if you've broken it, Sullivan, you're buying me another one. Got that?"

Matt only laughed. Things were working out a lot better than he'd expected, he decided. Which only went to prove that there was just no predicting Kate Hennessy.

Epilogue

Kate set her bags at her feet on the doorstep of her house in Atlanta and pushed a hand through her red brown bangs. She needed a trim, she thought. Her hair had gotten shaggy during the two weeks she'd been away on assignment. She fitted her key into the lock on the front door, eager to step inside.

It was always so nice to come home.

She had hardly gotten through the door when she was greeted with a shrill shriek of welcome. "Mom's home!" the little voice announced delightedly. "Mom's home! Hi, Mom."

Kate caught the running four-year-old in her arms and drew him close for a tight hug. A shaggy, floppy-eared dog of indeterminate breed barked and bounced around her feet, welcoming Kate home in his own way.

"Hi, yourself," Kate told her son, settling him in a familiar spot on her hip. "I missed you. Have you been a good boy while I was gone?"

The child emphatically nodded his sandy head. "I was very good," he assured her. "Dad said so."

"Did he? Well, I brought you a present from Czechoslovakia. It's in my bag. You can have it as soon as I unpack."

Jake grinned in anticipation and threw his arms around her neck to plant a smacking kiss on her cheek.

"Hey, Jake. Don't get all Mom's kisses," Matt warned from the doorway. "Save a few for me."

Kate had stopped to pat the dog, who was squirming himself into a near frenzy in his bid for her attention. The sound of Matt's deep, lazy drawl made her straighten quickly and turn toward him. As always, the sight of his lean, tanned face brought a smile to her lips.

"Hi, Sullivan," she said, reaching her free hand out to him.

"Hi, Sullivan," he repeated, catching her hand and drawing her close for a long kiss.

"Good to have you home," he said when he drew back. "How'd the assignment go?"

She smiled smugly. "Better clear a spot on the mantel for a new award to go with your most recent one."

He grinned. "I'm sure we'll find a place for it."

"Mom brought me a present from Checkerslobbia," Jake announced excitedly. "It's in her bag!"

And then he turned back to his mother, launching into a lengthy and not always intelligible description of everything he'd done for the past two weeks, including a movie he'd seen with his nanny and a pushing match he'd gotten into with a kid at preschool who'd tried to steal Jake's crayons.

Her gaze locked with Matt's loving eyes, Kate smiled and tried to hear her son over the still-excited yipping of Sherman, the family pet.

Matt had been right all those happy years ago in his predictions about their relationship, she thought contentedly. Their marriage had been noisy at times—but always spectacular. Like fireworks.

As though he'd read her mind, Matt tightened his fingers around hers and kissed her deeply as their son continued to talk and the dog to bark.

Kate wouldn't have traded the noise—or the love—for all the awards in the world.

* * * * *

A Note from the Author

There are so many roles available to women these days—and there are times when I think I've experienced them all. Daughter. Wife. Mother. I was, very briefly, a single career woman, and then a childless, married career woman. I worked outside the home until my first child was three. I spent a couple of years as a full-time homemaker after the birth of my second child, before beginning a new career as a writer, working from an office *in* my home. I wrote throughout my third pregnancy and completed a book when my son was only two months old. And I give full credit to my loving, usually patient and totally supportive husband, who has always been there for me when life sometimes seemed too impossibly demanding.

If I've learned anything during my sampling of options, it has been that there is no easy path in life. Each choice comes with its own special rewards, and its own sacrifices and disadvantages. Add to those complexities the

mass of expectations from society at large and one could
develop a severe complex—as did Kate Hennessy, my lat-
est "Special Woman."

Kate is competent, ambitious, gutsy, prickly, strong and
compassionate, and yet, when it comes to love, she is a
mass of contradictions. She has the same needs and desires as other women, but experience has taught her that
traditional "women's roles" are too restrictive for her active nature. She fears that having it all—for her, at least—
is impossible. It takes a very special and understanding
man to convince this skeptical woman that the challenges
of marriage and family can be as rewarding, and as con-
querable, as those of her career. Matt Sullivan, being a
typical male, takes a while to come to this realization himself, but when he does, he is just the one to help Kate learn
that valuable lesson.

Kate has found a mate who encourages her to be everything she can be—just as I did. I believe that makes the
challenges much easier to face and much more rewarding
to celebrate.

COMING NEXT MONTH

#919 MAIL ORDER COWBOY—Patricia Coughlin
That Special Woman!
Allie Halston swore she'd conquer rigorous ranch life, even if it meant taking on all of Texas! Then she faced sexy Burn Monroe—who was more than just a cowboy with an attitude....

#920 B IS FOR BABY—Lisa Jackson
Love Letters
Beth Crandall's single passionate night with Jenner McKee had changed her life forever. Years later, an unexpected letter drew her back home, and to the man she'd never forgotten....

#921 THE GREATEST GIFT OF ALL—Penny Richards
Baron Montgomery knew determined Mallory Ryan would sacrifice anything for her young child. But when her boundless mother's love was tested, could Mallory accept his help and his promise of everlasting devotion?

#922 WHEN MORNING COMES—Christine Flynn
Driven and dedicated, Travis McCloud had sacrificed his marriage for career. Now a chance reunion with Brooke compelled him to open his heart...and to take a second chance at love.

#923 COWBOY'S KIN—Victoria Pade
A Ranching Family
Linc Heller's wild, hell-raising ways were legendary. Yet Kansas Daye wondered if becoming a father had tempered Linc—and if he was ready to step into her waiting arms.

#924 LET'S MAKE IT LEGAL—Trisha Alexander
John Appleton gave up the fast track to become Mr. Mom. Then high-powered lawyer Sydney Scott Wells stormed into his life, and John knew he'd show her the best of both worlds!

Jilted!

Left at the altar, but not for long.

Why are these six couples
who have sworn off love
suddenly hearing wedding bells?

Find out in these scintillating books
by your favorite authors,
coming this November!

#889   **THE ACCIDENTAL BRIDEGROOM**
by Ann Major
(Man of the Month)

#890   **TWO HEARTS, SLIGHTLY USED**
by Dixie Browning

#891   **THE BRIDE SAYS NO**
by Cait London

#892   **SORRY, THE BRIDE HAS ESCAPED**
by Raye Morgan

#893   **A GROOM FOR RED RIDING HOOD**
by Jennifer Greene

#894   **BRIDAL BLUES**
by Cathie Linz

Come join the festivities when six handsome
hunks finally walk down the aisle...

only from

Dark secrets, dangerous desire...

Lovers
DARK AND
DANGEROUS

Three spine-tingling tales from the dark side of love.

This October, enter the world of shadowy romance as Silhouette presents the third in their annual tradition of thrilling love stories and chilling story lines. Written by three of Silhouette's top names:

LINDSAY McKENNA
LEE KARR
RACHEL LEE

Haunting a store near you this October.

Only from

Silhouette®

...where passion lives.

Premiere

The stars are out in October at Silhouette! Read captivating love stories by talented *new* authors— in their very first Silhouette appearance.

Sizzle with Susan Crosby's
THE MATING GAME—Desire #888
...when Iain Mackenzie and Kani Warner are forced to spend their days—and *nights*—together in *very* close tropical quarters!

Explore the passion in Sandra Moore's
HIGH COUNTRY COWBOY—Special Edition #918
...where Jake Valiteros tries to control the demons that haunt him—along with a stubborn woman as wild as the Wyoming wind.

Cherish the emotion in Kia Cochrane's
MARRIED BY A THREAD—Intimate Moments #600
...as Dusty McKay tries to recapture the love he once shared with his wife, Tori.

Exhilarate in the power of Christie Clark's
TWO HEARTS TOO LATE—Romance #1041
...as Kirby Anne Gordon and Carl Tannon fight for custody of a small child...and battle their growing attraction!

Shiver with Val Daniels'
BETWEEN DUSK AND DAWN—Shadows #42
...when a mysterious stranger claims to want to save Jonna Sanders from a serial killer.

Catch the classics of tomorrow—*premiering* today—
Only from

▼ *Silhouette*®

TM

PREM94

"HOORAY FOR HOLLYWOOD" SWEEPSTAKES

HERE'S HOW THE SWEEPSTAKES WORKS

OFFICIAL RULES — NO PURCHASE NECESSARY

To enter, complete an Official Entry Form or hand print on a 3" x 5" card the words "HOORAY FOR HOLLYWOOD", your name and address and mail your entry in the pre-addressed envelope (if provided) or to: "Hooray for Hollywood" Sweepstakes, P.O. Box 9076, Buffalo, NY 14269-9076 or "Hooray for Hollywood" Sweepstakes, P.O. Box 637, Fort Erie, Ontario L2A 5X3. Entries must be sent via First Class Mail and be received no later than 12/31/94. No liability is assumed for lost, late or misdirected mail.

Winners will be selected in random drawings to be conducted no later than January 31, 1995 from all eligible entries received.

Grand Prize: A 7-day/6-night trip for 2 to Los Angeles, CA including round trip air transportation from commercial airport nearest winner's residence, accommodations at the Regent Beverly Wilshire Hotel, free rental car, and $1,000 spending money. (Approximate prize value which will vary dependent upon winner's residence: $5,400.00 U.S.); 500 Second Prizes: A pair of "Hollywood Star" sunglasses (prize value: $9.95 U.S. each). Winner selection is under the supervision of D.L. Blair, Inc., an independent judging organization, whose decisions are final. Grand Prize travelers must sign and return a release of liability prior to traveling. Trip must be taken by 2/1/96 and is subject to airline schedules and accommodations availability.

Sweepstakes offer is open to residents of the U.S. (except Puerto Rico) and Canada who are 18 years of age or older, except employees and immediate family members of Harlequin Enterprises, Ltd., its affiliates, subsidiaries, and all agencies, entities or persons connected with the use, marketing or conduct of this sweepstakes. All federal, state, provincial, municipal and local laws apply. Offer void wherever prohibited by law. Taxes and/or duties are the sole responsibility of the winners. Any litigation within the province of Quebec respecting the conduct and awarding of prizes may be submitted to the Regie des loteries et courses du Quebec. All prizes will be awarded; winners will be notified by mail. No substitution of prizes are permitted. Odds of winning are dependent upon the number of eligible entries received.

Potential grand prize winner must sign and return an Affidavit of Eligibility within 30 days of notification. In the event of non-compliance within this time period, prize may be awarded to an alternate winner. Prize notification returned as undeliverable may result in the awarding of prize to an alternate winner. By acceptance of their prize, winners consent to use of their names, photographs, or likenesses for purpose of advertising, trade and promotion on behalf of Harlequin Enterprises, Ltd., without further compensation unless prohibited by law. A Canadian winner must correctly answer an arithmetical skill-testing question in order to be awarded the prize.

For a list of winners (available after 2/28/95), send a separate stamped, self-addressed envelope to: Hooray for Hollywood Sweepstakes 3252 Winners, P.O. Box 4200, Blair, NE 68009.

CBSRLS

OFFICIAL ENTRY COUPON

"Hooray for Hollywood"
SWEEPSTAKES!

Yes, I'd love to win the Grand Prize — a vacation in Hollywood —
or one of 500 pairs of "sunglasses of the stars"! Please enter me
in the sweepstakes!

This entry must be received by December 31, 1994.
Winners will be notified by January 31, 1995.

Name _____

Address _____ Apt. _____

City _____

State/Prov. _____ Zip/Postal Code _____

Daytime phone number _____
(area code)

Account # _____

Return entries with invoice in envelope provided. Each book
in this shipment has two entry coupons — and the more
coupons you enter, the better your chances of winning!

DIRCBS

OFFICIAL ENTRY COUPON

"Hooray for Hollywood"
SWEEPSTAKES!

Yes, I'd love to win the Grand Prize — a vacation in Hollywood —
or one of 500 pairs of "sunglasses of the stars"! Please enter me
in the sweepstakes!

This entry must be received by December 31, 1994.
Winners will be notified by January 31, 1995.

Name _____

Address _____ Apt. _____

City _____

State/Prov. _____ Zip/Postal Code _____

Daytime phone number _____
(area code)

Account # _____

Return entries with invoice in envelope provided. Each book
in this shipment has two entry coupons — and the more
coupons you enter, the better your chances of winning!

DIRCBS